THIS IS THE
WATER

YANNICK MURPHY

headline
review

First published in paperback in Great Britain in 2014 by
HEADLINE REVIEW
An imprint of HEADLINE PUBLISHING GROUP

1

Cataloguing in Publication Data is available from the British Library

ISBN 978 1 4722 1090 6

Typeset in Electra LT Std

Printed and bound in Great Britain by
Clays Ltd, St Ives plc

Headline's policy is to use papers that are natural, renewable and
recyclable products and made from wood grown in sustainable forests.
The logging and manufacturing processes are expected to conform
to the environmental regulations of the country of origin.

HEADLINE PUBLISHING GROUP
An Hachette UK Company
338 Euston Road
London NW1 3BH

www.headline.co.uk
www.hachette.co.uk

For my children, swimmers extraordinaire!

THIS IS THE
WATER

Part One

Part One

*T*his is the water, lapping the edge of the pool, coming up in small waves as children race through it. This is the swim mom named Dinah wearing the team shirt with a whale logo on it, yelling at her daughter Jessie to swim faster. This is Jessie who cannot hear Dinah because Jessie is in the water. Jessie is singing a song to herself: She is singing, "This old man, he played one. He played knick knack on his thumb." Dinah is red in the face, standing in the stands. Dinah moves her hand in the air as if to help hurry her daughter along. Behind the starting blocks the water comes up over the edge of the pool and splashes the parents who are timing on deck.

This is the facility. The long shafts of sunlight that come in through the windows and hit the water on sunny days. The showers whose pressure is weak, whose tiles need brush-cleaning in the grout. This is Dinah after her daughter Jessie doesn't win the race. Dinah is sitting back down on the bleachers in the stands. She is writing down Jessie's time. She is comparing the time to the last time Jessie swam that event. She is telling herself at least her daughter beat her previous record. This is how much she beat it by: one one-hundredth of a second.

This is the racing suit some of the swimmers wear. It feels like the skin of a shark when rubbed the wrong way. Rubbed the right way it's smooth and gives you the feeling that you can beat your old times, that you can beat anyone's times. The suits are supposed to fit tight, as tight as a corset probably. The suits, the girls all say, are terribly uncomfortable. They ride up their crotches. They cut into their legs. They dig into their shoulders. They flatten their chests. They make it difficult to breathe. But they love their suits nonetheless and after a meet they rinse them and hang them up dutifully to dry, unlike their practice suits, which they sometimes let stay in their bags overnight in a wet ball, and the chlorine from the pool eats away at the fabric.

This is the bathroom in the locker room where a girl changes into her suit. In the bathroom grunting can be heard. Many hands are on the girl and the suit trying to help her get into it. If you look under the bathroom door, you can see so many legs. From the stall you can hear the pull of the swimsuit fabric, the sucking sound of skin being pushed and shoved.

This is the mom named Chris who is timing with another parent she doesn't know from another team. Chris is not wearing the swim team tee shirt with the whale logo. She did not think to put it on when she left the house at five a.m. with her daughter in the car and her daughter's swim bag stuffed with towels to last throughout the long day of racing, and when the moonlight was flowing over the field, lighting up a deer and a doe nibbling at the edge of the forest. Chris does not cheer for her daughter. She only realizes her daughter is swimming in the race when she looks out across the lanes of the pool and sees someone who looks like her daughter swimming. She still doesn't cheer when she realizes it is her daughter because she knows her daughter would not hear her over all the other noise. Chris also thinks it's silly how many parents are so involved in their child's swimming and cheer so loudly, as if the cheering will make their child go faster, as if it were the Olympics or if winning or losing a swim down the length of the pool and back were a matter of life and death. Chris's daughter, Cleo, is becoming more interested in swimming every season, even though Chris doesn't ask her much about it. Cleo keeps a record in her journal of all of her past times and of the times she needs to qualify for certain meets. Cleo has begun sharing her times with her father, Paul, because he seems more interested than her mother in how she's able to shave off time by tucking tighter in her turns, or keeping her hips up in the backstroke. This is Chris, being splashed by the water when a swimmer dives in and liking the way the water feels through the leg of her blue jeans, making her feel cool when it is so hot in the facility. These are the windows of the pool, covered over in mist so thick it looks purposely sprayed on, as if what were being done behind the glass were not to be seen by anyone on the outside.

This is the outside. A bright New England day that is almost spring, but not quite. Snow still in patches in places surrounded by the pale green grass of last summer—last summer wanting to still be seen, even if its grass looks frizzy at the tips and is mixed with what looks like bits of straw. These are the two highways behind the lawn of the facility, the cars going by quickly, most of the drivers wanting to leave the area whose exits are congested with shopping stores and food chains. They want to get back to the areas where people actually live instead of shop. They want to get back to their homes on rural roads where what wakes them up in the morning is the occasional lowing of the neighboring farm's cows, or a woodpecker at work on the exterior siding of their cedar-framed house, and where the spring peepers peeping at night in the nearby ponds are the last sounds people hear before sleep. This is what's in front of the facility: a view of a small mountain gently rounded, a skyline often interrupted by vee formations of high-flying geese, a dirt road that loops around the facility and also branches off and travels to the south for only so long before it peters out and you see a field of scrubby grass surrounded by scraggly pines, unhealthy at their tops, their upper boughs the color of rust.

This is Dinah at the home meet talking to Chris when Chris's shift as a timer is over and she goes up into the stands. "How did your daughter swim?"

"She looked like she was having fun," Chris says. What Dinah hears is, "Chris's daughter did not swim well and she doesn't want to talk about it." This is Dinah telling Chris that her daughter, Jessie, lost one-hundredth of a second off her seedtime.

This is Chris needing the bathroom, thinking as she sits on the seat that she needed to sit down as much as she needed to pee. Chris has been feeling tired lately, she thinks, or maybe she's just been feeling tired for years now. She's not quite sure. Maybe she's been tired ever since she was a girl living down south and had a babysitter, a young woman named Beatrice who would stay with Chris in the evenings and make sure she did her homework and tucked her into bed, who was raped. Chris thinks she loved

Beatrice as much as she loved her parents, maybe even more. Her parents were too busy running the general store they owned to spend time with Chris in the evenings, but Beatrice would come over with her college texts, and Chris would have her math sheets and her ancient civilizations textbook out, and they'd sit at the kitchen table studying together, with music from the pop radio station playing. Beatrice would lean over Chris, helping with a fraction, smelling of fruity shampoo, and when Chris got the answer right, Beatrice would say, "Atta girl, Chris." After they studied for a while, Beatrice would announce it was break time, and she'd pull out her collection of nail polish and bend over Chris's toes and paint them with colors Chris had never even imagined existed, or had imagined existed only as precious metals that one could find deep in the veins of the earth. Gleaming, creamy, flecked metallic bronzes and coppers and golds and silvers in small bottles with price stickers from the drugstore stuck on their plastic tops. After seeing those colors, the realization came to Chris that anything could be replicated, even the insides of the earth. She imagined how fun it would be to be a painter, and to have those colors to work with all of the time and be able to paint anything you see before your eyes. Those evenings with Beatrice were some of the reasons Chris became an artist. Afterward, Beatrice would do her own toes, and the two of them would dance on the sloping farm kitchen floor with wads of cotton stuffed between their toes so that the nail polish would dry evenly. Then, at night, Beatrice would climb into bed with Chris. They'd pull the blankets up above their ankles and lift their feet up into the air so they could admire their nail-polish artistry and how their toes flashed jittery specks of metallic light when they moved them side to side in the falling darkness. It wasn't until later, when Chris's parents would finally come home, having finished closing up the store and making all the egg and tuna salads for the next day, that Beatrice would slide out from under the covers and leave Chris's side. One evening, though, Beatrice did not show up at Chris's house. Some men in their early twenties had followed Beatrice in a van while she was jogging on a dirt road. They slowed down alongside her, matching her pace, and slid the van door open. They pulled her inside, where she thrashed and tried to escape, and where they kept her for three days with tape on her mouth and over her eyes. When they were done with her, they shoved her back outside the van's sliding door and onto the same dirt road where they had first found her jogging. After that, Beatrice didn't come over anymore. Even after the men were caught and convicted of her rape as well as others before hers, Beatrice still didn't come over. The last Chris heard of Beatrice she had dropped out of school, and her family had moved, taking her with them, but no one knew where. Chris was alone then in the evenings. Her parents decided she was old enough to stay by herself and put herself to bed, but sleep never came easily. She would think about Beatrice and how much she missed her.

I have felt tired since then, Chris thinks. And my husband now too, makes me feel tired. Lately, Paul has being waking her up in the middle of the night because he's been coming home late from work. Yes, ever since Beatrice and ever since Paul I've been tired, she thinks. But it's not the kind of tired that sleep could cure, it's the kind of tired that gets in your bones and becomes a part of you, a thing you carry around, Chris thinks while she's on the seat in the bathroom, still not wanting to get up even though she's finished.

This is you, Annie, mother of two swim-team girls, Sofia and Alex, wife of Thomas. This is you at the facility, walking in the crowded foyer because a meet is taking place and there are swimmers and families of swimmers from teams all over New England lined up to buy tee shirts with the name of the swim meet on them, and there is the hot machine that presses and glues the letters of the names of the swimmer onto a tee shirt and it stinks up the foyer so that it smells like rubber burning. This is you checking the time, knowing that in half an hour you will have to go on deck and help time the racers alongside Adam, the father of two boys on the team. This is you looking around the foyer, seeing other parents and other swimmers talking to each other, buying snacks, and using the restroom. This is you looking for a second at the newspaper lying on the cheery Moroccan-blue front desk of the facility. There is an article about a woman found dead out west in Denver. The police were triumphant, though. They caught the man and he confessed to strangling five women in the city over the past ten years. You are thankful you don't live out west, with the smog, and the craggy dry mountains, and the stranglers. You are thankful your children are raised here, where they can walk down the back-country roads any time of day without feeling scared. Where the air is crisp with cold in winter and smells of moist green grass in the summer, where the mountains are covered in maple and pine, and where there are almost no strangers. Here is a place where the UPS man knows you and gives your dog a biscuit and lets your chickens hop onto the steps of his truck, where they peck at the bumps in the corrugated metal. Here, if your car is parked at the market, the UPS man knows it's okay to open up the back and put your package in there to save himself the trip on the dirt roads to your house. You are glad you live in a place where everyone leaves their cars and their houses unlocked, where the librarian calls you at home to let you know the book you have on hold is available, or if she doesn't call, she might swing by your house and leave it on your porch, along with a book that is new to the library and that she also thought you might like.

You don't read the entire article about the strangler in Denver. It's too grisly, too far away, and too foreign. Not like the facility, where right now there are so many youths looking well fed and fit, so many boys with perfect complexions and girls dressed in brightly colored suits, standing and talking to parents who wear fashionably understated and relaxed looking clothes.

You look around the facility. There is Kim's mother, who is nervous but tries not to show it, even though she is pacing in front of the glass window with a view onto the pool because she is scared that Kim won't win her event in her fly. Kim has wanted to win an event in the fly because it has been so long since she has won and she used to win her fly so often. Oh, and look, there is Sofia, your eldest, your pretty thirteen-year-old, running up to you before her event and telling you she is starving and that you have to buy her something to eat or she'll die. This is you telling Sofia that if she's hungry then she should eat part of the peanut butter and jelly sandwich you packed for her, and this is Sofia scrunching up her face so that her thinly tapered perfect eyebrows, which look as if they're painted on and which you wish you had yourself, form peaks so that now it looks as though two small mountains are perched on top of each one of her soft brown eyes. This is you looking into the pool through the glass windows and seeing the display board in the pool area that tells in bright lights which event the swimmers are on, and then this is you saying, "Don't you have the two-hundred IM soon?" even though you know her event isn't for a while. This is Sofia also knowing she doesn't have her event soon—but knowing your answer means she can't buy something to eat—turning on her barefoot heel, going back inside the pool area with her head raised, and holding her towel on her shoulders as if it's a stole and she's striding off into the cold air of night instead of entering a hot, steamy, and very crowded pool deck.

This is you, Annie, in the foyer, the smell of the burning rubber from the hot tee-shirt machine making you feel sick, making you wish for a moment you were back home instead, almost an hour away, taking a walk through your fields, noticing how the moss was already coming up in soft mounds in the shade by the stream where a layer of thinning ice, thin as a sheet of plastic wrap, still covered the small trout below.

This is you in the foyer, thinking about how the burnt rubber smells almost like gunpowder after a shot has been fired, and this leads to you thinking about how your older brother, who was fifty-four, shot himself in the head two years ago because his wife had told him that week that she wanted to leave him. This is you wondering how he was able to do it, having teenage children he would leave behind, and how much blood there was, and how fucking stupid he was. His family never guessed he was capable of it, but maybe there were previous signs. Your brother could not stand it when your father left your mother for another woman. He could not stand it that your father never visited you or your brother. Your father never came by or called, and your brother, being the only son in the family, thought it was up to him to be the man now. But he could not be the man. He was still a boy. He played baseball on a team called the Cougars and collected buffalo nickels inside of binders filled with blue-colored cardboard pages, fitting the coins into rigid slots shaped like half moons. He played trumpet, his lips after practice puffy and red, and your ears ringing with the brassy notes of "The Carnival of Venice" long after he stopped his practice session. He played monster in chase, you would scream when he ran after you, because he had that chipped tooth that looked like a fang, and he was so much bigger than you, you knew he could catch you. It was just a matter of time before he grabbed you and threw you down and tickled you until you cried. Now you are not so young, and being not so young, you think you shouldn't be thinking about milk that can't be unpoured, so you stop thinking about your brother, and think about the bathing suits for sale at the facility instead. There are suits so low in the back they look as if the dog from the Coppertone ad on the billboards were biting and pulling down on them.

This is you watching Kim, the girl who did not swim her hundred fly as fast as she thought she could. Her tears mixing with pool water dripping from her hair, which she just removed from her cap. Her shoulders heaving, the sobbing visible, even though the sound of it can't be heard. The voices so loud in the stands because spectators are cheering on other swimmers in a race after hers. The swimmer who wins in the race after hers raises her fist in the air, smiling.

CHAPTER TWO

*T*his is the killer. Our killer, not the killer from out west. He is in the stands watching Kim. He is a man with dark, wavy hair and a forehead with wrinkles so thick they look like steps. He has also read the article about the strangler out west. He thinks the killer was stupid to be caught, but he is also jealous of the strangler because it has been a long time since he himself has killed. He notices how even from far away he can see Kim's heart beating through her swimsuit. He can see how her cheeks are flushed from breathing so hard. He looks to see if her neck flutters. Can her pulse be that strong beneath her ivory skin? He notices how bright her eyes are, how the tears welling up in them have made her look so alive. Is there a way to have this light for my own? he thinks. This is Kim not noticing the killer. Not many people do. He is quiet. He does not cheer. He just watches what's down on the pool deck.

This is Kim thinking how much she wanted to win the race,

how if she had won she could go home and place the blue ribbon on the string that she has strung from one wall to the other across her room. She could hang it beside all of the other ribbons strung up on that string from all of her six years as a swimmer. After only her first year she was able to cover the length of the string with ribbons, and now she has so many that she tapes them to the bottoms of the ribbons already hanging. Her mother refers to it as her "wall of ribbons," and thinks that if Kim cared less about the ribbons and more about improving her technique, then she'd actually win more ribbons. To Kim it's not a wall of ribbons but more like a curtain of ribbons, because when the window is open, letting in a breeze carried across the tall grass and daisies that dot her side yard, the curtain of ribbons shudders and flaps. Kim likes the curtain, thinking how one day, when the ribbons reach down to her bedroom floor, then she might pull the curtain aside, step out from behind it, show the world who she is, but right now she likes hiding behind it because all that it says about her is that she's a champion swimmer, and maybe that's all she wants people to know about her because right now she's not even sure herself about who she is, and she learned long ago that you don't make the mistake of telling anyone how you feel. Once, when she was a girl of ten, she told an older girl she knew that she liked the girl's brother. Kim and the brother were friends. They lived down the road from each other and played in the stream for hours at a time, creating dams and waterfalls with rocks that fed into crystal clear pools where she could see the reflection of the two of them working, their knobby, scuffed knees sometimes touching. When the older girl told her brother that Kim liked him, he stopped coming over. After a big rain, the rocks they had moved to create the waterfalls fell out of place, and white water whooshed by full force, without stopping, without creating calm pools of water Kim could see her face in. It was then she joined a swim team and swam as hard as she could to forget.

Do you know how the strokes are performed? There are officials who know if you don't. They will tell you the rules. A child doing breaststroke has to double-hand touch at the wall. A child doing butterfly cannot kick like a frog. A glide to the wall in the backstroke can't start before the flags. A wiggling foot on the blocks at the start is a false start and allowed only once. A fall where the swimmer enters the water is also a false start and allowed only once. One false start in a relay is a DQ for the entire team, a disqualification.

This is you, Annie, at the facility, looking in through the glass windows at the pool where a boys' race is being swum. The swim team is coed, but there are not as many boys as girls, so the boys' heats are fewer in number. It must be a first heat you are watching, because so many of the swimmers are inexperienced and swimming poorly, and you see at least three officials in their white polo shirts and their blue shorts raising a hand in the air, letting the judges know a swimmer performed a stroke incorrectly. This is you with your thoughts wandering while watching the boys. This is you remembering how hard your brother laughed days before he shot himself when you saw him on his birthday at his house. Your parents, both dead a few years now, of course weren't there, but his children were, and you noticed how it was easy to see how your kids and his were related. They shared the same dark features and olive skin. Their laughter even sounded similar to you, their voices sounding in the same range. But whose laughter was like yours now? you thought. Your parents were gone and now your brother. You realized then you were the last one left in your family, and in that moment, where you were completely feeling sorry for yourself, you felt like an orphan.

This is you now bent over the water fountain at the facility. The hot air makes you so thirsty. You wish the water could enter your mouth more quickly. You wonder why water fountains have to move from the bottom up and why they can't come from the ceiling down, straight into your mouth, where gravity would probably be on your side and help quench your thirst that much faster.

This is you minutes later up in the bleachers, the boys' heats are over, and now you are watching your daughter Sofia swim a one-hundred free. You notice how she still isn't using her walls and streamlines, and those turns that when you straighten out and push off the wall you are not breathing, and it isn't until you are at the flags again that you come up for a breath. The turns are hard to do, but the coaches want the swimmers to use them because they save so much time. Even though Sofia isn't using those turns, she still has a faster time. You write her time down on the heat sheet you bought that lists all the entries and heats of the swimmers. The heats are being run with the slowest girls first and the fastest girls last, so that for example if you have sixty girls in the race and a ten-lane pool, you'll have six heats of ten girls each, the last heat being the fastest and the overall winner most likely coming out of that race. You like watching your daughters swim, but if they don't swim well in a race, you don't mention it. You are always proud of them, even when they don't lose time, because they always work hard in practice and try to swim their fastest in a race. Thomas, your husband, thinks that you have the girls on the swim team as much for your benefit as for theirs. This is true. You like being able to swim when your girls swim and you like talking to the other parents on the team. It's a social place for you. You also like seeing your girls progress and cheering them on at a meet and being involved in their lives and speaking their language about workouts and strokes and technique. You're even in their social sphere a little more because you know the other girls on the swim team they come home and talk about. You know Hayley's mother's a rock singer in a band and that Hayley can sing pretty well herself and takes chorus and that her class was invited to D.C. to sing on the Capitol steps. You know that Kali's mom gets migraines and that she's allergic to gluten. You know that Chris, Cleo's mother, is a professional artist, because your girls are friends with Cleo and you've been to Chris's house to drop off the girls and she's shown you her studio and her canvasses heavy with oil paints depicting dark assemblages of wildflowers sprawling on the surface without reference points, as if the flowers were stars almost, growing without being tied to the earth, and floating in space. When you want to talk about how you freelance as a wedding photographer in order to supplement the family income and be able to afford the family vacations, you can talk with Kali's mom. You can talk to her about how it's sometimes difficult to deal with soon-to-be brides and their families because Kali's mom is the owner of a five-star inn that hosts weddings and serves organic fiddleheads. When you want to talk about how the skiing was great over the weekend after a huge snowfall of heavenly powder, you talk to Emma's dad, who also skis. When you want to talk about the new curriculum the state is adopting for the school system, and the new assessment test they'll use that has to be taken on a computer and how you're nervous your girls don't type well enough, you can talk to Nick's mom, who's a middle school teacher. And of course, if you want to talk about swimming and your own children, you can talk to anyone around you, even the mothers and fathers you don't think you have anything in common with, because every parent there can talk swimming. They understand what a fast fly time might be. They can make a remark about how a certain stroke-and-turn official might be inattentive during a race and never catch a DQ. They can look at a set of twenty-one one-hundred frees on a 1:20 that the coach wrote on the board for her swimmers to swim and know that is a tough workout.

This is Dinah, seeing how your daughter Sofia out-touched her daughter Jessie in the one-hundred free, even though Jessie used her streamlines and turns. This is Dinah coming up to you while you're about to go down the stairs to the foyer saying that she did not see your Sofia using her streamlines and turns, and that she thought all the girls were supposed to be using them now. This is you shrugging, saying, "I suppose she'll start using them one day, but can you blame her? That's a long time to hold your breath and swim hard at the same time." This is Dinah thinking how when she talks to the coach after the meet, she will let the coach know that she noticed Sofia is not using her walls and streamlines. This is Dinah thinking how she hates it when others don't do what they're supposed to do, and how Annie and her daughters always seem to be doing what they're not supposed to do. For example, Annie, because she couldn't afford all the equipment, never bought her girls the required fins they need for workouts, and instead, before a kick set, lets them dig through the bin on deck filled with ones that were left behind from swimmers years before. Dinah thinks how that's not right, especially when it says right there in the handbook that the required equipment to purchase is a water bottle, a kick-board, and fins. Then there are the instances, Dinah thinks, when Annie asks the coach for special permission to age her youngest daughter up at a meet so that her youngest daughter can swim in the same session as her oldest daughter, just for convenience's sake, so that Annie won't have to be at a swim meet for two five-hour sessions back to back. This is frowned upon, of course, because it means Annie's youngest is swimming with older swimmers, and usually, therefore, faster swimmers. Dinah doesn't approve of this at all, since it means the afternoon session goes that much slower because there is a slower swimmer entered. Then there are the re-quired parent meetings that Annie doesn't go to some of the time. Instead, on those days, Dinah sees Annie swimming in a lane in the pool, while almost all the other parents are packed into a stuffy utility room off the pool, sitting on folding chairs and listening to a lecture by the coaches about volunteering for the team, or listen-ing to a guest lecturer about the importance of feeding your swim-mer carbohydrates and avocado the day before a meet, when that's the last thing Dinah wants to serve her daughter, Jessie, who, like herself, is already carrying too many pounds. Dinah once told the coach afterward that she saw Annie in the pool swimming while the rest of them were in the meeting. The coach sighed. "There's not much I can do," she said. Dinah told the coach maybe there was something she could do. "Maybe you could kick her kids off the team," Dinah said, to which the coach replied, "Dinah, it's been a long night and I am going home now."

CHAPTER THREE

*T*his is Mandy, the cleaning lady. She has always been concerned about her teeth. They cross over in the front so that they look like a row of theatergoers in the first seats with all of their legs crossed. Of course it would be a summer show, everyone in shorts with legs exposed. A showing, maybe, of *Showboat*, or some other summertime show. Maybe *West Side Story*. This is Mandy sweeping the floor in the locker room, seeing if what she should be sweeping into the dustpan can be swept down into the drain instead, thinking about Natalie Wood, how she drowned in the sea, and what a shame that was.

Some of the swim-team mothers talk to Mandy, and some pass her by, and some just nod slightly when they see her with her mop in her hand, pushing the water that has come off their daughters' bodies and onto the tiles. Some know all about Mandy and how she and her husband go fishing and how their daughter works at a clothing store selling clothes she would never wear because they are all clothes for outdoor enthusiasts and Mandy says her twenty-year-old daughter's idea of outdoor enthusiasm is firing up a barbecue and grilling a few sirloins. Some don't even know that Mandy's front teeth are all crooked because they have never looked up at Mandy to see her smiling. Some assume that because she's at the pool her income is the same as that of everyone else who can afford to pay the six-hundred-dollar individual membership for the facility, or can afford to pay over one thousand dollars just to have her child swim on the team for one season. Some confuse Mandy with the other cleaning lady, or even with the cleaning man, who is as round as Mandy and who also wears glasses. Some think Mandy is part of the coaching team and they ask Mandy questions like when is the next meet and what time does it start. Some think Mandy is another swim-team parent and they ask her which one is her child and which squad does she swim on: developmental, juniors, or pre-seniors? Some think Mandy works in the snack bar, and when they see her in the bathroom or in the hall, and there is no one working the snack bar, they wish she would just get back to her job selling snacks because they'd like to buy a bagel or a chocolate milk or an electrolyte vitamin-fortified drink for their swimmer. Some think Mandy works in the weight and exercise room and writes your name down when you enter the sweat-smelling room and adjusts the fans so that they blow on you while you run on the treadmill and programs the two overhead televisions so that one is always airing a talk show and one is always airing sports. Some think Mandy works the front desk and checks your ID card and holds the key to the glass case that sells goggles and water bottles for an exorbitant price. Some think Mandy is just a gym fanatic who comes every day but never looks any thinner, despite all that spinning and sweating.

This is Kim in the warm-down lane still crying over the race she just finished and trying to correct herself, trying to lift her rear higher out of the water thinking that because her sixteen-year-old body's changing, and her bottom half's getting heavier, it's causing her to sink more, but when she lifts her rear higher, her arms go deeper, which causes her chest to dive deeper, which makes her recovery all that much slower because her arms encounter that much more resistance.

This is you timing with Adam. This is Adam telling you how his boys don't even like to swim on the team but would rather play in the locker room and fill their swim caps up with shower water and throw the water at each other. You know his boys, you have seen how they like going down the slide in the water park next to the competition pool with their eyes closed and their arms crossed in front of themselves like dead people in open caskets, only they're alive and doing it for maximum speed. Together you and Adam look up at the timing board when the names of the swimmers appear, and you wonder what officials at Ellis Island would have renamed these kids if they had just walked off the boat. Lipshutz would be "Lips," you think. This is you forgetting to press the plunger and stop your stopwatch when a kid comes swimming into the wall for the touch because you are thinking of last names the kids will never have. This is you writing down a time for the kid anyway, looking at Adam's time and changing yours a few tenths of a second so that it looks believable, because even though the times of the swimmers are important to the swimmers, this swimmer will not have a competitive time. It will be enough for the swimmer to know that maybe she knocked off a few seconds from her seedtime, but that is all.

This is Adam asking you if you happened to hear the news about that awful strangler out west. This is you saying, yes, how awful. This is Adam saying, "Thank God we live here. I mean, that's why my wife and I moved out of Boston, to get away from exactly those kinds of horrors." He says in the rural town where he lives, a town similar to yours and also an hour away from the facility, the school board member is the greengrocer who is also the animal control officer who is also married to the postmistress, who herself is head of the recreation committee and whose brother is the volunteer fireman and the select board member and the general store owner, and that brother's wife is the town clerk and the PTO head and the notary, and her brother is the librarian of the one-room library that's open only two afternoons a week and boasts a working fireplace, one computer for browsing, and a perpetually filled barrel of oyster crackers for the taking of patrons who come up the porch and pass through the pleasantly creaking screen door. This is you agreeing, saying, "Yes, we are lucky to be able to raise our children here."

This is Chris outside, the air on her wet blue jeans feeling good. She breathes in deeply—all the other fathers are watching her breathe. Her jeans fitting well over a small round rear, over thin legs. Her blond hair blonder now in the spring sunlight that makes water droplets on new grass glisten. Her breasts through her thin jacket almost visible, she isn't wearing a bra, she doesn't need to.

This is Dinah telling her daughter, Jessie, that in her next race she has to swim harder than she's ever swum before. This is Jessie, a big girl whose practice suits stretch so tightly against her big belly that the polyester is almost see-through and one can see the white of her skin, telling her mother that she was singing, "This old man, he played one," in her head while she raced. This is Dinah groaning, and saying, "Sing something else. Anything else. Sing some rock. Sing some AC/DC." This is Dinah's daughter saying she doesn't know any rock or ADHD. This is Dinah saying, "It's AC/DC." Then saying, "Forget the song. Swim like a great white shark is after you." Dinah's daughter says, "But there isn't a great white shark after me." Dinah sighs, "Okay, if you drop your time I'll give you a dollar for every second." This is Dinah thinking how she cannot imagine how overweight Jessie would be if she did not swim. Dinah herself never did sports as a kid, and maybe if she had, she wouldn't be fat like she is now, and maybe she would have friends, because all of the girls on the team seem to have friends. She has seen Jessie and her friends stopping at the wall between sets, talking to each other, laughing with each other, and splashing each other. She has seen them before practice huddled next to someone's locker, showing each other their latest clothing purchase, the latest series book to read.

This is Dinah hoping her daughter Jessie doesn't turn out to be a bumbler like her father, Joseph, a man Dinah married years ago because she thought he'd be a good father, which he is, but that was the only reason she married him. This is Dinah hoping her daughter doesn't turn out to be like Dinah either, an overweight woman who has almost no friends and knows that she has almost no friends because she is critical of everyone else's behavior and doesn't understand why people can't live by high moral standards and beliefs the way she always has. To Dinah, all things carry equal weight: Writing thank-you notes by hand to people who give you gifts ranks up there with not stealing from a store. Hanging up on a telemarketer is just as disrespectful and deplorable as cheating on a spouse. The few friends she has made over the years were always subject to her wrath when they made the slightest mistake in her eyes—"What? You keep in contact with old boyfriends? You might as well be having an affair with them!"—and they gradually stopped being her friend. That was also a mistake in Dinah's eyes. If they were stronger people, they would see that she only made comments to help them become better people. Dinah knows she's uptight, but doesn't feel it's right to deny that part of her. It would be like cheating on herself. Dinah's husband is someone who always defends people like Annie, who don't see the importance of following all the rules to a T, and he says that other mothers on the team, who are so uptight about doing everything the team asks of them, could learn from Annie's more relaxed attitude.

It's work for Dinah to drive Jessie forty-five minutes to the pool every day after school and sit and wait for the two-hour practice to be over, but in the long run she feels it's the best gift she can give her daughter, like a get-out-of-jail-free card allowing her a disassociation from those twisted strands, those DNA, she inherited. Joseph is not especially handsome or smart or funny (he looks and acts goofy, always tripping on stairs and hitting his big square-shaped head on low doorways), but he has been a good father—always there to scoop their daughter up in his arms after a fall or to whisk her off to the doctor when need be, with a trip afterward to the ice cream parlor. But now that Jessie is older and doesn't need that kind of fatherly attention anymore, Dinah feels she doesn't need Joseph either. It's as if both daughter and mother have outgrown him. To make matters worse, he's losing his hearing, a condition caused by one too many deer hunting trips during which he's shot a rifle off close to his ear, and as a result he's yelling more because he can't hear himself and thinks no one else can hear him either, so now Dinah's yelling more too, trying to get him to understand everyday things like, "I'm taking Jessie to practice tomorrow, you make the dinner," or "We'll be home from practice late, be sure to take the roast out of the oven." What's made him even more annoying is that in the past few weeks he's asked that she become some kind of a translator for him. When he talks to people and he can't understand them, he turns to her and says, "What did they say?" His hearing is affecting his work as a real estate salesman, and he's asked Dinah to come along with him a few times on a showing to help translate, but she's now refusing to do it. A part of this has to do with time—being a manager of a prosthetic supplier, she has to work nine to five shipping off artificial arms and legs gently packed in Bubble Wrap and Styrofoam popcorn. A part of it has to do with her not wanting to have to take care of him in any way, and a part of it is her not wanting to have to meet rich couples touring high-end houses.

This is our killer. He drives fifteen minutes from the facility back to his home. He lives in an apartment he has lived in for twenty-five years. He has lines in his forehead so deep they could serve as stairs for a small doll. He has a washer and dryer in his kitchen, and when he eats meals he usually starts a load to wash or dry so that he has the sound of one of the machine's drums turning to keep him company. As a killer, he has pride, he thinks, and does not want to be caught, the way so many experts think serial killers want to be. He is not like that careless killer out west all over the news who, as a matter of fact, made this killer want to kill again, just to prove it can be done right. It has been so many years since the last time. It makes him hungry again. Why shouldn't I be able to once again see the light go out of a young woman's eyes? he thinks. He thinks about Kim. He has been watching her for a few months. He thinks how Kim's eyes, once she starts winning again, will be fever-bright with excitement and satisfaction. All he has to do is wait for that moment.

This is Kim at home at night watching butterfly technique videos and practicing, lying chest-down on the ottoman, trying to imitate the swimmer on the screen. The ottoman's fabric has a coarse weave almost like a burlap sack and is uncomfortable on her skin, and her little sister, who is eight, keeps telling Kim how she swims butterfly and that maybe Kim should swim it more like she does, which doesn't help Kim since her sister is like a rubber band and has such a flexible back she sometimes walks around the house in a backbend, reporting on what she sees on the ceiling, just for the fun of it.

While lying in bed that night, behind her curtain of ribbons, Kim thinks about how her dream for years has been to go to age groups, zones, sectionals, then junior nationals, then nationals, and then of course the Olympics. Things looked as if they were headed that way for a long time. Every season she improved her times, and every year she was going to more age-group meets and then zone meets, and sectionals, and even out west to California for juniors, but this season she's slipping backward. She thinks she should get out of bed and sit at her desk and study for her history test tomorrow, but she's too tired. Who cares, anyway, she wonders, if Caesar was a villain or just ambitious? "I care," she responds, and she means it. She wants to keep getting all A's in school, so she turns on the light, gets up, puts her robe on, and opens up her history book. When she falls asleep reading at one a.m., her pale blond hair, which she wishes were blonder, more the color of corn silk than what she thinks looks ghostlike and wispy, is spread across an illustration of Caesar crossing the Rubicon.

CHAPTER FOUR

This is you at home at night after the meet hanging up towels, wet and smelling like chlorine, and this is you with Sofia and Alex, looking at the swim videos you took of them earlier in the day, your girls stopping the frames now and then to see exactly where they started to slow down or when they reached out to touch the wall. They joke and make remarks like, "I wasn't going to let the girl in the lane next to me win. I thought, This is my race, all mine!" they say. This is you later, looking at yourself in the mirror and hoping to see Chris in the reflection instead. Chris who has the breasts she can wear with no bra, and the rear all the swim-team dads stare at when they should be watching the race they're timing. You know you will never be like Chris. You look out the window at the moonlight on the trees and on the rock wall. It makes the rocks glow. It makes the trees appear as though their leaves are made of silver.

You think about you. How if you were to describe yourself

to someone, you would empty out your purse on the table. You would not have to say anything. Your ChapStick that's never used will talk for you. Your receipts from another country close to the equator that for some reason you've left in there for almost a year will talk for you. Your picture of your friend from years ago will talk for you. The hairbrush with hair from not only your head, but also Sofia and Alex's heads, will talk for you. Then you sit on your unmade bed, the bed you never make except before you're ready to go to bed, and you wonder who that someone would be who would want to know about you in the first place. You cannot think of anyone who would want to get to know you that well ever again. You wonder if your husband, Thomas, knows what you have in your purse. If he even has any clue. When he comes into your room to brush his teeth in the bathroom you say, "Do you have any idea what's in my purse?" Thomas brushes his teeth for too long, you have always thought. He's going to abrade his gums and someday they will peel away from his teeth like a pink strip of stretched-out bubble gum that's already been chewed. He is brushing his teeth too long now, and of course not answering you because he is brushing his teeth. When he is finally finished he rinses his mouth and then takes a long time dabbing at it with a towel that is still wet and smells like chlorine from when the girls used it after their races during the swim meet. If I were Chris, the swim-team mom with the breasts and the rear, you think, I bet he would not wait so long to answer me. He would have talked through his brushing and his toothpaste foam to say in a mumble, "Yes, dear," or "No, dear." Apparently, though, Thomas never heard the question about your purse. "I've got a great idea how to make money," Thomas says. "Do you want to hear it?" he asks. Thomas does not ever wait for you to answer his questions, and starts telling you his ideas anyway.

This great idea is not so great, you think. He wants to develop a water gun that horse owners can use on dogs so that dogs don't endanger them when they're on horseback on the rural roads where you live. You think, why not just a regular water gun, the kind your daughter Alex has that blasts hose-sized streams of water more than fifty feet? You don't tell Thomas, though, that his great idea is not so great. Instead you turn away from him in bed, facing the window where you can see the moon on the birch tree making its bark appear frozen white.

This is Thomas in bed lying next to you, patting your arm once before you fall asleep. Thomas has dispensed with the kissing. You think this happened two years ago when the work he does in his research lab started becoming more difficult, coincidentally around the same time your brother shot himself. There is too much worry for Thomas now, what with managing the other researchers and creating the antibodies that he sells. You think that where his lab is located adds to his stress. It's near the local commuter airport, and wouldn't the constant screech of tires hitting the tarmac and the smell of airplane fuel in the air run him down? This is you facing the wall, wondering if the kissing would make a difference. In the morning, would you love him any better because he kissed you on the lips? Would you love him any worse? This is you wishing hours later when he wakes up and makes his way to the toilet in the thick, cloudy darkness of night that he hadn't woken you up. This is the house whistling, the wind coming in through windows not all the way closed. This is you wondering if there is such a thing as wife energy, and if you had it whether maybe you would love

Thomas more. Maybe Thomas would be kissing you at night instead of patting you on the arm. If you had wife energy, he would be complimented more often. You would tell him how smart he is. You would tell him you like the way his hair looks when it grows long. You would tell him he did a fine job with the mower, that the fields look like golf courses. You would tell him he is funny instead of listening to funny things he says and not laughing out loud, just laughing inside, because the outside laughter takes energy, and you have used the energy up already. You have used it when listening to your teenage daughter call you names. You have used up your energy trying not to get angry, trying not to care, so that she would eventually stop. You have used up the energy reaching behind you while driving and grabbing a book from your daughters that they were fighting over. You have used it up closing a window. Yes, just a window, you thought to yourself while doing it. The window was heavy and hard to pull down. You had to put your back into that window. What was the use of all that swimming you did at the facility while your daughters were practicing if you could not even close a window?

Outside the house the bats are catching moths and slamming into the windowpanes. There are many moths now that the weather is warmer. You saw one the last time you shot a wedding. You photographed a luna moth fluttering by the bride's face just as she said, "I do." It was a photo you liked, the luna moth covering the bride's mouth with its lime-green body. But the bride did not like the photo and said it was a shame you hadn't taken one without the moth, as if you were the one who had called upon the moth to come fluttering by at that moment, as if you were the one who was trying to cover up the evidence of the words "I do" being spoken.

You keep the photo anyway, in a drawer along with other photos you liked that the brides did not because they were not photos about their wedding day. Some are close-ups of flowers, a gardenia with a ladybug walking on its petals. Some are of the distorted, elephantine reflection of someone's legs in the steel gray side of a guest's car.

"It's great that the bats are back," Thomas said a few days ago, and then you took your wool coat off its hook by the door and stored it on a shelf in a glass case, afraid the moths would find it. Even the glass case took your energy. You had to lift up on the handle while shutting it or it wouldn't close all the way, and while you were closing it, Thomas was talking to you, or rather he was reading to you from his magazine. He wanted you to know how smart it was that he tutored the girls all year round because according to his magazine, schools were dumbing down textbooks, and dumbing down tests, and dumbing down courses in public schools. These were things you somehow already knew about. It wasn't an article that was shedding any new light on what you already had learned as a parent of two children in the school system. "Stop already," you said to him, "I know all this," but Thomas did not listen and he kept reading, loudly, his deep voice seeming to resonate through your own chest because he was standing so close to you, wanting you to listen, and he was so loud that you could feel his voice inside yourself, behind your rib cage, like the rumble of a nasty chest cough.

And you wonder if, like Dinah's husband, he too is losing his hearing from his hunting rifle going off by his ear so many times. But really he didn't shoot that often. You know this because years ago, before you had children, the two of you would hunt together on your property. He would sit high on a ridge overlooking the slender stream in your valley, and you, lower down, would face the opposite way, toward acres and acres of woods thick with nettles and scrub pines and tangles of blackberry bushes. You would sit very still and the few times you saw a buck, you would not shoot. You did not want it to die. You did not want to have to drag it home after chasing it in the woods, after following drops of blood and the sound of it stumbling. You did not want to have to eat its lean meat. You would let the deer pass by, and a few hours later after you learned to feel the quiet, and you became part of the quiet yourself, then your husband would rise from where he sat and come down toward you, and the sounds of his hard-heeled boots crunching on the leaves and his stiff canvass coat bending back and breaking branches were so loud compared to the quiet you were just a part of that it seemed as if there were an entire herd of your husband crashing through the woods. "Did you see anything?" he would ask, trying to whisper, but even his whisper was loud. Cradling your rifles as you walked back to your house, and then emptying out the bullets on the front lawn before you entered, you would shake your head. "No, not unless you count a few squirrels and a few noisy birds," you would say. Slowly, over the years, you stopped going hunting with him, and so he would tell your girls, "Just wait until you are old enough. I will take you hunting. You can take your mother's rifle." But he himself was less fond of killing the deer than he was of just sitting quietly on the ridge, and so he would come home with just the smell of the leaves on him, bringing in the cold air when he opened the door.

CHAPTER FIVE

*T*his is a qualifier meet weeks later when the weather is warmer. Driving two hours south to the away meet, you pass trees on the sides of the highway that look faintly green, the buds on the ends of their branches brand-new. You think how in a week's time there will be leaves on the trees up by where you live too. No longer will people driving in cars on your road be able to turn their heads and look up at your house as it sits high on a hill, the copper roof like the buds on these trees, just starting to turn faint green with age. Once again, the trees will grow leaves and the bushes and the blond, tall grass will grow, and no one will be able to see you and your family walking through the rooms of your house: Thomas on the phone with the lab that he runs arguing with a staff member because for months now, almost a year, batches of bacteria he's been growing to target a gene are failing and he can't figure out if it's due to a virus, contaminated water, or a temperature problem, and it's driving Thomas crazy. You at the sink staring at your face in the mirror thinking if you were a bride you had to photograph, then you would have a hard time finding the right light to photograph yourself in—you would have to pull far back with the lens in order to capture the slightest hint of youth, of beauty, of any camera-worthiness at all. Those people in the cars below your hill on your road on a sunny summer's day with the leaves and the blossoms in full riot would not be able to see your girls bent over homework, or standing tall, practicing, holding small chins over the warmly colored wood of old violins.

This is the dead pool at the away meet, a huge affair built years ago and named after a man who has been dead for years in a town that looks like it's dead, located on a college campus that looks like it's dead, where the people shuffling into the store at the gas station to buy weak coffee look like they're near dead. The dead pool, the moment you enter it, is so hot you feel your blood evaporating and your tongue thickening, and you're already wanting a drink of water. The course is long, twice as long as the swimmers are used to. This is the national anthem. Who can hear it being played over a sound system so old?

You eat grapes. The grapes have already become warm because the facility is so warm. You talk to the other parents. "Aren't we lucky," you tell each other. "We don't have to time today. The home team has enough timers." But you don't feel lucky. You like to time. You like to be down on deck doing something. The children, the young ones, need to be asked their names. They need to be in the right order. You cannot have someone diving off the blocks who is not in the right order on the heat sheet. The swimmers are nervous and they are bored standing on line at the same time. They play with their goggles. They put them on and take them off so many times. On line, the girls give each other back massages or they spell letters with their fingers on each other's backs and make each other guess what word they are spelling. They play a game called ninja, which you don't understand even though your daughters have explained it to you. The girls all jump together and then end up with their hands in different poses as if they were karate-chopping the air. It reminds you of the game of statues you played as a girl, only these statues always end up in a fighting stance.

Since you are not timing today, you have time to think, which is not always a good thing. The first races are the five-hundred frees, and Sofia and Alex are not in this event, and it is a long event. You look around at the crowd in the bleachers, and as usual there is someone who reminds you of your brother. You notice a man with a chipped front tooth and it reminds you of your brother, but your brother only had a chipped tooth for so long. When he was older, after he married, he had the tooth fixed, but still when you picture your brother, it's always with that chipped front tooth. Maybe it's because when you played chase with your brother, that tooth looked sharp, like it could tear the skin on your back, on your neck, if he caught you. You try to stop thinking about your brother. You are always thinking about him when you are alone, when Thomas isn't there talking to you about something he's read in a magazine, when your girls aren't there asking you questions, asking you to help with their homework, to tell them the difference between to, too, and two. You are alone because Thomas is too busy with work to come to most of these meets.

He works weekend days at the lab, bent over proteins, fussing over radioactive isotopes, hearing outside his window the screech of plane wheels grabbing tarmac, the roaring of engines, the voices of people in a hurry, trundling suitcases with wheels over long distances of asphalt from car trunk to check-in. You lower your head while sitting in the bleachers, looking down at your hands, your signature veins popping out as if you just had too much blood running through you and the walls of your veins were on the verge of bursting. You remember what Thomas told you about a phenomenon, that of all the matter in the universe, we only see 4 percent of it. "Does that include air?" you asked. "Yes, it includes air," he said. "We know what air is. We can see it. But there is so much we can't see, and we don't even know what it is. It's invisible to us." You knew you were supposed to be impressed by only being able to see 4 percent of what was around you and in front of you, but you couldn't help thinking that for you it was less than 4 percent, because you couldn't see air the way Thomas could see air. He could probably visualize water vapor and oxygen and CO_2, but you could not.

These are your fingers, sore at the ends from trying to pull up the competitive swim-team suit over Sofia's body when you first arrived at the facility and you stood in the stall in the bathroom. This is you, dialing Thomas, who you think by now has left his work at the lab and gone home. This is you telling him you have arrived at the meet, telling him you guess you are lucky, you don't have to time, and Thomas tells you he has been home already an hour and split wood, and that he has seen a fox come up close to the chickens. Already you have lost the duck and the rooster and a few hens to a fox.

This is the fox, down in the woods that are not so thick, but the maples grow thin, and the pines only reach up to the waist, and the sun has a clear path to hit strong and full on the fox's cinnamon-colored back. This is you telling Thomas that the girls here on the other swim teams look like Amazons, and that you are afraid for your girls, who are just of average weight and height, and the youngest, maybe not even average yet, maybe below average. This is the fox moving his ears from side to side, listening to Thomas's deep voice as Thomas stands out on the porch talking to you, smelling on Thomas the chainsaw oil that dripped on the knees of his pants. This is one of the Amazon girls diving into the water, going down, so far down, on her dive, as if she is too heavy to control it, and then she comes up, breaches, is what you think, and you're glad one of your children is not next to you, because if she were, you might say "breaches" out loud, and then your child would say, "Oh, Mom, how could you say that? You're not supposed to say things like that." Your children have been schooled in schools where guidance counselors give weekly lessons on bullying. Bullying is not what bullying was when I was a kid, you think. When you were a kid bullies were kids who threw another kid against the chain-link fence at recess and took the lunch money out of his pockets. Today, bullying is calling another kid a name, and bullies are kids who simply don't want to play with another kid because they don't like them. You know because Alex, your younger daughter, recently came home from school with a note saying her actions that day were considered bullying, because she and another girl openly agreed they did not want to play with another girl. The girls were overheard by a teacher. You felt then that you were only seeing a mere 1 percent of the universe. You reprimanded your daughter, and explained how that wasn't nice, but then later that night, talking to Thomas, you told him you needed clarification. Since when did all this become bullying? you asked. Thomas shook his head while reading his science magazine. You thought he was shaking his head with you, telling you he didn't know either when all of the rules changed, when what we could see in the universe started shrinking, but then he said, "Listen to this," but you didn't. You left the room. Some of his words, though, chased you down the stairs. You made out the words "quarks" and "particles" and "gluons." Your house is like one big ventriloquist. There are open parts everywhere, so that you often don't really know where a voice is coming from. You'd think a person was talking to you from the bathroom, when they were really in the rec room, or in the girls' loft. His words chased you downstairs, and seemed to get louder as you entered the kitchen, even though he hadn't moved from the bed. You had no idea what he was talking about and doubted that if you had read the article yourself you'd understand it any better.

You remembered to take a vitamin, and then felt guilty remembering, because you hadn't remembered earlier to give your children their vitamins, and they were the ones who needed them the most. All the growing of the bones, the laying down of the platelets, and your older girl, Sofia, who recently started her period, she would need more iron now, you thought. You thought of the other things she might need, things not for purchase, but intangible things like compliments, and feeling the eyes of others on her, noticing how she looks good in a dress. She might need you and Thomas to tell her how pretty she is, how strands in her hair in the summer sun look gold. You once had these things yourself, these compliments, and maybe it was not so long ago, but now they are gone, and you think maybe that is not so bad, because in a way it's as if you have given them to your daughter. They are hers now. You wonder what it was that your father once gave to your brother when he was a teenager, or was that the problem, he gave nothing to your brother at all, and your brother walked through his teenage years without this kind of passed-on gift from your father. Your brother did not take on the posture of a man who was proud. His shoulders stayed rounded. His eyes darted in conversation rather than frankly holding someone's gaze. His voice, even, still broke, rather than taking on a mellow, basslike tone.

This is the killer, our killer, at the meet watching Kim. He holds a heat sheet that he bought for three dollars from a parent sitting at a desk at the entrance to the bleachers. On the heat sheet he can see that her fastest time for her hundred fly was 1:08.74. He watches Kim behind the blocks. She is not like the other girls. She does not turn around and high-five other swimmers. She does not wave to someone who may be watching her from the stands. She stares straight out while waiting for her race, and she jogs in place and loosens up her arms, not seeming to look at anyone, not even when she hears her name being called by her teammates, who cheer her on before she gets ready for her dive. When she's on the blocks, she easily bends the top half of her body over and holds on tight to the edge of the block, so tight our killer is surprised that when she dives in the platform of the block doesn't come off in her hands and end up with her in the water. He watches how she moves, how her slender neck reaches up and out with every upswing of her arms. He wonders if today will be the day she beats her record, because that is what he is waiting for. He is confident she will do it soon. No one else focuses as hard as she does before her race. On her last lap, though, it is obvious this isn't the day. She seems to tire, either that or the other girls swimming with her get a burst of energy. She ends up touching the wall with a 1:09.75. She has gained time. When she gets out of the water she does not even go up to her coach for a bit of advice. Instead she goes right into the warm-down lane, her head sunk low between her shoulders. The killer sighs. He was looking forward to the way the blade of his knife would cut through that throat, sending all of that red blood that would be pulsing so hard from her athlete's strong heart down her shirtfront. (He couldn't understand why that strangler out west bothered to strangle. What a waste of an experience, not seeing the blood, not letting the blood do what it most wants to do—flow.) Especially, though, he was looking forward to how she would look, all of the excitement and satisfaction and energy in her eyes from having beat her record suddenly leaving, suddenly his for the taking.

CHAPTER SIX

S itting in the bleachers, trying not to turn around and yell at the parent sitting behind you who yelled at you in the first place, you imagine the sounds of the air conditioner that was in the house you rented on vacation at the equator almost a year ago. You close your eyes and imagine also the calm blue light that would come on the control panel of the air conditioner when it was turned on. You think how you loved that trip. Thomas surfed with you then. He wasn't thinking about his failing lab on the trip. You would see him riding a wave and then falling over backward when he had ridden the wave as far as he could, landing in the water with a yelp and a hoot at having had such a good ride. He walked with you on the beach at night, then stopped and held your arm. He was smiling, amazed, holding out a flashlight into the shrub-covered dunes, where hundreds of orange and purple crabs crawled, their movement sounding like pattering drops of unceasing rain. But now, since you've been back, and the problems at his lab haven't disappeared, the bacteria still aren't growing, the planes by his office at the airport are stilling screeching on the tarmac out his window, he hasn't reached out for you once, and what does it take, you think, to make him reach out to you again? This is when you hear, "Hello, Annie." It's Chris, with the perfect breasts and rear. "Hey, have a seat," you say. You then proceed to move your purse and your book to make room for her. Chris has no bags with her, not even a purse, as usual. Because you have known her a few years now you know most of her clothes. She is wearing her faded blue Levi's jeans rolled up to the ankles, tennis shoes, and a white V-neck tee shirt. Her hair is kept back with a simple black ponytail holder, and she wears no makeup. You think she is the most beautiful woman at the meet today, and then you turn around and look at all the other women in the bleachers and think you are right. Chris always smells faintly of mint, not like toothpaste mint or breath-freshener mint, but like the real mint, the kind that grows wild in your field by your house. Whenever you take a walk to the stream through the fields, you break a leaf off and pinch it and smell it.

"Cleo just told me she wants one of those suits," Chris says. "Like the ones Alex and Sofia have." With a lift of her chin she points to your girls, who are on deck.

"Oh, those," you say. "They are the biggest marketing scam. The least expensive of them costs a couple of hundred dollars, but do they really make the girls swim faster? They're so tight the girls sometimes say they can hardly breathe, but without them the girls don't think they can win the race, and if they don't think they can win it, then sometimes they don't," you say. Chris nods. You feel as if you've hurt Chris's feelings somehow. "I mean, that's great that Cleo's that into swimming that she wants one. Now you too can experience the joy of having to help pull, tug, squeeze, and jam your daughter's rear into a suit in time for her first event when her body's still wet from having swum warm-ups." Swimmers can't wear the suit during warm-ups and then also for their events that day, because that's too long to keep on a suit that sadistically tight and uncomfortable. "Welcome to the torture club," you say. Chris laughs. Her teeth are very white, in perfect rows. It is not a full-hearted laugh. It is a polite laugh. You've heard Chris make it before. She does it when she's not really listening, when she's worried, for example, about where Cleo is, if she has taken too long in the locker rooms and hasn't yet come out. But what did I expect? you think to yourself. That wasn't very funny what I just said. You pull out grapes and offer some to Chris. "They're already warm," you say. "It's so hot in here I think they're turning into wine." Chris nods, but she does not look hot at all. She is not sweating at the temples the way you are. Chris takes one grape, and then doesn't take any more. "Where's Paul today?" you ask.

"He couldn't make it," Chris says. "He's got papers to correct." You nod. Chris doesn't ask you where Thomas is, even though you are ready to tell her that he's cutting wood and splitting wood and stacking wood, and that really, for all you know, he could be eating the wood, because on any given day that he comes home from the lab, if he's not mowing the lawn, then he's doing the wood, because in the winter, all you heat with is the wood because wood heat feels warmer and saves money. This was Thomas's idea, not yours, as most things to do with the house and the family usually are, except the swim team, of course, and joining the facility, which were your ideas. Concerning the wood, you would have been happy with walking over to a dial and turning up the heat. You could have done without hauling in wood at six in the morning in the dark while trying not to slip over ice-encrusted snow. You could have done without always having splinters and small bits of wood embedded in the weave of your sweater fronts from holding the logs to your chest on your way to the woodstove. Who knew that your wrists would hurt from picking up the wood at one end and tossing it on a pile to be stacked after it was split, that it would make them inflamed, and that swellings the size of robin's eggs would appear on the inside of them? You could have done without never having the chance to read the entire paper because its pages were needed to start the fire every—

"What's the matter?" you ask Chris, because you have just noticed that Chris has a tear sliding down her cheek. Instinctively, you look toward the water, to see if it's Chris's daughter, to see if Chris's daughter, Cleo, has lost her race and that's why Chris is crying, because you remember from past meets how you have seen tears in parents' eyes. You have seen tears in the eyes of Dinah, for example, who cried with joy a few years ago when her daughter made it to age groups, a more competitive division, in the fifty breast. You thought then that for Dinah Jessie's success was more about her than her daughter. You've seen plenty of girls cry too, and even boys, when they've lost races. You have seen parents cry when their children who have lost a race cry. You have seen parents cry because the coaches have yelled at them, telling them they have not honored the swim-parent's code, that they have overstepped their boundaries and taken the sacred job of coaching into their own hands. The parents, apparently, were guilty of telling little Mary that she has to bring her arms up out of the water faster in fly. They told her in the car ride home that her rhythm was off, they told her that her legs were spread wide on the entry, they told her before a race to not forget the two-hand touch, they told her to keep her hands in prayer position for the pull out, and they told her to, for crying out loud, breathe on both sides in the free. But it is not Cleo that Chris is crying about, you realize. Cleo is just sitting on deck on her towel reading a book. She's not even swimming the event that's taking place. Chris can't answer you yet. Now more tears are sliding down her cheeks, and the tip of her nose is turning red. You don't have a tissue in your purse to offer her. Unused ChapStick, yes, but not one tissue. You try not to ask Chris any more questions. She will tell you if she wants to. You think how you have been friends for a while but never cried in front of each other before. You realize this has suddenly changed your friendship, turned it up a notch. You are now closer whether you want to be or not. You wonder if someday you'll cry in front of her too and she will look at you with those blue eyes and put her thin, long-fingered hand on your arm and tell you it's going to be all right. You look at the timing board. The five-hundred frees are over and now it's the relays. Your daughters are walking with their relay teams to the blocks. Your older daughter, Sofia, walks half the distance with her book in her hand, still reading. When she realizes she can't dive into the water with the book she runs back to her towel and leaves it there. Chris wipes her face with her hands, making her face appear shiny, and even prettier, you think, and then you think how when you cry, the skin around your eyes puffs up, and your whole nose turns beet red like a seasoned alcoholic, and the skin on your face and your neck gets red blotches in irregular shapes resembling the outlines of the fifty states. Once you stopped your crying completely because you happened to look at your reflection and saw the perfect outline of Texas, and could not believe it was there on the side of your neck. You thought maybe it was some kind of a sign, that you should go to Texas and start life anew, but then you realized you had no desire to go to Texas, and that life anywhere else, except maybe Florida, would be better.

"Darn," Chris says. "I didn't want to do this."

"Do what?" you say.

"Cry," Chris says. "It's just that there are so many people I can't tell, and it's so hard not telling anyone." You eat another grape, wishing this time that they really had turned to wine. You could use a drink. For a second you think about inventing a wine product in the shape of a grape, where the outside of the grape is made of something edible, and the middle is filled with wine. You could keep them chilled. You could take them with you and pop them into your mouth at sporting events. You could use them as ice cubes in seltzer to have as spritzers.

You are confused. You aren't sure if you want Chris to tell you exactly why she is crying. You get the feeling, the once-in-a-lifetime feeling, you think, because you've never had this feeling before, that what is going to come next out of Chris's mouth here at the dead pool is going to change the world as you know it forever. You watch your girls lining up for their relay heats. Your youngest, Alex, your ten-year-old, has her elastic goggle straps set way too long. You can see that they will drag in the water and hit your girl's arm as she swims, probably keeping her from swimming her best time. You are disappointed in yourself for not remembering to cut them earlier, when you were at home. Do you have something in your purse to cut them with now? No, of course not. Along with the ChapStick you've never used, you have click-button pens whose points are stuck in the on position so that the inside lining of your purse is riddled with what looks like a secret code of dashes and dots of black and blue ink. You have nothing that could cut. "Have you got scissors?" you say to Chris, or maybe you think you say it to Chris, but you can't be sure, because Chris doesn't answer you, and instead she says, "I think Paul is cheating on me."

"No, he's not," you say.

"I think he is," Chris says.

"I'm sorry, but I just can't believe that," you say, because you can't.

"Well, there's so much I can't explain," Chris says. "So much he can't explain. It's got to be the answer."

"You're wrong," you say. Chris swallows hard. You can hear the swallow. You are afraid the tears will start coming down again. "What man in his right mind would cheat on you?" you say.

"He's started working late. He comes back and it's after midnight. He says he's working, but he never used to work this hard."

"That's it?" you say. "He works late and you think he's been cheating on you? It doesn't sound like enough to hang the guy." You really don't believe Paul is cheating on Chris. You realize all of a sudden that your daughter Alex is swimming her leg of the relay. She's anchor and freestyling with all her might toward the wall for the win.

"I'm so sorry, but I just can't help thinking that it's a misunderstanding," you say, touching Chris on the elbow just after your daughter touches the wall for the win. "I'm positive."

You wonder why you are defending the man. You've never really had a conversation with him, you've never even talked to him up close, you just know him by sight—he's come to a few practices and meets and you've seen him in the stands—whereas you and Chris have known each other for at least three swim seasons. She's been to your house a few times to drop off Cleo to visit with your girls, and you've been to her house to drop off your girls to visit with Cleo. You've never seen Paul any of these times. Maybe he is cheating on Chris. Maybe he is banging one of his college students, a student who stays after class and leans over his desk asking him questions about things she knows he loves to talk about. It's just hard to believe, considering how all the husbands you know let their tongues drop to their knees when they see Chris.

Sofia is in the next relay. She is standing with her shoulders hunched, and you wish she would look up in the stands and look at you so you could mouth the words "back straight" to her, and so you could throw your shoulders back too, demonstrating. You think that ever since Sofia started her period her posture has been worse, and you wonder if it's just because the girl is that much more tired.

When she started her period she held out a panty liner and showed it to you. "Is this blood?" Sofia asked, and it was, the blood had stained the pad in the shape of an hourglass, and you looked at the design and considered how you were looking at it as if it were a Rorschach ink blot, and you wondered, if your girl kept showing you the bloodstains on her pads throughout the rest of her cycle, what more would you see in their shapes? Would you see a bird with its wings folded in? A hammer? A footbridge?

"I'm sorry to put this on you," Chris says. "It's just that I couldn't talk to my family about it. They all think Paul and I have a perfect marriage, and that he's a saint. They'd blame it on me."

"Don't be sorry, especially since I'm sure it's nothing at all," you say. "Sometimes I think Thomas is losing his mind. Just the other day he talked for hours about the decline of civilization, how he believes we're going through it."

Your daughter's dive is beautiful—high and long. She's the leadoff, and what a lead she's given to her team before she's even entered the water.

"How can I be sure it's nothing?" Chris says.

"Don't think about it, that's all," you say. "And watch Cleo swim. I see she's up next. She's a good swimmer. She's graceful, like you. Sometimes I don't care how fast a swimmer can swim. Sometimes I just like watching them move in the water. It's as if the water makes way for them, like it's taken aback by how good a swimmer can be. Do you know what I mean?" Chris looks at Cleo, and her daughter looks up at the stands, looking for her mother. "Wave to her, she doesn't see you yet," you say, and Chris waves to her daughter and then the daughter waves back and forth, smiling, and you think if you put your hand up in the air, in the space between where the two hands are waving at each other, you could feel some kind of a force, maybe Chris's mother energy. You don't know what the name of it is. Maybe it's something Thomas would know. It's a quark, a pulse, a gravitational field, a gluon of extreme magnitude.

CHAPTER SEVEN

Contrary to popular belief, we are not all geniuses," reads Floyd Arneson, our killer, while he's at school on his computer. Right now there is no teacher in his office and the principal is at a meeting for the day. Floyd Arneson is an administrative assistant in an elementary school and his boss is the principal. The school runs almost all year round, because it also runs summer programs. Floyd Arneson calls himself a secretary because he has promised himself that he will not go through life fooling himself. I work as a secretary, he thinks to himself. I am also a killer. I know perfectly well what I am doing. I know perfectly well how I have to keep my knife very sharp or it will not cut easily through the skin, the fat, the larynx, and the tendons. I know very well how I have to dispose of my clothes afterward, how even a speck on the top of my shoe is a reason to dispose of the shoe and buy a new pair. Our killer is interested in himself and there is so much written about serial killers that he likes to know what is new and has been shared in the media. "Like the rest of the population," he reads, "we range in intelligence from borderline to above average." We could have wives and children. We could belong to the church. We could be the head of the church. We could have wet the bed. So many of us have wet the bed as boys. We could have pulled the tails of dogs, have stuffed cats into sacks. We could have splayed open wide the bellies of just-stunned birds not dead from their crash into glass they thought was just more world to fly through. We could suffer from psychopathy, we could be doctors, and we could be nurses, lawyers, and cooks. We could be women working with men, burying bodies in our yard. We could be women working alone. We could be extremely clever and intelligent, or we could be just average or below. We could be school secretaries, or we could be truck drivers. As children, we could have been plagued by nightmares or slept like babies. We could have set fires, or stolen purses, or tagged graffiti all over school walls. We could have helped our mother with the dishes and played nicely with the cat and done our homework every night. We could be the kid in school now, walking through the halls, holding the snack tray, careful not to let the cartons of milk fall over. The biggest myth, our killer reads, is that we want to get caught when really we do not want to get caught and we feel we cannot get caught. The killer laughs, he reads a line Jeffrey Dahmer once said, "When I was a little kid, I was just like anybody else."

This is you driving home at night, nearing your house, where the tops of the pines on the hill shine metal-bright in the moonlight like sword tips.

These are the girls, running inside the house after you park the car in your driveway. They are after Thomas, jumping on his back and hugging him and wanting to know what he did without them while they were away. They want to know what food he ate, and Sofia bangs open the freezer, checking to see if he bought ice cream without them and left them some in the container. Alex shows him a sweatshirt she bought that has the name of the meet and her team logo printed on it, and then while Thomas isn't looking, she takes the merchandise sticker off the sleeve, pats Thomas's back, and says, "I missed you, Dad," and the sticker is now stuck to the back of his shirt. "I missed you too! It's good to have you home," he says, trying to get another hug from her as Alex steps back from him and then doubles over with laughter, pointing at his back, saying, "Dad, you're so gullible!"

Thomas asks you how the drive home was and you tell him there was construction everywhere and he says, "You know what they say. There are four seasons here: leaf peeper, winter, mud season, and construction season. It's now the start of construction season."

Usually, at night, in the dark, you tell Thomas the gossip you heard at the pool. You always tell him which coach was furious with which parent for overstepping that sacred boundary and taking on the role of coach. You tell him how Dinah's husband is getting so deaf that he doesn't even bother to talk to people anymore, and Thomas shakes his head while in bed. You hear his hair rubbing against his pillow while he says that's a shame. You tell him which parent showed up lit and smelling like hard liquor when she picked up her kid, you tell him about the parents who you know are paying their kids to come to practice, you tell him who lost their cool at a meet and went up to the officials and judges and demanded they retract a DQ, a disqualification, that their kid received. But you do not tell him about Chris telling you that she thinks her husband is cheating on her. If you told him, then maybe he'd start thinking Chris is available now, or maybe he'd try to make Chris feel better and start talking to her more, and isn't it bad enough the way he, and all the other husbands, look at her perfect breasts and her rear? So instead of telling Thomas about Chris, you tell him about the dead facility at the away meet, about how Sofia and Alex swam so well, and how it was so funny when one of the coaches slipped and fell into the pool because his own daughter happened to be swimming in a lane by the wall and he was running alongside her, yelling at her to "glide." All of it is true, you think. You haven't told Thomas any lies. The girls did swim well, the facility did appear dead, and the coach did fall into the water, afterward showing you the worn-down soles of his rubber shoes and how they did not afford him any traction on wet surfaces. Maybe another day you will tell Thomas about Chris, but now you are getting sleepy, the stars out your window seem blurry. You really must be tired, you think, and then you realize that Thomas has put the screens in the windows earlier in the day, and what you are seeing is the blur created by the mesh wires, and isn't it funny that all of the almost 4 percent you can see is a blur, and does that change the 4 percent somehow, does it turn it into a 1 percent instead?

You wake up in the night. You can't fall back to sleep. If only I had more wife energy, you think. You would turn to Thomas and touch him. You would do all the things you know you are supposed to do. You would do all those things those women you photograph do to their husbands on the sacred first night of their marriage. You would do what you did to Thomas on the night of your own wedding day. You would climb on top of Thomas, you would slide down the length of Thomas, you would kiss all the tips of him, every one, even the tips at the flare of his hips and his collarbone. Now, even when you are so tired, you do it anyway. Even though your arm is so heavy, like stone, you lift it and touch Thomas. You let your fingertips softly run down his back, like pattering raindrops. You let your fingers trail down the front of him, the pattering raindrops falling on his sleeping penis. When he stirs, it's not to stretch himself out flat on his back so you can touch more of him, it's so he can lift your arm off himself, and how easily he does it, it's not made of stone for him, for him it is a dried twig found on the trail, so easy to lift and let sail in a wind. He lifts your arm by the wrist, places your hand palm down on the cool sheet between you. There he pats your hand twice, and then he goes back to sleep. His sound of sleeping heavily comes amazingly soon. He can always fall asleep so easily. You hear the birds are chirping and it's the middle of the night. Whatever happened to birds rising with the sun? You can hear something walking outside. It could be a deer. It stumbles on the wide, flat rocks Thomas placed in a row forming a walkway from the driveway to the front door. You hear a snuffling sound. You hear your daughter snoring from the next room and wish that years ago, when Alex had tubes put in her ears for frequent infections, you had also had her adenoids removed, because the doctor said it was a good time to get them out, while your daughter was under, and that if she snored at all, it would help with the snoring, and she would concentrate better in school. This is why, you think, your brother didn't do well in school and why your mother was always having to tell your brother to study and do his homework, when really she shouldn't have had to tell him anything, he should have been doing it on his own, and nobody told you when you were a girl to study, to hit the books, to ace the exam. Now I really will never get back to sleep, you think, because you are hurt by Thomas not wanting you to touch him when it took what seemed like so much effort to touch him in the first place, and the hurt reminds you of your dead brother and you have started thinking about him again, and all of the things you remember about him growing up parade in front of you. You remember how at the beach one family holiday you were playing by the shore, and your brother and your parents were closer to the dunes, where a beach blanket lay, where a cooler sat planted in the soft sand. You were playing with small white crabs that burrowed into the wet sand where the tide was coming in. You could hear the voices of your parents from where you were, but you could not make out their words. Your parents were yelling or screaming at each other, you didn't know which. Your brother, who had been sitting beside them on the towel while they were standing and yelling at each other, suddenly stood up and sent sand flying up behind his feet as he ran toward you. "Let's go in," he barked, and grabbed you in his arms. You were afraid of the waves, and you told him so. "No, I don't want to go in!" you said, kicking the air while he held you around the waist with one hand. "Stop!" you said, and he told you not to worry, the waves weren't that big. He was holding you upright in the water when a big wave came over the top of you, and you could see him under water, where it was all green. Under water, you saw the look of surprise on his face, he didn't know the wave would be so big, and under water, you started screaming. When the wave passed, you started hitting him, and he laughed, and was still laughing after you broke free of his arms and ran back to shore. You can't believe that all of the memories you have of him right now are of him laughing, and is that a warning sign? Should you call helplines across the country and clue them in, let them know that if the person they're trying to save is on the other end of the line laughing, that's when you call the cops and get them to send a squad car to the bridge, the house, the cliff, wherever the man or woman is who wants to do themselves in?

And why was he running so quickly away from your mother and father that day? What was it he was running away from? You've often wondered this over the years, and more so since his death.

CHAPTER EIGHT

*T*his is the next day at practice. The rain is coming down hard on the facility and it sounds loud, as if the roof were made out of tin sheets and the place were a barn. Practices seem to be better when the weather is bad. Everyone happier to be in a place where it's warm, not minding being stuck indoors. The starts look better to you. Your girls go off the blocks in streamlines tight enough to fit through holes in doughnuts. They've also got spring in their legs that takes them almost to the first flag strung above the pool before they enter the water. Kim's butterfly kick looks so strong, it looks like she's getting as much speed from her down kick as she does from her recovery kick. It won't be long, you think, before she starts breaking pool records again. She must be done with growing, and now her movements are not so awkward. She has grown into herself. The coach, a woman who was a you-don't-know-how-many-time all-star champion in college, is really pushing them along. You admire the coach. Everyone admires the coach. The girls on the team all want her attention. Sofia tries to get her attention by being sarcastic and making the coach laugh. Alice tries to do it by crying and complaining over sore muscles and slight scratches that always seem to require the coach to fetch her an ice pack or a Band-Aid. Kim tries to get the coach's attention by swimming the fastest she can. Alex tries to get the coach's attention by being silly and showing the coach how she can make the muscles of her stomach roll like waves. The coach has days when she doesn't laugh, though. She can be serious, and those are the days your girls tell you practice was hard or practice was boring. At one meet, the coach raised her voice at Sofia, telling her that she didn't take it out fast enough in the first fifty, and your daughter came to you and cried. You agreed with the coach. You saw the race. It looked as if Sofia was daydreaming, which she probably was, having just put down a book before she dove into the water. She was probably still thinking about the book's characters in midair. She was still inside of the book. She was reading a book that took place in Afghanistan, and she was probably flying kites in Kabul during her entry. She was eating fresh fruit and lamb on the steps of a mosque at the turn. She was not thinking about how she should have taken the first fifty out as hard as she could, because if she had been then she could have won the race. The coach talks to you, the parent, about this. "Sofia has to take it out faster," she says to you. "And I told her so, and I'm sorry if I upset her, but maybe it's good I upset her. Sometimes I have to be harsh with the swimmers, or maybe there are just some swimmers I know I can be harsh with and Sofia is one of them, because I get the sense that she's not a head case. She won't get so upset by criticism that she'll ruin her stroke entirely. She mustn't be afraid of expending her energy. She doesn't realize how strong she really is, how much breath will be left inside of her even after the first fifty," the coach says. When you talk to Sofia about it, she says, "I know, I know," and then puts her head back into her book. In her world, strings of kites glued with shards of glass are cutting each other in half against a blue Afghan sky.

This is you in the water. You swim in a lane reserved for swimmers who are not on the swim team. You swim while the swim team swims alongside you. This is you thinking as you're swimming that it sounds as if the water is whispering to you. Swimming always calms you. You rarely think about Thomas or your brother while you're swimming. In fact, you started to swim more seriously to forget about your brother after his death. It's as if the water embraces you, lets you know that here is a place you can be without getting hurt. I will buoy you. I will caress you. I will soothe you and whisper to you, it seems to say. You hear the faint shush of the water going by your ears as you freestyle forward. You wonder what the water, if it could talk, could possibly be telling you about your stroke. Could it be telling you to lift your arms up higher, as if you were reaching over a barrel, the way you have heard swim coaches do when describing the stroke? Could it be telling you to kick harder? After all, your kick is barely a splash, barely a flutter. After you take a swim yourself, just a mile of freestyle, a two-hundred individual medley, and an IM kick, not even a quarter of the workout that the swim team will do, you look at your toes in the shower. They look like toes on a child. They are fat and rounded, and not slender and long, the way Chris's are. You wiggle them, letting them send up a happy hello to you from where they are on the tiled floor. You wash your hair that is thinning, thinking maybe

your brother wasn't so dumb after all, maybe doing yourself in before you're really old and useless is the right way to go. A boy who
is allowed in the women's locker room because there is something
wrong with the boy and he is in a wheelchair and has a woman
who helps wash him, is in the next shower stall. The boy says the
word "water" over and over again. "Yes, you like the water," the
woman says. You can hear soap or shampoo going through the
boy's hair in the next shower stall, as if the woman were playing
with the boy's hair, lifting it up into peaks like a troll, or creating a
long blade of it through the center, like a foamy Mohawk.

When Paul, Chris's husband, shows up after practice to pick
Cleo up, you decide you'll go and talk to him. Maybe there's a way
you can tell just by talking to him if he's really cheating on Chris.
"Hello, Paul," you say, coming up to him, getting his attention as
he's turned away from you looking out the door. When he turns
toward you smiling, you feel as though a light is shining back at
you. Even the facility seems brighter, as if up above through the
high skylights clouds have made way for sun, but it's not the sun.
The sun is on its way down. "Hi, Annie," he says, his whole face
opening up to you, as if the sole purpose of him standing there and
waiting were for you to come by and talk to him. Has he always
been this good-looking? you think to yourself. You don't remember
ever standing this close to him before. Usually it's the mothers who
have the kinds of jobs they can leave early to pick up the kids and
drive them from school to practice whom you regularly see, not
the fathers. You see Kim's father sometimes waiting at practices,
he's always working on his computer, or you see Keith's father at

practices, always reading a war novel. You see Catherine's father, a man who watches the entire practice attentively as if it were as exciting as a meet. You've seen Jonathan's father sometimes driving up in his pickup with the lawn care logo on the side and driving off again after Jonathan's gotten out of the truck with his swim bag, but again, it's mostly the mothers you see. Maybe it's because it's been so long since Thomas, your own husband, has touched you in the night, and because when you tried to touch him last he patted your hand instead, that Paul suddenly seems attractive. But you are no spring chicken, and you would be very surprised if Paul even looked at you twice. You decide he will probably notice your graying hair first and then the wrinkles by your eyes that are so pronounced they look more like the head of a serious garden rake than the proverbial crow's feet in lines of three, which to you sound almost dainty in comparison. You decide, when he looks at you, still smiling, that you can see why Chris, his beautiful wife, married him, and why any student of his would probably lean over his desk a little too far, revealing a little too much, in order to get his attention, and to get him to smile at her the way he has just smiled at you. You decide your friend Chris should maybe be more worried than you thought. You realize a few things.

You realize it has been a long time since you have met another man who you thought was attractive. You realize how you are probably a good wife, never talking to men other than your husband, never thinking maybe there are men you could flirt with, men who would talk to you about things other than the decline of civilization, and particles in the air you can't see. You realize your eyeliner may be smudged and that you should run the tip of your finger under your eye so you don't look as though you've been crying. You realize that when you speak, your voice sounds gravelly, as if all these years you've been smoking cigarettes instead of exercising almost daily, eating healthy food, and drinking from BPA-free containers. You realize that when he, Paul, smiles back at you it seems as if his eyes are twinkling, and as if they're sending out points of light you can feel animating your face, making you smile back. You realize you have the urge to toss your hair out from where it lies on your shoulders, to give it fullness. You realize that you hold back that urge to toss your hair out from your shoulders because you realize it would be sending a type of signal you haven't sent in a long time, a signal that you can be attractive if you want to. You realize that the sun is really down outside the facility, and that the pavement is turning dark, almost as dark as India ink. You realize you are thinking that maybe without the sunlight shining on you, you might not appear to have lines like garden rakes at the corners of your eyes. You realize you are staring at Paul's lips as he talks. They are sensual. You realize now that you are standing close to him that he is taller than you previously thought, and that you have always been attracted to tall men. You realize you are asking Paul how he is enjoying being the parent of such a good swimmer on the swim team, and you realize he is answering you, and choosing his words carefully, saying he likes it just fine, that he thinks Cleo is the one who is really enjoying it, which is the way it should be. You realize you like the sound of his voice. It's a deep voice that makes you look at the skin on his chest that you can see between the collars of his shirt, where the top three buttons are open. You look at his chest after hearing his voice, wondering what his voice would sound like if he were talking softly and you were laying your head against him.

You realize you are stepping back, telling him you are glad you met him. You're afraid of how much you're imagining being closer to this man. You wonder where Thomas is. He came with you to the facility. He does come sometimes to work out or to watch the girls swim, but it's rare these days, his work being more important. Even though you've asked Thomas to come more often to help at the meets, he says he'd rather work on the wood at home or spend extra hours at the lab. Now when you see Thomas coming down the hall from the men's locker room, after having just showered and changed, you realize that you are relieved. You wish that Thomas, in his infinite wisdom about space and particles, could speed up and get to you faster. You realize Thomas is tall too, and has a deep voice, and eyes that sparkle, and that you are lucky he is all of the things that Paul is, and that you don't have to toss your hair for Thomas. All that you have to do is go get in the car with Thomas, and go home, and at night, after he has patted your hand, and after images of your brother have paraded in front of you, all you have to do is sleep.

At breakfast alone the next morning when Thomas has left for work and the girls are upstairs, you are bent over. Hunched, you are folding in on yourself while you eat your raisin bran, thinking about how you aren't supposed to think about the death of your brother since there's no forgiving him and no getting mad at him, there's just no more him. You don't have the energy to lift your head up. It's not the weight of the world pressing down you feel so much. It's more like the weight of the world is sucking you down from below, pulling you into its fiery reaches, its melting core. The raisin bran tastes like cigar ash, and you think you've swallowed a bug.

This is you calling Chris, feeling bad that she's upset about Paul, and asking if she'll be driving to the next swim meet, and wanting her to come, telling her how nice the facility is, how even the hotel is nice. You know because you've been there before, for meets in the previous years. This is Chris saying, "No, I'm letting Paul take Cleo. At least he'll be with Cleo, so seeing the woman he's having an affair with won't be an option."

This is you coming home that evening after picking up the girls from practice and after a meeting with a potential client in a café to discuss her wedding-day photo shoot. You tell Thomas, while the girls go upstairs, and he's reading at the kitchen table because there he can bask in the last light of the day, how this client wants all of her photos done in black-and-white, even if it's a bright sunny day and even though her wedding sounds riotous with color—tangerine-colored bridesmaids dresses and tiger lily centerpieces on all of the tables and ring bearers in fuchsia. "Isn't black-and-white cheaper? She sounds practical to me," Thomas says, and then he tells you about the article he's reading, about people who are hypersensitive. The slightest touch hurts them. The slightest noise deafens them, and they can't help it. It's in their genes. You wonder, while Thomas reads to you from the article, if he's ever noticed the picture of your own wedding day framed on the wall in your bedroom, in direct view from where you lie on the bed, where it can be seen first thing when you both open your eyes, and last thing before you turn off the light. In the picture your bridesmaids are in red, holding bright red bouquets of roses, everything contrasting nicely against the white lace of your dress and Thomas's black tux. In the picture your lips are the same red as the bridesmaids' dresses and your cheeks are flushed red from all the excitement of the day. You think how much of the color would be lost if the photo were in black-and-white. The red of the bridesmaids' dresses just looking dark, and the white of your dress looking colder, not as warm as it does beside the red dresses. In black-and-white Thomas's tux would just be dark like the red dresses, nothing setting him apart from the bridesmaids at all, as if Thomas matched them, as if he had been more connected to them than he was to you on that day. This is you noticing how when the sun has gone down completely, Thomas still works at the kitchen table. In the growing dark, his outline becomes more solid, his light-brown hair now almost black, a different man altogether than the one you married. These are the girls coming into the room, Alex whistling and Sofia turning on lights, changing the mood very quickly. Thomas's hair now light brown again, his eyes flecked with sparkling green. Pans get banged around in the shelves because Sofia is starving as usual and wants to bake herself cookies. Alex turns the radio on loud. The dog comes to walk between everybody, brushing you with the end of her tail, reminding all of you that soon she's to be fed. This is Thomas telling you the girls should stay home and study instead of going off to the swim meet, and this is Sofia banging a tray on the countertop, saying no. This is Alex saying forget it, saying she wants to go to the meet. She's at the top of her age group and doing well in breast, beating out almost everyone else in the fifty and hundred. This is you thinking, as Sofia preheats the oven, how it will warm up the house, and how soon, in a few weeks when summer's fully arrived, it will be almost too warm outside to want to bake cookies inside and the dessert of choice, as it does every summer, will turn to ice cream and smoothies. This is Thomas later, telling the girls to grab their jackets and come out and see the stars. They take out a sleeping bag and lay it on the front lawn, and from the open window upstairs you see how with one girl up under each of his arms Thomas points out how stars don't really twinkle, it's our atmosphere deflecting their light that makes them appear as though they are changing in color and intensity. He tells the girls that almost every star we see is really two stars, and that from so far away they look like one. Sofia says, "Does that mean when I wish upon a star I'm really wishing on two and that my wish has double the chance of coming true?"

"Yes, I suppose that could be right. I hope it's true for you, at least," Thomas says, and then you see how when he says it he brings your girls closer to him, hugging them tighter under each arm.

CHAPTER NINE

*T*his is you days later taking the girls to a league meet an hour away, pulling out of your dirt driveway in the cool dusk, turning on the heat that won't kick in for two miles, and seeing a coyote the size of a German shepherd jogging in a slant on thin legs in front of your headlights. Look, you say to your girls, but it is too late. The coyote is gone, and is now probably hunting somewhere in your front field, where a lone tall pine grows and where there is cover by a falling rock wall for small chipmunks and rabbits to hide. This is you, forty minutes into the drive and still on back roads before you can get on the highway. That's how far back you live in the country. You can see families in homes on the sides of the road. People turning on their televisions, working in the kitchen, some just walking across the room and shutting a window. The people you happen to see outside are closing barn doors and putting horses in for the night, or standing in front of their doors in triangles of light cast from lamps in the hallways and calling for their dogs out in the fields to come home. This is you finally on the highway, your mind wandering. Although wander is completely the wrong word, you think, because it always seems to go back to you thinking about how Thomas hasn't been touching you at night and how your brother shot himself in the head. These are guilty thoughts of how maybe you weren't even close enough to your brother to be mourning him for so long. You were eight years apart. You had gone to his room as a girl and talked to him often. You listened to him play guitar, the same refrains over and over again, trying to get them right, but he never seemed satisfied. You sometimes looked at yourself in his mirror, seeing him there too, sitting on the bed bent over his guitar, his back in the shape of a C as if he were melting and would end up like silly putty stretched out over the strings and the neck and the frets. Sometimes in summer you just stood in front of his air conditioner, his was the only room that had one, and lifted your arms, letting the wind flutter the wisps of hair by your temples wet with sweat. You sometimes heard him talk on the phone, but he said very little, and he still held his guitar on his lap while holding the phone to his ear, every once in a while strumming a chord softly. His was a conversation of yeses and nos. You assumed he was talking to girlfriends, because sometimes he would smile saying yes, and sometimes he would smile saying no.

This is your brother with the gun in his mouth. This is your brother forming a cauliflower head on the carpet with his blood. This is his wife, hearing the shot downstairs in his office set up with sound mixers and stereos and computers. This is your brother's teenage son, hearing the shot too, colliding with his mother as both of them try to run down the stairs together, barely fitting that way, abreast in the stairwell as they run. This is the mother using all of her force to hold her teenage son back from opening up the door. This is the teenage son calling out for his father and banging on the closed door. This is the father answering with just the sound of his blood as it pours out of him. This is the crime-scene tape being looped around the beech trees in front of the house, a yellow web forming that will keep people out.

CHAPTER TEN

The air conditioners in the rooms in the house you rented at the equator made a lovely sound every time they were turned on. You wish you could hear the sound at times like this when you had thoughts of your brother. The air conditioner made a small series of space-age-sounding, relaxing notes whose decibels were in the perfect range, neither too quiet nor too loud. You would feel cooler the moment you heard the sounds, even though of course it would take a while for the air to circulate and the temperature to drop. You thought on the plane ride home that the one thing from the equator you would have liked to bring back was a recorded sound of the air conditioner. You were not interested in bringing back shells from the beach, or crafts made by local artisans. You just wanted that series of notes.

When you finally arrive at the hotel and you and your girls bring up your bags, you hear a knock at your door. It's Cleo wanting to know if your girls want to go down to the hotel pool. Your girls, of course, want to go. You go with them, knowing you should get some exercise yourself. When you get to the hotel pool, it's already a swirling mass of kids from all the swim teams who came to the meet. You slide into the whirlpool instead, realizing with an emotion you can only identify as the horror of embarrassment that Paul is in there too. You didn't recognize him at first, his hair wet and not in a ponytail now but hanging down loose at the base of his neck.

You feel like wet clay in your bathing suit. Your breasts, your rear, are not perfect at all. "Is Cleo excited about the meet tomorrow?" you ask him. You are hot in the water. You wonder how long you can last before having to get out and dive into the cooler pool with the swim team kids. You think Paul says, "She can't wait," but you cannot be sure. The children are yelling so loudly. They have started doggy-paddle races now in the kidney shaped pool, and you think to yourself that here is a conglomeration of all the eastern states' best swimmers and here they are doggy-paddling. Paul invites you and your girls out to dinner. You say yes, and thank you. You say you know the girls would love that. You think how you would love it too. You wonder what you will wear. You hear him say, "But maybe a better idea would be to order a pizza. Everywhere will be crowded." You are relieved that you can wear anything. You are getting used to the water. You could now stay forever in the whirlpool. Have the pizza in the whirlpool, why not? you think. You hear Paul say he is too hot. He would jump into the pool with the kids, he says, but he is afraid the dose of chlorine in the hotel pool would asphyxiate him. You hear him say he can already feel the chlorine drying out his throat and tearing up his eyes. You look at him and his eyes are red and tears are sliding down and you think that this must be how he looks when he is really upset. You wonder what could make him really upset. You are glad when he gets out first and heads up to his room. You did not want to have to rise from the water first and let him see your body in the suit. You see Dinah and her husband walk into the pool through the door at the same time Paul and Cleo are about to leave. Paul calls to you, "Come to our room in thirty minutes. I'll order the pizza." You see Dinah look at her husband and then look at you. You tell Dinah you like her swimsuit before she can make a snide comment about you and Paul. You tell her it's very Marilyn Monroe. Dinah's husband smiles at you. He does not even try to have a conversation. He can't hear anything above the swimmers' voices, amplified in the small room of the pool. He sits down in a chair next to a rubber plant that is really made out of rubber. You know because one of your girls has already pointed out its almost indestructible leaves to you. Dinah looks down at her suit, or really at her breasts coming out of the suit.

You head upstairs in the elevator with your girls. You had to tell them twelve times to get out of the pool, before finally throwing the Styrofoam lifesaver that hangs on the wall onto their heads to make them hear you. In the elevator you see how they are dripping pool water on a cheap knock-off of an oriental-design carpet. You let them take long showers when you get to your room. You are thinking that at least you are getting your money's worth from the hotel in the way of the hot water bill. You think you can hear Paul in the next room clearing his throat.

When the pizza comes, the girls and Cleo eat in your room and Paul invites you to eat in his room. This is Paul's black leather coat on the dresser, looking like an extension of Paul himself, the arms of the coat slightly folded, the elbows holding wrinkles in the leather that were created by the constant flexing of his arms, the cuffs looking gently worn and gray compared to the black of the rest of the leather. This is Paul moving clothes off one bed so that you can sit while you talk. This is Paul asking you questions about yourself that you're not used to answering. You are used to Thomas talking to you about what he thinks is important. You are not used to having to speak for so long in front of a man. This is you thinking that it feels a little like you are emptying your purse out in front of Paul, even though you are not. You are telling Paul about where you grew up and you are telling Paul about your brother, about the good and the bad of your brother, and Paul laughs once in a while, at the parts you mean to be funny, because you try to be funny telling him things you think that you have never even told Thomas about your brother because Thomas never wanted to hear about your brother, even when your brother was alive. When it's late, and you think you should go, you wish you could pick up what you let fall out of your purse. Is there a way to put back all the things you said, as if they were just your ChapStick and your hairbrush, and zip them inside? When you get up, Paul rises off his bed at the same time. This is Paul saying he wishes you could stay longer, saying he has enjoyed talking with you, saying he is tired of hearing himself lecturing all day at school, and that sometimes he thinks he has lectured for so many years that his voice would continue on talking without him if he could just take himself outside of himself while he was teaching and sit down in a chair in the lecture hall with his students and, like the rest of them, text on his phone. This is you laughing and this is you thinking you should say something about Chris, because Paul and Chris are married and you want Paul to know you are aware of that, and that you talking to Paul was not about you wanting to be with Paul in any other way than just two swim-team parents talking, but already you know the conversation has gone beyond that. You haven't mentioned the team or your daughters' swimming once. This is you sitting back down in such a way that you can pull your shirt away from the muffin top of fat on your belly so it doesn't look as bad. It's something you only do when you want to look presentable, when you first meet a client whose wedding you may photograph, for example. It's something you never do at home when you just sit in the chair at the kitchen table across from Thomas, because he's always reading a magazine and wouldn't notice anyway. This is you asking how Paul first met Chris.

He tells you he first met her in Greece on a trip he took right before he started college. They were both just eighteen years old. You listen to how beautifully he describes how they met at an archaeological site in front of a figure captured in ash during the eruption of a well-known volcano. You can hear your girls and Cleo in your room next door laughing at a show on the television. Outside it's getting dark, and you notice that Paul has not gotten up to turn on the light. He looks gray in the fading light and you imagine he could very well be the man frozen in volcanic ash come back to life.

You gasp so quietly, almost to yourself, when he leans over you to take a picture from his wallet, which is behind you on the bed. You think you should stand up now and leave. Your gasp frightened you. You had no idea how it would feel to have him so close to you. You wonder if there's something the matter with you. If all of a sudden you've developed the disorder Thomas read about in the article where you're hypersensitive to everything. Or maybe there's nothing wrong with you, and this is the most normal your body has felt in a long time. Normal because you want to be close to someone and you want them to touch you. You feel warmth coming off Paul as if he were pavement on a hot day. You wonder, for a moment, if it's the room. But then you realize the heat is coming from you as much as it's coming from him. You look at his wallet pictures instead of leaving. Chris with long hair blowing in a breeze. Cleo as a baby being held up in the sky by Chris as white, puffy clouds float by. Chris from behind as she's looking at a cathedral. Of course, you think, he would take a picture of her from behind. What man wouldn't? Paul is smiling as he shows you the pictures. You accept the wine he has brought out of his bag. You drink from a hotel cup that still tastes like the plastic it was wrapped in. You do not expect the phone call from home. It's Thomas wanting a recap of the day. You do not tell him you are in Paul's room. You do not tell him you are looking at a picture of Chris's great rear taken by Paul, and that you feel as if you are see-ing Chris's great rear through Paul's very own eyes. You tell him you're in the middle of dinner. You tell him you'll call him later. "Wait," he says. "Make sure the girls do some of their studying while they're there," he says. You can hear him running the water from the kitchen tap as he talks. You hear him swallow. You are amazed that you know the sound of his swallow, its timbre and tone. You would know it anywhere, the way a mother knows the sound of her own child's cry. "Talk to you later," you say.

Paul tells you more things that night than you have ever told Thomas, or anyone else. They are things from long ago, the embarrassing things that Thomas would not have listened to you talk about, because to him they would sound trivial. You tell Paul these things and he laughs. His laughter makes you even funnier. You really are quite funny, you think to yourself. You feel as if you have turned that darned purse upside down, you have turned it inside out, you have shaken it and let all the lint float down onto the hotel linen. You let him touch your cheek, you turn your face as if you would kiss his hand, your lips on the flesh of his palm. The TV next door gets louder, the show is a comedy. Now, in addition to the children's laughter, you can hear the canned laughter of a popular show. "Is this how you handle all those students who come to you with questions about their prose?" you ask, your words spoken into his hand. He laughs. He keeps his hand on your cheek. He is looking at your face.

"I have confessions of my own," he says.

"That sounds ominous," you say, jokingly. The canned laughter gets louder.

"No, I mean real confessions. Ever since that news piece about the serial murderer killing all those women in Denver, I've been on edge. I have to tell someone about what happened to me once—well, really, what happened to someone I met."

"Tell me," you say.

"All right," he says.

This is Paul's story. This is him telling the story in the room with the lights still off and only the light from the parking lamps outside coming into the room. This is him interrupting his story, just for a moment, to find another bottle of wine in his bag, and opening it and pouring it for the both of you into your plastic cups. This is him saying, "This is a story I've been trying to write, because I thought it would lessen my guilt." This is him giving you the facts. This is you thinking this is a joke, or this is him trying out a story on you that he hasn't finished yet because he wants to know if it will hold your interest.

"It happened a long time ago, just after Chris and I came back from Greece. We were so young. We were taking it slow. She wanted to separate for a while. She suggested we date other people, to see if we were sure about dating seriously." He doesn't look at you when he says this, sitting next to you on the bed. He is looking at nothing or he is looking down at the wine in his cup. He is wearing a white tee shirt. You look at his chest, seeing his heart beating slightly beneath the cotton. His voice sounds quiet. It is a voice you think he uses when he wants to capture the attention of his students. You think he is probably the kind of teacher who never has to reprimand his students to get their attention. All he has to do is whisper, and they lean in closer to him to hear everything he has to say. You do lean in closer. You can feel the breath from his words blowing across the hairs in your ear, and the sensation sends shivers down your spine. You learn that he knew a woman named Bobby Chantal. You try to picture her. She looks just like Chris in your head, blond and perfect. You try another picture of her, because she couldn't possibly look like Chris. There couldn't be two perfect Chrises. You picture Bobby Chantal with dark brown hair and a curvy body. Paul is quiet. "Go on, I'm listening," you say. He nods. "This is difficult for me," he says. He takes a deep breath and continues. You would like to take notes. You would like to reach over him and pick up the hotel stationery and the hotel pen loaded with the barest minimum of ink and begin to write what he's about to tell you because you have the feeling that you'll want to replay his words in your head later, when you are apart from him, and you don't trust yourself to remember them well. Today you have already forgotten to remind your youngest to pack an extra pair of goggles for the swim meet, and at the last meet her one pair broke right before her event, and she had to borrow her friend's that were too big, and when she came up from finishing her race you could see the water sitting in the eye cups, the wavy line of it going halfway up her eyes.

" . . . I said yes, and then we went for a drive," you hear Paul say, and then you could kick yourself, because you realize you have already forgotten a part of the story he is telling. What he said yes to you can't quite remember. Yes, now you remember, Bobby wanted to go for a drive. He had just met her that day, not far from his college campus. It was a cool summer's day. Fall was in the air, but it hadn't yet started to change the colors of the leaves. She met him after he had just gotten out of his creative writing class, while they were both standing on a long line at a coffee shop. The cool temperature made everyone want an afternoon coffee. He had joked with Bobby Chantal, saying by the time they were served they could have had a coffee sitting down at the nearby restaurant. "That's a good idea. I'd like to sit down for a while," she had said, and she got off the line and started walking toward the restaurant. "Do you mind if I join you?" he asked. They had a coffee at an Italian restaurant where the odors from the kitchen were so strong that even their coffee smelled like garlic and basil. She was easy to talk to. She was older than he was, but still young, and very attractive. She told him about growing up in a small house on Cape Cod, and how she used to bandage her little dolls so that they looked like mummies. She didn't call her dollhouse a dollhouse, she called it a doll hospital, and then when she was older she went off to nursing school. He pointed out how beautiful the sunset was going to be. He could see pink clouds rolling in. She suggested going on a drive. He recommended they go up the highway a bit, and then to a lake where there was a place to sit and talk. As they drove, she told him the stretch of highway they were on was the stretch that was famous for making Vietnam vets have violent flashbacks, its rolling green hills reminiscent of Nam. What was stranger, she said, was that many vets came from far away just to travel the stretch, to see what memories it could stir up, as if stirring them up could somehow vanish them. Paul found this fascinating. "I might use that in a story someday," he told Bobby. She held out the flat of her hand to him. "Don't forget to give me a percentage of the royalty check," she said. A little ways up the highway there was a rest stop and a lookout. "I bet there's a good view up there of those mountains that look like Nam," she said. "Let's stop here instead of going all the way to the lake."

They stopped the car at the rest stop parking lot and hiked up a short path to the lookout; as they walked, he held her hand. At the top they sat on a picnic table. She told him to close his eyes and imagine he was in Nam, even though he'd never been there. At first it was difficult. A woodpecker was pecking a beech tree nearby, as rhythmically as if he were pounding nails, but then somehow the noise faded, and when he opened his eyes again, he really was in Nam. He could almost make out helicopters flying over the ridgeline, and huts with straw roofs, and thin threads of smoke rose from the ground that he could imagine were from cook fires. "Unbelievable," he said to Bobby. They stayed sitting on the picnic table until dark, and then he kissed her. She drew him down on her as she lay flat on the table as if it were a bed. And well, Paul says, one thing led to another. Afterward, she excused herself and said she was going to use the rest stop bathroom. "I don't think she ever made it through the door," Paul says. While he waited, he could see the black outlines of the mountains, and he imagined again that he was a soldier in Nam, only now it was night and the enemy was all around. At first when he heard a scream he figured that he had let himself imagine for too long that he really was in Nam and that what he had heard was just an owl screeching in a nearby tree and not a human screaming for his or her life. When Bobby didn't come back, and the owl never called again, he went down the path toward the restroom to check on her. When he found her she was facedown, the white of her hospital dress easy to see in the light coming from the entrance to the restroom and making it look as if her dress were glowing. He called her name, but there was no answer. He turned her over by her shoulder, and the front of her white hospital dress was anything but white now. It was stained with blood and dirt, and even her face and her forehead were covered in a mixture of blood and clods of dirt and bits of grass. He felt for a pulse, but there was none. There was no point in even calling an ambulance. He could see, as he held her, that her neck had been slit. He looked in the parking lot, but there were no other cars aside from his. He ran around the back of the restroom and along the edge of the woods, but no one was there either.

While standing at the edge of the woods, and looking into the darkness, he realized that if he called the police, he would become a prime suspect. They would check for signs of rape. They would want to know how he knew her. How was it that he had just met her that evening and then she was killed? "It was not like I could help them with the case," Paul says. "I hadn't seen or heard anybody. I figured the best thing, the least complicated thing, was for me to get out of there, so I left. I took off. I left her there all covered in blood." Paul puts his hands over his face in the dark hotel room. You feel like maybe you missed something. Wasn't it just a second ago that the both of you were laughing about a silly college anecdote you were telling him about the time you ate brownies and didn't know they were laced with pot, and you had never even smoked pot, and you were so hungry and ate so many that it was as if you were tripping and the EMTs had to come and calm you down and then everyone on campus the next day knew what had happened. Wasn't it just a second ago you were feeling overwhelmed by his body leaning over yours? Weren't you just thinking about him touching you?

And now he is talking about unimaginable things, horrible things, blood and rape and a throat being slit. It feels as though you are being sucked down into that evil abyss you always seem to fall into whenever you think about your brother and his suicide. You are standing now. You are heading out the door. You feel a strong urge to check on your daughters, no, to be with them, to hold them. How reassuring it will be to have them in your arms and smell the shampoo in their hair and the faint smell of chlorine that lingers no matter how many times they shower after swimming. When Paul stands and grabs your arm as you are going, you almost let out a scream, but he lets go, so you stop. "I'm sorry. I didn't mean to scare you. I've never told anyone before. I should have guessed your first reaction would be to run away."

"Turn on the light," you say, and Paul mutters, "Sure," and flicks the wall switch. You are relieved to see it is still him. You had the strange feeling that after telling that terrifying story, he would have changed. You would be looking at someone with a disfigured face, someone totally unrecognizable, but he is the same. Handsome, and tall, his gray eyes looking into yours, obviously wanting very much for you to understand him, and to stay. "Don't go yet. The girls are fine," he says. And, as if on cue, the girls' laughter is heard again through the wall of the hotel room, confirming that they are fine, if not better. Then he reaches up and touches your face, moving some hair away from your eyes. You back away when he does. "I'm sorry. I have to go," you say, and you do, entering the hallway at the same time the ice machine makes a crashing sound while emptying its ice into its bin.

CHAPTER ELEVEN

*T*his is you in your hotel bed waking up from a dream where Paul and you are having sex, and you not believing you just had that dream, not after the story he told you about Bobby Chantal and how he left her and never told anyone he was there at the scene of the crime. You realize as you get up from the bed and go to the bathroom, not turning the light on so as not to wake your girls, that it doesn't matter what Paul might have done so long ago when he was so young, you still like him. It would even be tempting right now to go knock on his hotel room door, because he was just inside of you in your dream, and you feel like you're humming down there. Thank goodness, you think, Cleo is sharing a room with him, otherwise you just might really find yourself knocking on his door.

*T*his is the rest stop on the highway. This is the grass on the lawn. It remembers the feel of Bobby Chantal's body, how hard she fell and smashed its slender blades, releasing a just-cut smell the way a going-over with the blades of a lawn mower would. This is the light above the restroom entrance. It remembers lighting up the face of the man who held the knife to Bobby Chantal's throat. This is the metal doorknob on the restroom door. It remembers reflecting the murderer's face, and every time someone comes and uses the restroom, the doorknob wishes it could show that person the murderer's face again so that the man, who was never caught, would be caught.

When Dinah says to you the next morning, "I saw that you and Cleo's dad stayed up late talking last night," you're not sure if you should respond or not.

Do you say, "Why, yes, and talking's not all we did—we also fucked our brains out," to shut her up, or do you remember Dinah is another swim-team parent and if the coaches expect the swimmers to be civil to each other, then you should be civil to Dinah as well? Do you just smile at Dinah and let her think what she wants about you staying up late talking to Paul in his hotel room, or do you say nothing because her husband's going deaf and she's overweight and you feel sorry for her? Do you say, "He's an interesting guy," letting her know you're defending yourself, and letting her know that maybe she too should have been staying up late talking to Paul? Do you say, "It wasn't really that late," and then launch into a conversation about how terrible the waffles are at the free buffet breakfast? Do you talk about Dinah's daughter instead, because you know that Dinah loves talking about her daughter's racing and that she would talk to you for the next thirty minutes about her daughter if you gave her the chance? Do you decide you couldn't possibly listen to Dinah talk that long about her daughter? Does a part of you feel good that someone noticed you and Paul becoming close, and does that make it somehow clear that Paul likes you as much as you like him? Instead, do you fix your eyes on your daughters, who are already on deck for their afternoon events and take note of how they look? i.e., do they look alert, are their backs straight, are they arranging the straps of their racing suits so that no bit of material interferes and increases their time, are they standing playing ninjas or giving other girls back rubs, or are they curled up in a corner with a book? Do you jump when your own cell phone rings even though you've had the same ring for years and you shouldn't be surprised by it? Do you answer, in front of Dinah, knowing it's Thomas, as if you know it's Thomas, or do you answer as if you don't know who it is and say, "Hello," and not, "What's going on?" which is what you would usually say to Thomas when you know it's him calling? Do you tell Thomas the meet is going fine, that everyone slept as well as could be expected in the hotel room that felt more like a fish tank because the windows didn't open? Do you tell him the waffles tasted like cardboard, that one girl, from a team you don't know, lost a tooth while biting into one of the hotel's lousy, hard bagels? Do you let Thomas tell you all about the history book he is reading that he keeps saying is the world's best history book because it explores history not through the usual lens of religion or wars, but through agriculture? Did you know, he has told you, that during the Industrial Revolution, the natives living in the Amazon jungle were eating a healthier diet than we were? Do you let Thomas tell you more about how the Chinese depleted their soils and couldn't grow crops, and that the primitive Andeans, in comparison, were better farmers and knew to place troughs of water around their raised garden beds because the water regulated the temperature and extended their growing season by months? Or do you just tell Thomas the girls are about to race and you have to get off the phone even when the girls are not quite up in the bull pen yet, where they will wait to be sorted into their lanes, which would really, essentially, basically, be lying to Thomas? Do you prepare answers for Thomas asking you about the meet so far, about who is attending and which parents showed up? Do you prepare to tell him Cleo showed up, but fail to mention the fact that just Paul came with her and that you and Paul stayed up late talking about things that you and Thomas either never talked about with each other, or talked about together long ago, before Thomas became the head of the lab at work? Do you think how you should be prepared to tell him you don't blame him for the distance that has grown between you, that either you're both to blame, or it's not worth the blame?

What you end up asking Thomas about is the wood. How many logs has he cut through? He gives you an answer that makes you picture your house, the log pile he stands over and cuts with his chainsaw, wearing his protective chainsaw chaps that are mesh and meant to stop the moving blade. They were bought at a discount and when he brought them home you knew why they were on sale. They are bright orange with dark spots on them and look to you like the animal-skin clothes the cartoon characters in *The Flintstones* wore, and you were afraid for him then, thinking how could anything that silly-looking prevent a life-threatening slice to a femoral artery? He says he is at the point in his history book where the author is discussing the Potato Famine, and you say what about the Potato Famine, and he says oh my god, the Potato Famine, but you never get to hear why the Potato Famine was anything other than what you knew from school, a blight that starved so many in Ireland, because now the national anthem has started up, and this time it's not canned music, but a bunch of girls from the team, including your youngest, who is singing off-key into the mike. Of course, it's a hundred times better than the canned music because it's your daughter, Alex, and you can hear her voice amongst the others—it's out of tune, and you love it, and wonder if you pull out your little video camera now to tape her will it be unpatriotic, and do you care? And you wonder why some put their hand over their heart when the anthem is played and why some just put their hands behind their back and why you yourself put your hand over your heart when you're not in the least inclined to show patriotism. You're certainly not inclined to show patriotism by having troops go off to war, and you start wondering how strange it is to live in a world where so much of what other people do and what your government's doing is something you wouldn't do at all, and it makes the living you're doing seem as if it isn't living at all, at least not in the big sense, only in a small sense, in the way the goose you have at home lives, knowing only what's in the immediate area, not thinking beyond the fox by the pond and the hawk up above. You wish you could think of the bigger picture sometimes, how to come up with a solution to poverty, the dilemma of thinning ozone, the inevitable threat of worldwide drought, and not always be concerned whether the swim towels you washed can come completely dry in a forty-minute cycle or do they need sixty. Not always concerned whether the swimsuit you bought online could have been purchased for less on a different site. Not always concerned that if you hadn't let your daughter go to the public library a week ago during story time when all the preschoolers were entering the building, then she wouldn't have caught a cold and had to miss three swim practices in a row, possibly causing her not to be at the height of her conditioning now. Not always concerned about the fact that Thomas never touches you, and that maybe it really doesn't matter. Like you said, there's no blame, there's just the next morning with his body taking up your side of the bed, and you being pushed closer to the edge of the bed, where there's a gap almost wide enough for your body to fall through, and if it did you'd hit cobwebs, dead flies, balls of dog hair, and books you started but never finished, and maybe you'd be sucked down even farther, into that void where the horrors of everyday life swim around in some primordial stew you could never pull yourself up and out of.

CHAPTER TWELVE

T his is weeks later. This is how the summer has been passing, with you thinking about Paul, and taking the girls to swim practice, and sometimes seeing Paul at the facility and talking with him, and Thomas still not touching you, and you thinking about Paul even more. This is the air filled with the scent of the knee-high grown mint. This is your stream, lower now than in the spring, bordered by baneberry and pink lady-slipper, the flowers past bloom but the leaves full. This is your road in front of your house hardly visible through the hanging vines of the Spanish moss tree and the leaves of the tupelo and the old hemlock blocking the view and the sounds of passing cars. These are the storm clouds gathering from the south, sitting over the pond heavy with algae the color of forsythia and thick with tadpoles about to grow legs, turning the surface water dark gray.

This is you at a wedding, taking pictures of the bride, trying not to take a picture when she's swatting at the mosquitoes feasting

on her bare arms. This is you remembering your own wedding
with Thomas, when he grabbed you by the arm right before you
said the vows, holding up his index finger to everyone seated, letting them know he just wanted a moment. Then he took you back
behind the barn on the property where you were married. "What?
What?" you said, wanting to know what was going on and seeing
your white shoes disappearing into grass that hadn't been mowed
because no one expected anyone from the wedding party to be
walking around there next to the old barn boards, a rusted tractor,
and the rock foundation. What was wrong? Did he want to stop the
wedding? He kissed you there. It was a long kiss, as if he had all
the time in the world, and there weren't one hundred people waiting for the both of you and wondering what had happened. When
he was done, he said, "That's the real kiss I want to give you. It
won't be the same in front of all of those people. Remember this
kiss when we're old and gray," he said, and then he grabbed your
hand again and the two of you ran back up to where the judge was
and you stood in front of him. Everyone seated cheered then. You
knew you were married at that moment, saying the vows wasn't
even necessary. Now this is you thinking how one of the grooms
looks like your brother. He's got the same eyes that appear half
asleep. The groom is probably high, you think, and then of course
you start thinking about your brother, and about how he shot himself, about how the blood . . . You can feel yourself slipping into
thinking about him. It's almost as if you're ducking in through a
door with a sign on the front that says "Dead Brother Door." You
are relieved when you realize there's a way not to think about him.
All you have to do is think about Paul instead. This is you looking
at the road every few seconds, thinking you'll see Paul driving by

because the wedding is not far from Paul and Chris's house. This is you missing the chance to take a photo of the groom having his lapel straightened by his mother because you are too busy looking at the road. This is you also missing the chance to take a photo of the bride hugging all three of her bridesmaids at once—they're huddled together like teammates about to break into a cheer—because you think you actually do see Paul at the wedding, with his ponytail hanging down, and with his back facing you as he's getting a drink. You know it would be highly coincidental if he were at this wedding, but just maybe he is. You run up to him, and then almost drop your camera when he turns around and is somebody else, somebody with large nostrils and a deeply receding hairline. He doesn't have the thick hair Paul has, or the fine aquiline nose. This is you later, leaving the wedding in the dark while the father of the bride sets off celebratory fireworks in a field. You consider driving to Paul and Chris's just to look in the window and see if he's there, but when you look down at yourself, in the glow of an especially large display of palm and willow fireworks with bursting light that falls in tendrils, you see that your dress is rumpled, your sandaled feet covered in bits of grass wet with dew, and your hair is hanging in strands about your face like drooping antennae. This is you deciding that if you did drive to his house, on the pretense of saying hello to Chris, and he was there by himself, you'd be too embarrassed about the way you look to talk to him. You wouldn't even get out of the car. You'd drive away and he'd think you were stalking him, which, of course, you probably would be.

This is you the next day thinking you'd like to think that it was the hot summer lightning you just drove through on the way to practice that's giving you the urge to reach out and help Chris, but odds are it isn't. It's not like the lightning struck you or the car. The only things hitting your car were the giant marble-sized balls of hail. The lightning was only close enough to make you and your daughters' fingers feel tingly at their ends for a while. When you arrive at the practice, your fingers still a bit tingly, and your shoes wet, you realize you should help Chris. Your realization comes in the form of some kind of energy. Maybe it's a form of "friend energy." Your mind telling you that what is more important than your obsession with Paul is your new friendship with Chris. After all, she's in the same boat you are right now—a sinking one with a husband who's half there—and she can probably understand what you're going through. You've been feeling horribly guilty when you see Chris at the facility. You feel so guilty you haven't even talked to her the last few practices. You've collected your girls in the lobby and run out the door, hoping you wouldn't even see her in the parking lot. Today you will change. You will get Chris involved in her daughter's swim life. It will get her mind off her delusion that her husband is cheating on her. Over and over again you have seen mothers and fathers who can rattle off the times of their daughters and sons, and know exactly what they need to break in order to move up the ladder, and enter age groups, zones, sectionals, and even nationals. Those parents, like Dinah, even know the times of other people's kids. Those parents go to every single meet and outfit their vans with mattresses and in pitch-black predawn carry their sleeping children out to the car bundled in blankets so that they won't have to lose any sleep and have their fitness compromised when they swim their races. Those parents don't have time to fight or quarrel or accuse each other. Those parents, maybe those parents are really smart, you think, and then you think for a moment that maybe you should be one of those parents too, but then you dismiss that thought quickly, knowing that you can barely remember your locker combination, or your age, or the birthdates of your children, so how could you possibly remember both your daughters' times and the times they need to beat? How could you possibly lift your children out of bed and put them in the car while they're sleeping? You aren't strong enough, and your oldest girl is already taller than you are. Christ, she's menstruating already, and you know that Thomas won't get up in the morning to help carry them, he would laugh at the idea of you being so serious about swimming. "To what end?" he would say. And both of you have agreed that the worst thing you can imagine is having to go to college for swimming, having to maintain a scholarship and good grades and swim every morning when you could be staying up late working with a group of friends in the library, having sex, or going to keg parties. You picture Thomas laughing, throwing his head back while he laughs at you for turning into an über swim mom, which is what every swim mom has the potential to become the longer her children are on the team, and the closer her children are to reaching an age when they could get into college with a swim scholarship.

The place to start is with the swimsuit, of course. That is what Cleo wants, a racing suit. The racing suit means that she is serious. She is hungry to win. On your computer at practice, you show Chris all the racing suits to choose from. Some are low drag and some change flow conditions along the swimmer's body. Some have fabric splices that allow for greater flexibility, some are neck to knee, some are johns, some are tanks, some are thin straps, some are wide, some are scoop backs, cross backs, V-2 backs, wing

backs, super backs, fly backs, spider backs, diamond backs, butterfly backs, extreme backs, and max backs. Some have maximum
compression aiding in blood flow and improving stability, some
have minimal permeability, some have undergone a technical
heating process to produce an ultra-smooth, lightweight surface,
some have flatlock stitching, some are hydrophobic, some are
coated with Teflon, some . . . "What?" Chris says. "Teflon?" and
then she groans and tells you how a few years ago she threw out
all her old Teflon-coated pans because she could see the coating
was scraping off each time she used the spatula to turn food in the
pan, and she realized the coating was ending up in their mouths.
"Now you're asking me to have my daughter race in Teflon?" Chris
asks.

"I know, who would think anything associated with heavy
metal pans could make your daughter swim faster, but it does,"
you say.

"And what's this about hydrophobic suits?" Chris asks. "Isn't
hydrophobia associated with rabies?" You tell her you don't think
it's the same thing. Hydrophobia in this case is what you want. It
repels the water, lessening the resistance. In the end, Chris finds
a john she likes for Cleo and they order it for overnight shipping.
There's another swim meet in a week, and it is important for Cleo
to wear the suit during practice to see how it feels, so there won't
be any surprises when she has to wear it all day.

You wish, for a moment, you were swimming instead of technical suit shopping with Chris. You watched a video at home on how
to perfect the fly, and you want to practice bringing your hands
up earlier in the recovery. You have always dragged your hands
far behind yourself, as if waiting for someone to grab on to them

and keep you from completing your stroke. Who? Maybe someone who could convince you that all the swimming you are doing is pointless, that maybe you should be trying to get your daughters to pay more attention to improving their own swimming since they are the ones with potential and not you, or maybe you should be at home instead or out in the world trying to make a difference. A difference to what, you don't know. You aren't one to volunteer in your town or work at the food shelf or be a driver for the meals-on-wheels program. You prefer to stay at home when you can. When it is a warm day and the clouds are far away from each other, you go outside and lie on a blanket and feel the sun on your face. You aren't thinking about making a difference in the world when you're lying on a blanket under the sun. You are mostly thinking about the kind of bug that is trying to land on your face. Is it a deerfly? A mosquito? A stray hair from your own head mimicking a bug as it blows in the breeze? And what about that bird blocking your sun for a moment? Is it a raven? A crow? And what is the difference?

CHAPTER THIRTEEN

Some swimmers don't shower at all after practice. They dry off and get dressed right away. Later, at home, they shower. Some swimmers spend forever in the shower, wearing their swimsuits the entire time. None of the swimmers stand naked under the shower. You don't understand how they can spend hours in bathing suits in front of crowds of people at swim meets wearing suits so tight the outlines of their pubic bones and the clefts of their vaginas can be seen, but then in the shower be so modest amongst each other and never reveal themselves. Even the little ones, from an early age, learn how to put their bathing suits on without taking off their shirts first. Your Sofia is one of them. You are convinced no one has ever seen Sofia's breasts, except Sofia herself. You have never seen them either. In the locker room, after she's showered still wearing her suit, she lowers the straps of her bathing suit down just to her shoulders and then pulls her shirt over her head. That way she can remove her suit from under the shirt. When she comes out of the locker room her shirtfront is wet from having touched the wet suit, and her posture is poor. She looks as if she is doubling herself over. You're not sure why she does this. Maybe it's to hide the fact that her shirtfront is wet and that she has breasts large enough now, they're noticeable beneath the cotton cloth of the tee shirt she wears. You hope she is not caving in on herself, trying to curl up in two to protect all of the feeling parts of her. This is you hoping she doesn't end up like your brother someday, someone who never felt good about himself, someone who would try to fold himself in two if someone he loved stopped loving him in return. This is you telling Sofia to keep her back straight, but this is Sofia shooting you a look that could freeze water. This is you thinking what you should have done instead was asked how practice was, or told her how good she looks in that sky-blue-colored tee shirt she is wearing. What if, you think, your father, instead of yelling at your brother to do a chore, had told him how well he played the trumpet, how like the rest of us he enjoyed the sound of the notes that landed so pleasantly on our ears with a ring of authority and a tone of respect at the same time. Would your brother have been different as an adult then? Not that your father ever paid you compliments yourself, but your mother did, and that's all you needed maybe to face growing up. That's all any girl ever needed, maybe, a mother telling her how beautiful she was.

Some of the swimmers stay and practice their dives and their strokes after practice, asking the coaches for extra help. Kim is usually one of these girls, and today after practice she says, "What am I doing wrong?" to Coach, and Coach tells her what she's been telling her for a while now: "Your rhythm is off, that's all. You'll get it back." Kim wants to stay longer and practice with Coach, but she has to go home. She's taking an online advanced chemistry course this summer, and she has an exam to study for. At home, after studying, she replays a race in her mind. She remembers all of her races and sees them as clearly as if she were racing them again at that moment. She replays a race that she won, trying to see what it was she was doing right at the time. She cannot figure out why it was such a good race. She wasn't doing anything that different from what she's doing now. She begins to think it's the water itself. Her chemistry teacher posted a video lecture on how all molecules were once parts of something else. He held up an orange. "What you see here could have been the molecules that made up George Washington's hat." She imagines the water at that pool she won the race in was made up of the molecules that maybe once made up her relatives, people who would have a reason to care for her and help usher her along the lane as speedily as possible. Other pools where her times were slow had water molecules floating in them from people who maybe were not so nice. Lizzie Borden and her ax, maybe, are making up the water in those pools, she thinks before drifting off to sleep, wondering whose molecules are in the pillow she rests her head upon now.

This is the killer watching Kim again at a dual meet against a team from the southern part of the state. She swims her hundred fly and she breaks her record. She comes in with a 1:08.72. He wants to shout. He wants to call down to her and yell her name. She has given him such a gift. He looks to see what she looks like coming out of the water. He wishes he had brought binoculars so he could see her eyes more closely. Why isn't she smiling? Why isn't she raising her fist up in the air the way he has seen other girls do when they have beaten their times? And her eyes, why do they look dull from up in the bleachers?

This is Kim, who has just swum her hundred fly again, and she thinks she saw an official raise their hand while she turned at the wall. Did she DQ because she was submerged on the start longer than fifteen meters before she took the required pull with both hands that brought her to the surface? After all these years doing it correctly, could she really have misjudged it? Has she grown in height and that's why? What's changed about me? she thinks, and she looks at herself in the reflection of the windows of the pool and she sees her waist and thinks she looks thick, as thick as the old maple that used to be in her yard, and she looks at her legs and thinks they look fat, as fat as the logs cut from that old maple in her yard after it was struck by lightning. She looks at her hair and it looks as if she doesn't have any. It's so pale around her face she might as well have been struck by lightning, and she's a ghost at this meet who doesn't even ripple the water's surface or have enough weight to set off the touchpad so that it reads her finals time. When she goes up to Coach, Coach tells her that she DQ'ed after the start, that she stayed submerged underwater way past the first flags, and that it might have been sixteen meters that she stayed underwater instead of fifteen.

"What was it you were thinking, or were you thinking?" the coach says, and affectionately puts her hand on top of Kim's head. Kim shakes her head. It's hard to tell if her eyes are red from the chlorine or from crying or from just being tired after staying up late at night studying, but then when the coach sees the tears welling up in Kim's beautiful light-blue eyes, she wants to put her arms around her but knows she should not. If she puts her arms around Kim then she will be encouraging Kim to cry and there is no crying at swim meets. We don't get upset or get too excited. We don't throw our goggles down in rage if we lose. We don't jump up and down for joy if we win. We don't run up and let our teammates hug us. We don't curse or kick the post that supports the balcony with the bleachers with all the parents and the grandparents sitting up in them who are knitting or talking or yelling out their children's or their grand children's names. We don't run to the locker room and wish we were still small enough to squeeze ourselves into a locker and hide. We don't run into the shower and let the water course down our faces as we cry, letting the shower water take our tears down the drain. We don't lash out at our parents and say, "No, I won't!" when they tell us that we will do better next time. We don't run outside into the parking lot in our swimsuits and gulp in the cold air to get away from those inside who are staring at us and not believing how we could have gained so much time in a stroke we thought was our best. We don't do these things, but of course, we have all seen them done. Every big meet there is someone who cries, there is someone who drops their head after they get out of the water, there is someone who whoops for joy, there is someone who proudly raises their fist toward the sky.

*T*his is Kim at the meet the next day. She is less stressed about her butterfly being rhythmic enough because she has been thinking about driving. Being sixteen, she can now drive a car. Her parents have just bought her a new compact car, and she drove it to the meet by herself. She drove for two hours with her own music coming out from the speakers, and she sang to her own music the whole time without anyone telling her to lower the volume. She drove with all the windows down and her hair flying behind her because the summer wind on her face felt great, and made her feel just as good as when she'd last achieved her personal best time in the hundred fly. Now, at the meet, she stands on the blocks, ready to try the hundred fly in a time-trial just to see if she can come close to the time she could have had yesterday if she hadn't DQ'ed. This is Kim registering how the blocks are a different height than the blocks at the home team's pool, and realizing that her dive will have to be different to compensate for them.

This is Kim on the takeoff, exploding and then extending up and out over the water. This is Kim in the lead, this is Kim thinking of herself as a rock skipping over water, this is Kim at the turn, feeling her feet touch the wall and plant themselves firmly, but not for too long, just enough to get the turbo boost from the wall that she needs to dolphin-kick and shoot to the surface. This is Kim at the finish, jamming her fingers into the wall, not feeling the pain in them until later, after she's seen her time of 1:08.62 posted on the board, not until she's gotten a high-five from her coach and hugs from all of her teammates, not until she has called her mother from the pool, telling her through tears how she broke the pool record, not to mention her own personal best record. And it's not until later, a few days later, that the mortician who will be looking at her fingertips will wonder why they almost look as if they were burned by a flame.

This is Kim, stopped at a rest stop on the way back from the meet thinking as she is being grabbed from behind and feeling the knife at her throat that it isn't fair. She wants to live because she knows if she does she could beat her personal best time once again. She knows she could increase her speed. It was as if her new car had been her coach. Just driving down the highway with all the windows open had shown her the feel of the speed she would need to go faster than she had ever gone before.

This is the killer, putting his lips on each one of her eyelids as they close and she loses consciousness. Kissing her in, he thinks. The taste of the salt and chlorine on her and the warmth of her skin on his lips is the energy he has been waiting to call all his own.

CHAPTER FOURTEEN

*T*his is you at night getting into bed before Thomas does. He stays up with Sofia and teaches her math. I must remember to buy her more sanitary pads, you think to yourself, and you do the math, remembering when your daughter first started her period and when your daughter may get it next, and isn't it hard enough, you think, to remember your own cycle, and now you have to remember your daughter's, and in a few years, and maybe even sooner than that, you will have to remember the cycle of your other daughter. You remember your own first period when you were eleven. How your mother, too concerned with your brother, who was just twenty and still angry about your father leaving the family nine years before, hadn't gotten around to telling you what to expect. You had some vague idea about needing to use sanitary pads, but you were so young you didn't even realize that your period arrived every month, and so the second time it came you were shocked, thinking you only had to go through the cramps and the blood and the paraphernalia that came with it just once. Your mother was busy helping your brother lick his wounds from a girlfriend who left him. She worried so much that he would hurt himself in his grief that she hid the twenty-two rifle that was in the house and she gave him spending money to go out and have fun, and paid for him to take a college trip with an oceanography class to Bermuda, where he scuba-dived and snorkeled and was chased by hammerhead sharks. The hammerheads came from all directions, and when he tried to climb back into the boat, his classmates were trying to climb up the other side, and they made the boat sink down on their side, and on your brother's side, the bottom of the boat rolled up and exposed a barnacled underside that your brother had to drag himself up against in order to climb back safely into the boat. He came home with a chest full of cuts from the sharp edges of barnacles and still a bad outlook on life. By then you had accepted the plight of your sex, its horrible regularity, and you questioned for the first time, really, whether your brother would ever get over this girl who dumped him, and realized that if it weren't for this girl making him miserable, then something else would, because that's how he was going to be in this world.

Your daughter doesn't even need for you to explain how or why the body has cycles. She has learned it all through reading some young adult book, or through some swim-team friend. When you offered to explain it to her she said she already knew and for you to go away because she wanted to be left alone to keep reading a book. Well, that was easy, you thought sadly, descending the stairs of her loft where she slept. Not that you really wanted to demonstrate tampon use or describe PMS, but you were almost jealous that she was having such an easy time with the change. She didn't have to contend with a divorced, financially struggling mother worrying about her emotionally messed up son. Life is peachy for your daughter. She has her books and her swim team and her violin lessons and her beauty. She's tall and thin, with soft brown hair and high cheekbones. Only the hint of blemishes appear on her nose, and they can only be seen in certain unforgiving forms of light, whereas you and your brother, of course your brother to a terrible extent, suffered acne. On the other hand, your daughter's shyness is also a point of concern, and maybe her teenhood is not all that ideal. Her dislike of using the phone even to call the local library and ask for a book, or to call and order a meatball grinder at the general store, borders on the extreme, you think. Oh, is this something you have to worry about too? Do you have to watch your girl and make sure she is not the type who will one day end up like your brother on the floor with the bloodstain taking the shape of cauliflower? In the boards on the wall by your bed you see a face in the knots in the wood. You see two eyebrows and two eyes that look happy. No-see-ums fly between the pages of Anna Karenina, the book you are reading, and to kill them you simply close your book and then open it up again to the page you were reading so that now the letters, even though they're in English, have smashed bug parts on top of them and look like letters in a foreign alphabet, as if you're reading the original Russian. Thomas's voice booms up through the floorboards. He is saying polynomials and factoring very loudly, and it is making it difficult for you to read a book where you have to remember all of the characters' Russian names and nicknames, and you would like to concentrate on the book, on the plight of poor Anna, who has just sneaked back into her former home to visit her son, whom she was forbidden to see, but you can't concentrate because of the math going on beneath you. Now the children are in bed and you are in bed and the day is finally becoming dark, and the last bit of light can be seen going down in the sky over the back field. Thomas, from the bathroom, where he's brushing his teeth, starts talking through the foam of paste in his mouth about how he learned from his history book that the Taino Indians, the very natives that Columbus and his men encountered, slayed, and sickened with contagion in Hispaniola, kept ants from climbing up their beds by placing the posts of their beds in pots of water. He says this is further proof that civilization is in decline, since that is such a smart thing to do, and do we do anything today as smart as that? He answers his own question. "No, we pollute everything," he says. "We cause global warming. We have that horrible radio station." And you know the horrible radio station he is talking about. It is the one that records conversations of people who are having a joke played on them. It is the one that played the joke on the mother where the eighteen-year-old son calls to tell her that he needs money, that he got drunk and spent the last of it on a tattoo. Where is the tattoo? the mother says, and the tattoo is on the son's penis. You remember laughing at that one, and now you think you are definitely adding to the decline of civilization.

You turn off the light and wait for Thomas to come to bed. When he does come into bed, he faces the other way. There is not even a patting of your hand tonight. Just before you fall asleep an image of your brother comes into your mind. Your brother was angry. His girlfriend had decided to leave him. He lifted his guitar and smashed it onto the desk and against the wall in his room.

The guitar strings resounded. The neck of the guitar broke off. The body was splintered. You yelled at him to stop, but he wasn't listening to you then. The same way he didn't listen to you that day at the beach when you told him you didn't want to go in the water, but he took you there anyway. He just kept banging his guitar, even though all that remained to smash was the neck, and even that broke into pieces so small he could no longer destroy them. All that was left in his hand was the headstock and tuners, some of them still wound with strings that were sticking out in all directions, and bobbing in the air. You want to forget that scene. This is you thinking you can forget if you think about Paul instead. This is you imagining Paul, him leaning over you in order to kiss you. This is you thinking that the way his tongue would feel in your mouth would be an indication of how he would feel inside of you.

CHAPTER FIFTEEN

*T*his is Thomas the next morning saying, listen to this. This is you wanting to put your hands over your ears, because you are not in the mood to listen to observations about the decline of civilization or how Alzheimer's is transmissible or how some people have more chimpanzee DNA than others. You are going up the stairs while he talks to you from down below. You have to put together all of the photos you took of the last wedding you shot. You have to go on your computer and fix and crop what you can. You are known for your portraits, people in this part of New England have asked for you specifically to shoot their weddings, and you have to make sure you have a few that look good up on a wall or on a shelf for a lifetime, even on those long winter days when the snow outside has covered the windows and turned the house dark. When you're done, you have to send them off to the bride and hope that she likes the photos of herself that you like, but just in case, you will send her some where you think she doesn't look that attractive. You send her these because you are always surprised how when you just send the women the photos where you think they look their best, they ask if there are any others, and often pick the photo you would never have guessed as their prize portrait. "Listen to this," Thomas says again from below. He reads to you from the newspaper. "A sixteen-year-old girl named Kim Hood was found outside a rest stop with her throat slit on a stretch of interstate highway close to exit thirteen." You miss a step and go down, hitting your shin on the stairs with wide stringers. You turn and sit down on a step, rubbing your shin, whose first layer of skin has been peeled off, looking like a sunburn peel. Where you sit, the sun streams in from the window at the top of the stairs, lighting you up with a shaft of light. If you were a bride or groom, or guest at a wedding, it would be the perfect dreamy light to photograph yourself in. "Say the name again," you say, but you don't need to hear it again because you heard it right the first time. You are just asking to hear it again because you need a moment to put it all together. The girl is someone you know from the swim team. The interstate rest stop is the place where Paul told you Bobby Chantal was killed. "Kim Hood," Thomas says, and this time his voice sounds as if it's coming from far away, but really Thomas is closer to you now, and it is the strange effect of the way the house was designed, making voices sound far away when they're coming from somewhere close. Thomas is coming around the corner of the stairwell with the paper to show you the picture of Kim Hood. "No suspects have been found," he reads, and close enough to you now, he places the folded paper in your lap, where the beam of light falls against the words, as well as a droplet of what you think must be milk and must have dropped from his spoon as he slurped up his cereal. This is Kim's face in the picture. Her smile looking friendly, her clear blue eyes not looking blue but just vaguely clear, since the photograph was reprinted in black-and-white. Her hair looking wet, making you think that perhaps the photograph was taken right after a practice in the pool, the same pool you all swim in.

This is the coach, a woman who, when she hears about Kim's death, almost falls out of her chair in her office with the big windows that look out over the pool. She grabs onto the armrest of her chair as if she's about to take off on a plane and doesn't like flying. She says "oh, no" so many times while she listens to someone tell her the story on the phone. Mandy, who is mopping the deck, sees the coach saying "oh, no" and holding her hand to her head, and thinks she will go inside once Coach is off the phone and ask her if she's all right. When she is off the phone, Coach thinks of canceling practice that day, and then she thinks she will have a mindful practice for the team instead, a practice where the swimmers are mindful of what they're doing. Only today they will not be mindful of how they are kicking or stroking or breathing. They will have a practice where they think continuously of Kim. They will think of her generosity, her team spirit, a time when they talked to her, a time when she made them feel good, because Kim was always making her teammates feel good and cheering for them. They will think of how hard she swam, how much she tried in practice to get the strokes right. They will be mindful of how she was such a good student. When Coach comes out of her office and onto the deck, Mandy asks her if everything's all right, and when

Coach starts to tell her, she starts crying and Mandy hugs Coach and Coach says, "I think I better just go for a walk," and Mandy walks with her to the front entrance of the facility and pats her shoulder before Coach heads for the dirt path that loops around the facility and meets up with a dirt road that has deep holes in it filled with standing water and hovering mosquitoes.

*T*his is our killer. He has no interest in going to jail, or being punished for his crimes, or being recognized and publicized. I am the most dangerous kind of killer, he thinks to himself while using a paper towel to slowly wipe his face of the crumbs that have collected there from eating his turkey-and-sweet-pickle sandwich. So many experts would hypothesize, he's sure, that he kills young women because of some deep-seeded psychological reason. Perhaps he had a mother who beat him. But none of that's accurate. He simply likes to kill young women. The last girl, Kim, was strong. He could feel her fighting against him, the muscles in her back toned as hard as wire cables from doing the butterfly. He liked how her hair smelled like a mix of chlorine and shampoo, the smell of both those things coming through his nose and trying to compete with each other to define her overall scent. He liked how young Kim was. He especially enjoyed watching the light go out of Kim's eyes when she died in his arms. He feels he has that light inside of him now because he kissed her eyes. He feels special because of it, and growing up, he never felt special. He always felt anything but special. His parents were addicted to heroin. The only thing special to them was their fix. They would get high on the couch together in their trailer home that was on stilts and did not have a foundation. Beneath their home there was garbage—empty bags of snack-size chips and beer bottles with faded, peeling labels. Watching his parents, he would notice how dull their eyes became when they were high. Sometimes he would go up to them on the couch, next to the coffee table with the syringes and the spoon and the lighter, and he would tug on his mother's hiked up skirt or his father's loose jeans. "What's to eat?" he would ask. "Are you really hungry?" they would say, and they would let their heads fall on the back of the couch while they smiled, their eyes cloudy, looking as if they were swimming in milk. I'll never be that way, he thought to himself, and still does.

He stands and puts his clothes in the dryer after they're done with the wash cycle. I am just like any other man, he thinks. I perform domestic duties. I have a job. I pay my taxes. I curse in heavy traffic. I floss my teeth with floss that glides. I will never be caught. My last thought, before I die, will be congratulatory—I will say to myself, How clever you were. No one ever found out. There is something reassuring about knowing what your last thought will be right before you die. As if, somehow, you have cheated death. All those women I have killed, they had lives ahead of them they looked forward to living, but I cheated death by taking them before natural death could. Doesn't that make me just as powerful as death itself?

*T*his is night at Chris and Paul's house. Chris can hear cars on the road because their house is on a main stretch. Their road leads to the shopping malls and to the facility, about twenty minutes away, but after a certain hour, no one travels the road and you can only hear the sounds of animals, sometimes the chattering and trilling of a raccoon in a treetop talking to a mate, sometimes the grunt or hoot of a black bear come to bat at the hanging bird feeder to knock it down with its sharp claws and eat the seeds. This is Chris, when Paul gets home late at night, lying awake in bed and listening to the door swing open and closed, listening to the dog's nails clack on the floor as she goes up to him, probably stretching first and yawning, the dog going in for a pat on the head before returning to the corner and falling back asleep. This is Chris wondering if Paul's going to stay in the kitchen or the living room for a while and read before he comes to bed. This is Chris wondering if she should get up and put her robe on and walk out of the bedroom to wherever he is and ask him where he was. This is Chris wondering if she really wants to know where he was and if maybe, as she's standing there with her robe on, she should just go into Cleo's room and check on her, or maybe she should go into Cleo's room and lie down next to her and fall back asleep with her arm wrapped around her daughter's side and the outline of a mobile of our solar system clearly visible as it turns slowly above their heads. This is Chris already knowing the answer she will get from Paul if she asks him where he was, because it is the answer he has been giving her for weeks now. "I've been writing in my office at the college," he says. He doesn't explain any more than that. He doesn't say he really works better there and that's why he's doing it. This is Chris turning over when Paul finally does come into bed so that she is not facing him. This is Chris closing her eyes and breathing in deeply, thinking that what she's smelling could very well be the smell of another woman, or the smell of his office, or the smell of the air freshener that dangles from his rearview.

This is Chris thinking that most likely what she's smelling is not even him, but herself, the garlic on her fingertips from when she sliced it to put in the pasta sauce she made for herself and Cleo for dinner, or the conditioner she used on her hair, or the lilac bush she brushed against when she went for a walk. This is the night, getting darker and quieter, and the moon and the stars hiding behind clouds so thick they seem more like walls and not mere water droplets you're supposed to be able to walk through. This is Chris listening to Paul's breathing beside her, wondering now as he falls into sleep what or whom he'll be dreaming of. She remembers how when they were first married they would fall asleep on their sides, her front facing his back. The only way she could fall sleep was if her arm was draped over him, hugging him. Now she can't fall asleep if their legs are even grazing each other. Tonight, though, it doesn't matter that she's all the way over on her side of the bed and not even close to him. She can't sleep at all. She has read the paper, about the girl named Kim on the team who was killed. She is so angry with the killer. She is angrier with him than she is at Paul, who she thinks might be cheating on her. It is an old anger that she feels. Anger with a history. From what? she thinks, and then she knows. Anger with having Beatrice taken away from her when she was a young girl. Anger with those horrid rapists. It's what's inside of her. It's what Chris mistakenly thought all this time was a feeling of tiredness she couldn't get rid of. Suddenly she realizes what the feeling is: pure anger. It's almost a relief now, not to be angry with Paul any longer and just to be angry with this killer, but in the same moment she fears for Cleo, hoping the killer doesn't decide to target another girl on the team. What would she do if Cleo were murdered? She doesn't even want to consider it, but her mind, going too fast for her to control, throws images together, almost all at once, of Cleo running from the killer, her blond hair flashing white in the dark, of Cleo with blood pouring out of her neck, of Cleo being lowered into a grave white with frost. That killer better be caught, she thinks, and it isn't until she goes to wipe a tear from her eye that she realizes she's been grabbing her blankets the whole time, keeping a corner of them clenched in a ball in her fist while imaginary images of the death of her daughter keep coming at her.

Part Two

CHAPTER SIXTEEN

You can lie in bed after Thomas wakes up and goes downstairs to eat breakfast, and think about all that has happened. You can look around your room at the knotty pinewood that resembles, in some places, faces of people who are laughing, or a bird looking up, its beak raised. You can put your hands behind your head and say to yourself you don't understand how it came to be that you are smitten, and, yes, this is the word that you think is appropriate, smitten with another man. You'd like to call Paul and ask him if he's heard about Kim, the girl from the swim team who was killed on the highway. You wonder if he thinks that, after all these years, it could be the same man who killed Bobby Chantal. You get yourself up and then you get your girls up, it's getting late now, and you have to be at practice at seven a.m. and it is now 5:50 and it takes you at least forty-five minutes to drive there. At this rate, the girls will end up having to take their cereal bowls into the car, and they will most likely spill their cereal as you go around the tight curves and over the potholes the flood left from the year before, and as you try to avoid the roadkill that seem to be everywhere these days. You wonder, as you're getting into the car and reminding your daughters at the same time to make sure they have their swimsuits and goggles in their swim bags, if Chris would have married Paul if she had known he left a woman for dead at a rest stop. You wonder how come you're so forgiving yourself. You can't believe you're so smitten. What happened to maturing with age and placing the family first? Is this what Anna Karenina felt when she was cheating on her husband with Vronksy? Did she feel that it was beyond her control, that a pursuit of love and emotional honesty overrode her obligation to be dutiful, and that if she didn't follow her heart then she just wasn't being true to herself and would rather die than live a lie? Or did she not think at all, was she not capable of analyzing her situation, but only able to act and react? All you know is that when you last saw Paul at the pool at a practice you felt light and giddy, your heart skipped, and you think even your feet felt elevated off the ground. You talked quickly and you laughed often and you gestured using broad, embarrassing strokes with your hands. When you caught sight of your reflection in a window glass while talking to him, you saw that you were flushed and your mouth was curved up in a smile, even if what you might have been talking about wasn't funny at all.

Paul leaving that woman at the rest stop was so long ago, you think maybe it doesn't matter. You think how it is easy to make mistakes when you're young. You remind yourself of mistakes you made yourself—things you said to people you wish you hadn't. When you get to the pool and you see Chris with puffy eyes coming up to you wanting to talk, you wish it were Paul instead. You wish you could talk to Paul and not Chris, who says, "Can I talk to you a minute?" and you know it will be much longer than a minute. You sit with her at the tall café table with the tall stools that are by the windows looking into the pool. In the pool, when you're swimming, you're not thinking about your brother at least. It's as if the water is trying to protect you from those thoughts. When you swim, you are thinking about swimming. Whether your arms are straight enough out in front of you after a flip turn. Whether your kick is strong enough. Whether your head should be tucked lower on your entry with the fly. You sit with your swim bag on your lap because you would like to jump in the water soon, and by holding it on your lap you think you will be that much closer to feeling the cool water waking you up.

You don't know how to keep Chris from crying. Her tears slide down her cheeks. You see things in her eyes you've never seen before. Rods and pie shapes and flecks in her irises. It's as if her eyes were in the middle of exploding, and you were seeing all the bits and pieces shooting off in all directions. She tells you it's not about Paul, it's about Kim. She can't believe how awful she feels. She didn't know the girl well. You tell her, of course, she's been going through a lot lately, and after all, it is tragic. It's all only normal, you say. You feel your swim bag in your lap now feeling very heavy, as if it just got heavier to remind you that you should jump in the pool and do some laps, and work on your fly, and work on your free, and work on your breast, and work on your back. There is so much to remember. With the fly, keep from diving deep. With the free, keep your kick strong. With your breast, remember to glide. With your back, move your body, not your head, from side to side. With Chris, keep telling her everything will be all right.

You watch Chris shaking her head. You wonder why she's smiling. You think it is maybe because she is trying to be strong, but she can't, and she knows it, and so all she can do is smile, laughing at herself. You reach out and grab her hand and cover it with yours. You tell her to go on up to the bleachers and watch her daughter in practice. Tell her you've noticed how Cleo has improved her breast. She's using the rocking motion much like the motion she uses in butterfly to give her the forward thrust. Tell her you've noticed that the girls who do that are the ones who seem to win all of their races, mention other girls on the team who do this, lower your head when Kim comes to mind, but don't mention the name Kim because it's just too sad right now to think of the poor girl who was killed at the rest stop.

While swimming an easy five-hundred free to warm up, you see Chris in the bleachers watching the team. There's a sad smile on her face and even from far away you can see how beautiful Chris is. You can also see how men sitting in the bleachers just reading books or working on their computers while waiting for their daughters to finish practice glance up from what they're doing once in a while to look at Chris and smile at her. You feel slow in the water. You must be tired. You remember waking up in the night when Thomas woke to shut the windows, and you remember flashes of lightning breaking up the darkness over the hillside. You remember the dog barking for a little while, a bark that made you think there was someone coming up to the house, but then you fell back asleep, telling yourself it was probably just a deer. You live far out in the country. You live so far out in the country that a while back your dog had run to the low kitchen windows and barked at a moose that was a few hundred feet away, standing by an old burn pile where Thomas had set some brush on fire to get rid of it. The moose was a cow, and did not have the signature antlers, but she was big, and the barking did not send her tearing off through the woods back to where she had come from, as a skittish deer would have done. Instead the moose stumbled around for a while, grazing, and then she lifted her head in the air and turned to the left, ambling off. Through the window you could hear the clomp of hooves the size of dinner plates as she tread over the burnt ground.

You break into fly. It feels good to feel your heart pumping faster. You swim two laps without taking a breath every time you bring out your hands, but then you switch to taking a breath every time. Fly was always a challenge. The swim-team girls practicing in the lane over from you make it look easy, though. You try to watch them underwater while you swim next to them. How was it they could kick while their hands entered the water, and then kick again as their hands exited the water, without looking spastic, the way you knew you looked when you did it? You think you hear the water sigh. You wonder if it was you sighing instead. Then you wonder if it could possibly be the water sighing, and you wonder what it was sighing about. Was it a sad sigh? Did it miss the streamlined body of Kim Hood moving through it? Then you think you hear the water whispering again, only it's more like the sound of a strong wind that has been recorded through a microphone and played back. The sound whips about your ears as you swim, sounding as if it is repeating one word with each gust. It sounds as if it is saying "stop, stop, stop," and you wonder why. What exactly should you stop? But that is not so difficult to figure out. There are so many things you should stop. You should stop bringing your right arm in close to your body on your pull in the freestyle. You should stop kicking as if you weren't really kicking at all. You should keep your head higher. You should stop diving so deep in the fly. You should stop thinking about Paul. You used to think about your brother too much, and you'd swim to forget him. Now you think about Paul in order to forget your brother, and thinking about Paul is like diving too deep in the fly. It makes the recovery that much harder, you have that much more water to lift yourself out of, that much more time wasted before you can lift up your head and breathe. Instead you should be thinking about your girls. You should be making sure Sofia really doesn't need your help getting used to menstruation. How can you assume that everything she needs to know she read in a book or she learned from her friends? You think how you should be trying harder to listen to Thomas when he tells you about articles he has read in magazines. You think how it's his way of talking to you, and it's always been his way of talking to you. It's not as if there were a time when you were first married or before you were married that he sat down with you and asked you to tell him all your deepest feelings. Even before you were married he would say, "Hey, listen to this," and he would tell you an idea of his or about some article he was reading. When you responded, or just understood what he was trying to tell you, you knew he felt closer to you because you now shared a common language with him, and it was his favorite language. For him it was better than intimacy. You tell yourself you will stop thinking about your brother and Paul and then you do stop, because the susurrations you hear from the water telling you to stop aren't stopping. You get out and think that if you just go to the bathroom and jump back into the pool, maybe then the sounds will stop. When you go into the locker room, you see Alex sitting on the bench.

She is holding her head and crying. "It hurts, Mom," she says. Ah, this is why the water told me to stop, you think. She hit her head coming up for a turn at the wall on the pole that extends under the blocks to hold onto before taking off on a backstroke start. There is a little blood, but she will be all right. You hold her. You get her an ice pack. You tell her to sit out the rest of the practice.

When you go back into the water to finish your swim, the water no longer tells you to stop. You have a good workout, doing a set of ten fifties on the fifty easily, until you see state troopers walk onto the pool deck. They look stiff in their uniforms and overly dressed compared to the swimmers on the team, who wear their low-backed practice suits, and compared to the coach, who wears a team tee shirt and shorts. You see the coach tell the swimmers to keep going on with their set, and then she talks to the troopers. You wish you could hear what they are saying, but of course you cannot. Swimming in the pool with everyone now doing a kick set makes it difficult to hear anything but splashing, and also the music is blaring away. It isn't until you are out of the water and grabbing your bag to go into the showers that you overhear one gray-haired trooper, with a nose that looks as if it has been bashed in more than once, say that he was on the original case years ago when a young nurse was murdered at the same rest stop, and since then, he says, there have been several other women murdered, and he thinks the cases are all related. Even though you are warmed up from doing your swimming, you suddenly feel cold, as if the facility's skylights have opened up suddenly, letting in a cold draft that runs over your wet skin and makes you shiver and makes you walk quickly to the locker room and into the warm showers. The boy in the wheelchair is in the next shower again. He is repeating "water, water, water," and his aide is telling him again, "Yes, you're right. We're in the shower. This is the water." You close your eyes under the hot shower, and an image of Paul comes to you, and then you know you must wipe the image away. I will not think of him anymore, you tell yourself. "Water, water, water," you hear the boy in the wheelchair say, and then to stop yourself from thinking of Paul you say to yourself, Stop, stop, stop, and somehow, for a while, it works, and you do not think of Paul.

CHAPTER SEVENTEEN

*T*his is Mandy sweeping the facility deck, thinking how can so many people, who must have some money because they can afford the facility membership, be such slobs and be so careless? There are candy wrappers left in the lockers and a pair of brand-new sneakers forgotten under the benches. Where she's sweeping now, on the other side of the glass wall where one can see the lazy river, there's a wad of chewed-up gum some pig spit onto the floor. Even if there are some members who haven't been raised with money, at least they should keep their facility clean and throw away their garbage. While she's trying to remove the gum from the broom's bristles, a little boy comes up to her and asks her what is under the big metal grate at the bottom of the lazy river. "That? That is the entrance to the tunnel that leads to where I live!" Mandy says. "Really?" the boy says, and Mandy nods, thinking she misses when her daughter was young and gullible, and she reaches out to pat the boy on the shoulder and reassure him it's all right when the boy runs away screaming, "She's going to kill me!" and the boy's mother marches over to Mandy and tells her, "Don't touch my child ever again," and Mandy, holding the broom, thinks how she'd like to shoo the mother away with the bristles of the broom as if the mother were a mangy cat who had wandered inside the doorway. Now this is Mandy sitting in the facility director's office being read the riot act, which she doesn't listen to, instead looking at framed photographs on the wall of skiers going down mountains that look too big to be in this country, and she wonders why an aquatic facility director has pictures in his office of snow-covered mountains, and not pictures of large bodies of water that are tempting to swim in. This is Mandy not being fired, but being close to fired, and going back into the locker room to mop, but then going into a bathroom stall instead and sitting down on the uncovered seat while still wearing her jeans. She shakes her head, and cries a little, and then shakes her head some more. She cannot help but think of the girl Kim, who was murdered. Mandy has stopped at that rest stop many times before, usually when she and her husband were on their way to the lake for the weekend. She remembers the girl, Kim. She always smiled at Mandy, and said hello when she saw her. Mandy thinks how the next time she drives up along that stretch of highway with the rest stop, she will stop and leave a bouquet of flowers in a vase. Maybe she can even get her husband to make a wooden plaque with Kim's name on it and the date of her birth and death.

The dancing hippos enter the locker room noisily. The dancing hippos are a group of older women who take a swimmercize class. No one likes the dancing hippos, because they could just as well do their workout in the smaller pool with the lazy river, but instead they come into the competition pool and take up lanes and space and their hair spray gets mixed with the pool water and the cloying fumes get inhaled by all the lap swimmers. In the locker room they talk about Kim, how awful they feel for the mother, how they have told their own grown children to stay off the highways at night and, whatever they do, never to stop at a rest stop. Then they start chatting and laughing about something you don't want to know about. They can carry on that way for long stretches of time, discussing inanities such as where they bought a potholder or how to rid the garden of blight, all the while blow-drying their hair at the sink and spreading on lipsticks the colors of corals and flamingos and baby blankets. You don't have a garden, and anything to do with gardening usually makes you sleepy right away. You don't know how to recognize different plants raised for eating unless the fruit or the vegetable is hanging right off them. You don't know you need stakes for tomatoes or twine for training snow peas. You don't care. Why don't the dancing hippos just shut their mouths for once? Why are they always so loud about nothing? Why do they take so long to get dressed? Don't they have families to go home to and chores to be done? You know that the minute you enter the door at home you have to start cooking dinner and feed the dog that will be barking continuously until you do. You know you have to empty the dishwasher to load the dishwasher before you even have enough counter space to be able to chop the vegetables and start the dinner for the family, and your girls will be starving, of course. They'll tell you they are starving, and if you tell them to be quiet, they will tell you how many yards they have swum, and it will be in the thousands, and then you will feel bad for them because it is such a long way to travel, all those yards, without eating. Sofia will tell you exactly how far she has swum. She has been tracking how far and recording it in cyberspace. Already she is rounding the southern part of the island of Saint Kitts, and heading back north. You imagine her really swimming in the Caribbean. You see her amidst the blue and green clear water. You see her from up above. She is smiling. She is not concerned with taking out her first fifty faster, the way the coach has been telling her to do. She is just swimming at her own pace, occasionally turning her head to the side, admiring a nearby breaching dolphin, a pelican's impressive dive.

The dancing hippos cackle, at least that's what you hear, a high-pitched cackle that sounds like blackbirds or angry seagulls. You wish you were back on your vacation at the equator and not in the locker room with the dancing hippos, who are now talking about church. At the equator, from a great height overlooking the ocean, you saw a pod of whales that looked just like a breeze ruffling the water here and there. You ate a strange red fruit that looked like the inside of a fig when you bit into it, but almost tasted like a tomato. You used soap on your body provided in the shower that was in the shape of a seashell. You never wore a sweater at night or a wrap. You saw a snake rising from its own coiled body on the driveway to look at you in the headlights of your rental truck. You picked up a crab on the beach with a body as yellow as the sun and legs the color of Japanese eggplants. You stepped on stingrays that slid out from under your feet and made you jump on your surfboard and paddle hard away from them in any direction you could. You breathed in the air deeply while watching stars, and thinking what you were breathing in was some of the light from the stars as well. They were vast, expanding breaths that you thought made you think more clearly.

Now the dancing hippos are talking about food, which they always do after their aerobics class. They trade recipes back and forth that do sound good. Swedish meatballs and Brie cheese baked in puff pastry. This is not the talk of the swim-team parents. We, the swim-team parents, talk of roasted edamame beans for quick protein. We compare organic chocolate milk brands that come in convenient containers. We cook fava beans. We make quinoa pilaf. We flavor with sea salt. We bake with flax. We fry in cast iron. We create salads with fiddleheads found on our land or in our neighbor's fields. We berry-pick at local farms. We meet the steer we'll consume throughout the year. We raise our own hens. We raise our own turkey. We make our own ice cream. We know the horrors of the levels of the saturated fats in the nearby chain's doughnuts. We extol the local Japanese sushi joint. We do not talk of the bag of peanut M&M's we buy to get us through the long day of working at a swim meet. We will not talk of the Diet Coke we drink, perfectly timed to be drunk after our coffee and before the lunch hour, but never in front of our children, lest they see how we drink soda, and we never let them drink it themselves unless it's soda water flavored with natural juice high in some kind of element or vitamin they wouldn't normally get in their daily diet and packaged in a can whose design wipes out any image of an industrial facility spewing smoke, spinning the dials of the electric meter, and hiring immigrants at low wages. Instead the can design screams healthy, whole, natural, good for you, flowers, fruit orchards, and sunshine. As if the cans themselves were just plucked from trees.

You wish the dancing hippos would talk more of food. You'd like to ask them the perfect recipe for a piecrust. You have been trying to perfect your own. One recipe you know calls for vodka instead of water (vodka doesn't evaporate during baking). One recipe asks for lard, not butter. One recipe asks specifically for vegetable shortening to ensure flakiness. One recipe says keep the butter cold with ice before you use it. One recipe asks for baking soda. One recipe asks for ground almond bits. Which recipe do you choose? you want to know, but don't know how to interrupt. Do you just barge in on the conversation, smiling, asking if they could share their favorite piecrust technique? Do you not interrupt, because you feel guilty that when you saw them in the pool, in the end lane, smelling up the water with their hair spray, you wished them, and their ludicrous weight belts for jogging and their foam noodles wedged between their legs for floating, out of the pool and back where they came from.

Now the dancing hippos are singing. It is from a musical. It is from *My Fair Lady*. "With a Little Bit of Luck" is the song. It is from when Eliza Doolittle's father danced through the streets, weaving in and out of bars, singing that all he needed was a little bit of bloomin' luck. You dress so quickly to get away from them that you don't even bother to brush your hair in front of the mirror. You brush it while running out of the locker room door. You are fighting a knot in your hair so snarled it seems to have claws and be fighting back, when you see Paul waiting in the foyer. The minute you see him you want to do an about-face and go back into the locker room and finish brushing your unruly hair.

You want to apply eyeliner and lipstick to spruce yourself up. You'd even use a coral-color lipstick like the dancing hippos use, anything to avoid having him see you the way you look now. Your graying hair bushy around your temples and your eyes with rings around them from the impressions your goggles left on them. You don't turn around, though, and he waves to you and smiles and walks toward you. You can't help but smile back. Maybe your hair doesn't look that bad after all. He puts his hand on your arm when you get close enough. "Hey," you say. You begin to blush. You can feel your face turning hot, even though your hair's still wet from your shower and the rest of you feels refreshed. "What are you doing here? I thought Chris dropped Cleo off today."

"She did. She left early, though, and asked me to swing by and pick Cleo up after work. It's on my way." Just then, the troopers walk out of the facility, their radios crackling against their hips and their shoes squeaking loudly on the polished floor.

"Did you hear about the girl on the team?" you ask Paul while watching the troopers as they leave. The old trooper, the one with the nose that makes him look like a prizefighter, gives one last look at the people working at the front desk before he leaves the facility, as if wanting to memorize their faces.

"I did," Paul says. "It's incredible. The same rest stop, and everything."

"Do you think it's the same man?" you ask.

"I don't know what to think. The car's got to be different, though. That was a long time ago."

"What do you mean, the car's got to be different? Did you see a car that night?"

"Yes, didn't I tell you? It was a red Corvair. It would be a classic by now. It was probably a classic then."

"But you said you didn't have any information to give the police. You said you wouldn't be able to help them in any way," you say, suddenly feeling very tired, almost sick from feeling so tired, and thinking maybe it has been a while since you have eaten, but the last thing you want now is to eat. The facility smells like onion bagels being toasted at the snack stand, but toasted too long, almost burning. You wish you could go outside, but you have to wait for your daughters to come out of the locker room.

"Paul, a car? Really? You saw a car all those years ago?" you say, almost with a pleading tone in your voice, wanting him to tell you the truth, to clear things up. You are confused. If only you were back on vacation at the equator, on that long stretch of beach where at night the stars were so bright that when you breathed in they seemed to clear everything up for you. The coach of the team then comes out of the pool area. She has a duffel bag over her shoulder and a light jacket on. She is obviously done for the night and going home. She doesn't say good night or anything to Paul or you as she walks out. She walks with her head down and her lips pursed.

Paul speaks quietly. "I think we should talk about this some other time. Not here."

You are waiting for him to suggest another time and place. What if he asks you what you are doing later on? Sleeping, I'll be sleeping, you think, and for a flash of a moment you think of your bed with the flowered cotton sheets that look like wild flowers and vines and you wish you were in it right at that moment, on the verge of the sweetness of sleep. You are not in the least bit free later on. You have to go home and make your family dinner. You have to do dishes and put clothes in the dryer and a new load in the washer. You have to choose photos to send your client from your last photo shoot. You see the hours spanning in front of you. You have to read about what's going to happen to Anna Karenina. Of course you know the ending, everyone knows the tragic ending, but maybe somewhere along the way, in all of that text, you'll find there's a way she could have avoided her death—a place where she could have changed herself. You sometimes feel that reading books is the only way you can think, as if the reading occupied one part of your brain and this allowed the other part to go free and become more active. You need that time to read in order to think. That's all there is to it. Paul never suggests when and where another time would be. "All right, some other time," you say. And then your eye begins to twitch. It sometimes does this when you are tired, or when your goggles have pressed on the side of your eyelid for too long. You turn away so Paul won't see it and think you are spastic or have neural problems. Luckily, Cleo comes out of the locker room. She is showered and dressed, her swim bag slung over her shoulder. Paul smiles at you. "Have a good night, then," he says, and touches your arm before he looks at Cleo and asks her if she is ready to leave.

Driving home your girls ask about Kim. You decide that what is best is that you answer them as truthfully as you can. You are so thankful they are not old enough to drive yet, not while this killer is still at large. Alex wants to know if Kim knew the man who killed her, and Sofia wants to know what Kim was doing at a highway rest stop at night, anyway. Didn't everyone know they were dangerous and you weren't supposed to stop at those

things? "Really, they should rename them kill stops," Sofia says.
That night Alex wants you to snuggle with her in bed. You move
the assortment of books off her bed and climb in next to her. You
slide Alex inside the space you make when you are curled on
your side and you stroke your girl's hair and together you stare
out at the sky and the trees that are lit up by the light of the stars.
Alex says their coach kept making mistakes that day. She would
assign them six fifties to practice and then stop them after the
fifth fifty, or she would assign them eight one-hundred IMs and
then insist they hadn't done all eight of them and make them do
an extra.

"It's hard on her," you say. "She was close to Kim. She coached
her for years, and now she's gone."

"Mom," Alex says, "she's not just gone. She was murdered. She
had her throat slit. Do you think when your throat's slit and you're
bleeding to death that you can still see and hear and think?"

"Maybe, for a second, but that's a lot of blood to lose very
quickly. I'm sure she just passed out."

Alex shuts her eyes and then opens them and says, "You know
how you can see the silver outlines of shapes under your eyelids
even after you've closed your eyes? You know how it looks like a
photo? Do you think the police can get that image off the insides
of Kim's eyelids? I mean, maybe from her eyes they can get a picture of what Kim last saw. Maybe it was a picture of the guy standing over her, making sure she was really dead. Wouldn't that be
cool?" You agree it would be cool. "We'd be rich if we could figure
out that process," Alex says, sounding just like Thomas. You wonder what the last thing was that your brother probably saw. The
telephone in his room, where the last phone call was to a friend?

The stereo system knobs before they were splattered with blood? A picture of himself on a shelf as a boy holding on to his favorite stuffed animal? It was a dog he named Doggy Dear and its coat was bald in patches from her brother plucking the fur and twirling it between his thumb and forefinger in order to comfort himself.

CHAPTER EIGHTEEN

A week later there is a memorial for Kim in the auditorium at her school. Students are invited, the coach, as well as a few older girls from the swim team. Kim's mother wishes the girls from the team weren't there, only because seeing them reminds her so much of Kim, and also because they look so strange wearing clothes and not their swimsuits. Kim's mother hardly recognizes some of the girls with their hair brushed and dry. They also wear dark dresses and are crying, their heads lowered. The girls she's used to seeing on the team hold their heads high and laugh, but these girls are bent over as their shoulders shake with their sobs. Kim's mother wishes the coach, who is also shaking with sobs, would just do what she does best, and go down the line, facing these girls, telling them they've got to dig in and push themselves harder than ever before. The coach should be high-fiving the girls and wearing her athletic shorts and her team shirt, not this heavy dark dress just past her knees and covering her arms, her hands low in front of her clasped tightly together. Who is this woman? thinks Kim's mother, and then Kim's mother is also lowering her head, the sobs coming again as they have been coming for days, her shoulders even sore from them. Kim's father puts his arm around Kim's mother, but instead of it feeling comforting, it feels weightless, as if he were a small bird just alighting on her for a moment, and she can sense how any moment he will remove his arm, and fly off, and she will be left feeling only the absence of warmth.

This is an evening at home. This is one of Alex's violin strings breaking in the middle of an étude, and Thomas helping her feed a new one in through the peg holes. This is Sofia curled in her bed, using a stuffed bear as a pillow and reading and rolling her eyes every time Thomas tells her to come downstairs and start doing math work. This is you staring at the photos you took at your latest wedding shoot, thinking how if it weren't your camera the photos came from you would say the photos weren't yours. You barely remember taking them. It seems so long ago because everything prior to the death of Kim seems long ago. This is a strong wind coming up, and the old sheets of aluminum that Thomas uses to cover the stacked woodpiles sail off and sound like thunder, startling everyone, making Sofia look up from her book, making Thomas and Alex turn their heads to look out the window, making you lift your head from looking at photos you could almost swear you never took.

This is the night, when you first close your eyes after turning off the light. This is you in the dark asking Thomas how his work was at the lab today, and this is Thomas not even answering, but falling asleep so quickly you can't believe it when you start to hear him snore. This is you thinking about your brother. That time at the beach when he scooped you up and ran. Why did he do it? you wonder. What was the rush? Why did he run so fast? What was he running away from? You don't know, but you think maybe it holds the key that will unlock answers for you as to why he killed himself years later. You push the thoughts of your brother aside. You remember Paul at the pool instead. You are thankful you've been running into Paul at the pool these past few weeks since you last saw the trooper at the pool. This is you seeing his face at the pool the last time you saw him at practice. He was smiling at you. You want to keep the image there a while, but then Thomas turns on his side, facing away from you, and you are reminded you share your bed with Thomas, and the image of Paul fades, and you are just left with sleep. Sleep is rolling over you, closing off images and voices you have seen and listened to throughout the day. The last voice you hear, though, is Paul's, from that day a few weeks ago when he was saying, "It was a red Corvair. It would be a classic by now. It was probably a classic then." You can't believe how his words are coming back to you now. It's as if after the first time he said them, you deliberately forgot them. But now you remember, and it jolts you awake.

In the morning, while the girls are still sleeping and Thomas has left for work, you don't even sit down to eat your cereal. You hold it standing at the counter. The voice of Paul saying it was a red Corvair plays over and over again in your mind. You stand because you don't want to have the feeling of the floor beneath the chair sucking you down and you having to hold on to the armrests just to keep yourself from sinking. And what if I just call the police and tell them that information? you think to yourself. Aren't there anonymous tip lines? A tip that's not going to implicate Paul? But no, he should be the one to leave the tip. It would only be right. It could be helpful, really helpful. Maybe this is the same guy, and maybe years ago he owned that red Corvair and there's a record of it and his name could be discovered. Before you realize it, you have finished your cereal. You don't even remember eating it. You've been so lost in thought. You don't remember if you fed the dog either, so you feed her again, even though Thomas always says the dog is fat enough, and that if anything you should let her skip a meal.

That evening you drive the girls quickly to practice. When you're going past the house that looks as if it's folded in half, you forget you're in a thirty-mile-per-hour zone and go forty-five instead. You're all set to tell Paul what he should do. Call the police tip hotline. You even copied the number down on a Post-it note for him. Your daughters look up from the books they are reading. "Jeez-um," says Sofia. "We're almost at the pool already. You must have speeded all the way here."

"Look at this booger, Mom," Alex says as you pull up in front of the pool.

"Do I have to?" you say.

"Yes, look, it's got three of my hairs in it!" Alex says.

"Oh my God, she is not my sister," Sofia says. "You're all not related to me. Tell me I was adopted, please. Anything but knowing we share the same gene pool."

"Not only do we share the same gene pool, Sofia, we share the same swimming pool!" Alex says.

"Yuck, I am not looking at your hairy booger," you say to Alex, laughing. "Go, go, get out of the car and get to practice."

After the girls leave the car, you wait in the parking lot for Paul to pull up so you can talk to him outside the facility, away from the eyes of the other parents, such as Dinah, who you see has now taken to bringing small binoculars with her to practice, supposedly to be able to watch her daughter, but every now and again you see the lenses of the binoculars focused on you when you're talking to Paul. Usually some parents park and let their kids walk up to the facility, but now you notice that more are dropping their children off at the entrance, afraid the killer might just grab them and force them into his car. Some parents are even getting out of the car and walking their children into the facility and helping them undress in the locker room. In small groups in the foyer, parents talk to each other about the death of Kim. You have seen them hugging each other more often. You have overheard the words "terrible" and "tragic" and "such a beautiful girl" so many times in the past few weeks. You have said those same words yourself when talking to the parents while you are standing shoulder to shoulder, staring in at your children through the glass window and watching them swim, almost afraid to take your eyes off them for minute, not even daring to run errands while they're practicing, because what if? What if one of your own was now in the grave?

It's Chris who drives into the parking lot after dropping off the girls at the facility's front entrance, not Paul.

"Hi. What happened to Paul?" you ask.

"He had work to do at his office, so I brought Cleo instead," Chris says.

This is you in the parking lot with a slight breeze blowing by, blowing through your hair and making it come up around your face so that it gets in your mouth and your eyes, but blowing through Chris's hair and making it blow back behind her head as if she were an actress on some movie set and not in the facility's parking lot where there are stains on the asphalt from members dumping out the remains of their morning coffee. This is Chris asking you if you've heard any more about Kim's murder. This is Chris saying all she's heard on the news is that the cops don't have a clue, but that they think it may be the same murderer who killed a few nurses at rest stops years ago. "I hope that bastard gets caught," she says. "I have a feeling he's not done killing young girls, and the next one could be one of ours." This is you thinking this is the first time you've ever heard Chris say a curse word. This is Chris saying she's tempted to go and hunt the guy down herself. This is you laughing, because she must be kidding. This is her laughing too, saying, "Right, I can't even catch my husband cheating on me when I know he is. How could I possibly catch a murderer?"

This is the wind blowing so that strands of your hair are thick in your mouth, while Chris's hair is still blown back perfectly behind her. These are the mountains around you, storm clouds gathering at their peaks, and next to them there is a hillside of exposed black granite that looks slick with rain, even though it isn't.

This is Kim's mother, at home in Kim's room, touching the silky ribbons on the curtain Kim created with all of the ribbons she ever won. This is Kim's mother wishing she had never asked Kim to take the wall down because she thought it made Kim think winning was more important than improving her technique. This is Kim's mother touching each and every silky ribbon on that homemade curtain because she knows at one time her daughter touched each one of them and maybe touching the ribbons is like touching Kim again.

This is Sofia about to practice with not one, not two, but three suits on for optimum drag. They are three of her oldest suits, the elastic giving way and the inside linings giving out. She has decided that if she swims with three on, then, come the next meet, when she's only wearing her skintight racing suit, she'll be that much faster, and maybe she'll be able to go faster in her first fifty the way Coach has wanted her to do. Everyone on the team is trying to swim harder now that Kim is gone, and now that Coach reminds them so often of how Kim was such a dedicated swimmer and how they should all follow her example. The coach has been reminding them so often that Sofia thinks to herself that it's not the swim team she's on any longer, but the "Kim team," with the swimmers' every stroke, every breath, every turn, and every kick taken in memory of Kim.

In the pool, the water gets trapped in the stretched-out seat of Sofia's outermost suit and makes a balloon. Swimming the practice and making the intervals is difficult with all of the suits on, but Sofia manages to do it. When she's finished with practice, she goes into the locker room to change, and when Mandy, who is cleaning the sinks in the locker room, sees Sofia walking in, she thinks how there are so many straps crossing over Sofia's back that it looks as though she's wearing a lattice fence. She's wearing a wing back, a fly back, and a vortex back all at once. It takes her five minutes in the bathroom stall to peel all of the straps off her shoulders. She breathes loudly when she does it, and even grunts and whimpers a few times. "Everything all right in there?" Mandy says on the other side of the stall, but Sofia is too shy to answer and maybe, just maybe, Mandy isn't talking to her but to someone else in the locker room.

CHAPTER NINETEEN

*T*his is you at the indoor facility, swimming in the water that's cold today, and slightly bumpy from the dancing hippos swimming in the lane beside you. You see Chris up in the bleachers, and you're glad it's not Paul up there watching you swim. You feel out of shape, even after swimming so often. You feel that besides the rest of your body starting to sag, your eyelids are starting to droop, and maybe it's reducing how much people can see of your eyes. Isn't it bad enough that you're only seeing 4 percent of the universe without looking as though you're seeing even less of it? This is you getting such a strong whiff of the hair spray from one of the dancing hippos that you feel it going down your throat and causing a burning sensation. These are Chris's words coming back to you, as your throat burns, and you feel a headache coming on from the perfume of the hair spray, that the next girl he kills could be one of yours. Something has to be done. The water seems to say it too. *Some-thing-has-to-be-done*, it says over and over while you kick a six-beat free-style kick. The police have to know what Paul knows. This is you getting out of the pool early, not finishing your warm-down of a two-hundred free that you like to do after a speed set. You're out early, rushing through your shower, putting conditioner in your hair even before all the shampoo's completely rinsed out, just so you can get to the phone and call the police hotline. You hate leaving your girls in, but you know they'll be fine while the coaches are there, and this is something you have to do because in the end it just might save another girl's life. You don't want to use your own phone. You want the call to be anonymous. You decide to drive to a nearby gas station where you remember seeing a payphone. You can't remember the last time you were in a payphone booth, but the one you're standing in now feels as though it was just set there this morning. It wobbles back and forth as you shift your weight, nervous and impatient while you hear the phone ringing. When you start retelling the story, that you know someone who was at the rest stop that night Bobby Chantal was murdered so many years ago, the woman taking the information starts talking to someone else. "I'll take a Homewrecker," the woman says, and a man's voice says, "You want chicken or beef in it?"

"Beef, here, take some money," the woman says.

"Are you listening to me?" you say. "Isn't this a police tip hotline? This is important."

"Yeah, sure, go on, oh, and Jimmy, get me a Coke with that Homewrecker too," the woman says.

Slamming a hard plastic phone back on a payphone's metal cradle is much more satisfying than pushing a button on a cell phone, you think to yourself as you slam the phone down. You've heard about tip hotlines before, how half the time the person taking the call is spinning their finger by their ear as if the person giving them information is crazy and can't be believed. What you really must do is get Paul to go in and give a detective the information that he knows.

Since you're out early from practice, you decide to go see if Paul's in his office at the college. He's not hard to find. You know which department he teaches in and his office address is listed. You wish you weren't going to his office but someplace else, someplace quiet, maybe even to the beach where you vacationed near the equator. You imagine watching incoming waves with Paul and sparks of phosphorescence in the water at night. You'd like to ask him more about his teaching. You know he teaches writing, but what exactly about writing does he teach? Does he have suggested methods? You once taught a class for students who were studying for college entrance exams, and in the training for the class you taught them tricks. You taught them that guessing is always better than leaving the answers blank. Does he have that sort of thing for his students? A checklist of sorts they can go through that helps them write well? You want to know what exercises he gives them to get their juices flowing. Does he tell them to keep a hat filled with favorite lines they have heard and then to close their eyes and pull one of the lines out and start with that? Does he tell them to triple-space their lines so they can see their mistakes more easily? You once had a teacher in a college composition class who told you to do this, but you had to stop after a while because you couldn't afford the paper it was using up.

When you're standing at Paul's office door, you can hear him talking to a student. The student is asking what Paul means by writing from the heart, and he says it means a lot of things, but the thing it means the most is to write something that she feels strongly about. Something that if she were denied the opportunity to write about, she would feel she couldn't go on. You slide down against the wall next to the door. This could be a long meeting, you think. You start thinking how you would do if you were a student in Paul's class. Would you even know what writing from the heart means? The only things you think of writing down are things that are not easy to describe. You want to write down how a sunset looks sometimes, but it is impossible for you to put it into words. Some sunsets to you feel different from other ones. The way the clouds sometimes pass quickly over the setting sun gives you a feeling of sadness, but how boring would that be to put on paper, and it's really not an image at all, is it? you think. Sometimes you want to describe the stars, how their incessant shining can make you feel claustrophobic. Where you live there is no other source of light from buildings or houses to diminish their glow, and sometimes you'd like them to stop winking. Sometimes you'd like to describe how the sound of a loon feels as though it enters through your chest, as if that's where you hear it first instead of through your ears. You realize why you take photographs for a living instead. It's so much easier when you don't have to describe what you feel and can just take a picture of it. You remember how when you first took a photography class in college, you were so excited to see what stories you could tell just with the shots you took. The teacher assigned everyone the task of putting captions of what the people were saying beneath the photos, and you couldn't bring yourself to do it. You received a poor grade for that class, but it made you want to become a professional photographer. You realized how much you wanted to be able to tell a story without words, and you realized you never wanted anyone to come along and ask of your photos, "And what is that person feeling?" You wanted them to be able to feel an emotion from just looking at the photo, and if they couldn't do it, then the photo wasn't worth taking in the first place. From then on you majored in photography. When graduation day arrived, you didn't even sit in the audience so you could take photos of your classmates, the bright sun shining down on their mortarboards and making the silky cloth look from up above like waves sparkling on a rippling sea. Oh, no, I would be a horrible student in Paul's class, you think, and you begin to feel sorry for the student too, until the door swings open and out comes this young, beautiful girl with long brown hair in tendrils that curl far past her shoulders and brush the hem of her shorts, which are so short they look more like bikini bottoms. A scent of jasmine seems to be coming from her skin as she walks by.

You can still smell the jasmine in Paul's office when you knock on the doorframe.

"Prof, I've got a problem," you say. "I can't write from the heart. It's all closed up. Can you help me?"

Paul smiles. "Hey, look who's here!" he says. "What brings you here? Aren't you supposed to be at practice? Sit down." He pulls out the chair that the beautiful student must have sat in. The seat is still warm.

"Practice isn't over yet. I still have time to pick the girls up. I, I . . ." Paul is leaning in close, and the smell of the jasmine seems to be surrounding you now. You start thinking maybe he's drawn to you because he just had the beautiful student in his office, and now he's aroused. "Paul, you've got to do something. You've got to talk to the police about what you know about that red Corvair. It could mean something to them, and that poor girl Kim from the swim team, well, in a few years that could be Cleo or my girls."

You notice while you're talking that Paul's office is decorated with different plaques. There are framed diplomas and framed awards, all with his name on them. You didn't realize how academic he was. He wears a white tee shirt and blue jeans most of the time, and for crying out loud, he wears his hair in a ponytail! How would anyone believe from meeting him outside of the college that he wasn't just some house painter or bartender?

"Have you been talking to Chris?" Paul says. "That's the same thing she said to me, that in a few years it could be Cleo that this man goes after. I don't think either of you realize what a huge coincidence that would be. It's just not going to happen to our girls. The odds have it."

"But it could happen to some other woman, and very soon."

"Listen, the incident just occurred a few weeks ago. We don't know, there may be plenty of witnesses who come forth in the coming weeks and who remember something suspicious from that night. Let's give them a chance to come forward with relevant information. The information I have is over twenty-eight years old. Whatever I tell them about a red Corvair with Illinois plates could even be a red herring and keep them from following a solid lead."

"You don't want to dig this all up, do you? Be honest, you're just covering your ass." You wish for an instant that you had swum your entire workout earlier, because right now you feel tense, and you don't have that dreamy feeling you usually have after you've swum a full hour and change.

Paul doesn't answer you. He covers his face with his hands, but just for an instant, letting his long fingers slide down his aquiline nose until the tips of his fingers rest over his lips. You stand up, ready to go. You know the answers now to your questions. Paul stands up with you. You think he's stood up to open the door for you, being just as anxious to have you out of there as you are to leave, as if somehow you're putting to shame all the plaques that line his walls, but instead he pulls you close to him and kisses you. You're overcome by how good it feels to kiss someone. It's like being handed a glass of water and drinking it all down, not realizing how thirsty you were when the glass was first handed to you. It has been so long. It has been too long. His lips are smooth and his tongue exerts just the right amount of pressure against your own. You'd like to go on kissing for a long time, because what's the harm in kissing? You'd like it to be this way forever because you never want it to go farther than this. When you start thinking of Thomas, you force him out of your mind. If Thomas kissed you more often, you'd never be here in this jasmine-smelling office in the first place. You will not let Thomas take away this moment, this one kiss, because that's all it will ever be, and its memory will have to last such a long time.

It's the ringing of your cell phone that interrupts the moment. It's not a number you know. When you answer the phone it's Sofia's voice. She must have borrowed a phone from a friend. "Mom, where are you? We've been waiting ten minutes. Practice ended early," she says.

"I'm coming. I'll be there soon," you say. "Oh, and be safe. Don't go outside. Wait for me in the foyer."

Paul locks up his office and walks out with you to your car. "Have a good night," he says, before you get in. You cannot look at his face. You're afraid if you do then you might want to continue with the kiss, right here in the parking lot, where someone might see him who knows him and knows he's married. Funny, you think while driving, that you consider the kiss interrupted and not ended, as if it were a thing to be continued at a later time.

Before Kim was murdered, some parents would drive their cars up to the entrance of the facility and wait for their swimmers to hop in the back. Some parents would sit in the parking lot and wait while reading a book. Some parents would park their cars and go into the facility and wait in the foyer, talking to other parents, about swimming or about school, or about anything, considering how they are all friends and see each other so often they can talk about anything, or sometimes they would just complain about how long it takes their swimmers to get out of the shower and get dressed. Some parents would barge right into the locker rooms and yell at their swimmers to hurry it up, while their swimmers were drying off and struggling to put on socks over wet feet, or while their swimmers were fooling around, the little ones hiding inside the metal lockers, bursting out like jack-in-the-boxes and screaming, "Surprise!" and the older ones chatting away with other girls about books and clothes and teachers. But now, since Kim has been killed, all the mothers have been going into the locker rooms and making sure their children are escorted into their cars. You would usually wait in the foyer for your children, but today Sofia and Alex are waiting outside for you as you drive up, and waving you down frantically, annoyed with you because you happen to be late, when recently, ever since Kim's death, you have picked them up straight from the locker room. You're annoyed with them too. You told them to wait inside and not go outside. It's then, when you see them waving as if they've been marooned on an island, that you remember what Paul said to you in his office, that the red Corvair had Illinois plates. He hadn't told you that before, you are almost sure of it. Wouldn't you have remembered that they were Illinois plates? Why is it that he keeps layering on the details about something that he at first said he knew nothing about at all? And why did he kiss you then, right after he said it? Was it to make you stop thinking about Bobby Chantal? You realize that the kiss made it difficult for you to understand what really happened that night he was with her. The kiss was like a layer of fog that crept inside of you, clouding up what might otherwise be clear, and masking whatever you heard.

"I'm starving!" you daughters say in unison when they get in the car, and to keep them quiet so that you can think about the kiss and the Illinois plates on the long drive home, you stop and let them buy doughnuts, only briefly thinking about what an unhealthy food they are.

homas says the universe is expanding like a balloon, and that every year we are twenty-two miles farther apart from other celestial bodies. You wonder, for a second, if he's making an analogy between you and him—that every year the two of you are drifting farther apart, but of course you know that's not how he thinks. He doesn't think about relationships. He thinks about actual celestial bodies. You want to know, then, why we bother trying to visit other solar systems when it's just going to be harder to do so every year. We should just give up now, you think, while looking down at the goose. The goose is two stories below on the ground and you can see the goose turning her head and looking up at you with one eye while you look out the window. "Hello, there, goose," you say, and the goose tilts her head some more. The goose, you think, does not care about the universe, or the expansion of it, and neither does she care about the neighbors or the road beyond. The goose maybe cares about the two chickens that eat her food, and the dog that eats her food, and maybe she cares about the fox that trotted off with the rooster in its mouth a while ago. The expanding universe is not on the goose's agenda, you think. This is you thinking that you need to stop thinking about Paul, Bobby Chantal, and the red Corvair, that those things shouldn't be on your agenda, because they are expanding your universe beyond proportions you can understand or are comfortable with. In order to keep your universe small, the way you like it, you start folding the towels. There are always so many towels, and you like to feel the nub of the terry cloth against your dry fingertips because your fingers are always dry from swimming in chlorine. You have to put away your clothes and Thomas's clothes, and then the girls' clothes, and then the rags that go in the rag chest, which are really not rags but just an assortment of napkins and dish towels you keep by the dining room table. Often, a stray sock or a pair of underwear gets thrown into the rag chest too and someone during a meal will go get a rag to wipe their face and dig into the rag chest without looking carefully at what they are picking up and they will end up wiping their face with a gym sock or a flowered panty instead, which gets everyone laughing at the dinner table, but not for long, because the meal has to be finished quickly, you and the girls have come back from swim practice so late and now there is violin to practice and now there is homework, and where are the protractors, the rulers, the colored pencils for filling in land-masses and rivers on maps? And how did this happen, Thomas asks you before bed, that Alex swims more than she studies? How did we let that happen? The swimming won't get her anywhere in life. How is it that our daughter knows nothing about how the plates move? About how magma was formed? About what igneous rocks are? About what sedimentary means? And you don't say so, but you are not so sure yourself. Sedimentary sounding awfully similar to sedentary, and does this mean they are rocks that formed by barely moving, and is such a thing even possible? Thank goodness it is night now, the lights are out, the dog has settled against the door, the engine of the car out in the driveway has finished making its tick-tick-ticking sound, the owls have begun their calling, the swim suits and towels are all hung up, your daughters have practiced their violins and have completely memorized "Perpetual Motion." And your mind's suddenly able to recall that sedimentary means rocks formed by layers, so now you can go to sleep with one less thing on your mind. This is you thinking what a fine job you're doing keeping Paul and Bobby Chantal and that red Corvair out of your mind.

This is Chris at home, looking through boxes in the attic at three in the morning and finding the handgun her father once owned and kept behind the counter of his store just in case there was trouble. This is Chris remembering Beatrice, the babysitter she had as a girl who was raped. This is Chris finding the box of bullets alongside the handgun. This is Chris remembering Beatrice, how every night she would fall asleep next to Chris. This is Paul asleep downstairs, having a nightmare that he has found Bobby Chantal again. He is holding her in his arms. Her throat is slit. "Oh, Bobby," he is trying to say in his dream, trying to bring her back to life, but to anyone listening to him it sounds like "Oh, baby" instead, because words you say in a dream sound distorted to others who are awake. In short, it sounds like a dream he'd want to have, not a nightmare. This is Chris in the attic, hearing through the floorboards Paul saying, "Oh, baby," and thinking to herself that he is dreaming about the woman he's seeing. This is Chris not caring so much now. In a world of ten thousand things, what's more important? Her husband with another woman, or a killer who's killing young girls, girls on the same swim team as Cleo, girls almost as young as Cleo, even? She takes the handgun and the bullets with her down the rickety attic ladder. She hides them in her bedroom, where she keeps her winter sweaters folded up and encased in a plastic garment bag. Again Paul moans in his sleep. She doesn't mind it now. She is thinking of how she will find that killer.

During the day, out your window, you can hear what must be tree limbs rubbing against one another in the wind and squeaking, but it sounds like a new kind of animal, or just an animal you've never heard before.

In the shower, while thinking about how Paul kissed you, you keep saying "water, water, water," imitating the boy in the wheelchair at the facility whom you often hear showering in the next stall over. Maybe the drain hears everything and Thomas has figured that out already and that's why he does most of his talking in the shower. Someone's listening, someone who gives him the time of day. Someone who says, "Yes, tell me more about quarks, quasars and pulsars. Tell me how we are moving away from other planets at twenty-two miles per day. Tell me how Pluto was sent off course by a stray meteor and now has a wobble."

This is Paul asleep while Chris gets up from bed and gets dressed. He is not someone who snores, and Chris often has to go right up to him and watch his breathing in order to tell whether he's asleep or not. She can tell he's sleeping when his lips are slightly parted, as if he's just about to say something, or he has just pulled away from a kiss. He is sleeping now. She knows the rest stop that Kim was killed at, and when she drives by it she can see that there are police barricades blocking the entrance road. This is Chris driving farther up the highway, liking how she has the lanes to herself, liking how she can use her brights and not have to worry about blinding an oncoming driver because there is no one else but her on the highway. This is Chris pulling into a different rest stop, farther up north, in the dark, hearing her tires make a crumbling sound over the blacktop. This is Chris going into the bathroom, where moths fly by the light above the door and where a cricket is chirping in the corner by the sink, whose pipes sweat beneath the basin. This is Chris finished in the stall, and now standing at the sink washing her hands, realizing there are no hand towels and wiping her hands on the skirt of her dress instead. This is her hand sliding over her pocket, sliding over the hard handgun she can feel beneath the cloth. This is Chris looking in the mirror, looking to see who could be standing behind her looking at her looking in the mirror, but there is no one behind her. The door is behind her and it is shut, but not all the way, and wouldn't it be easy, Chris thinks, for someone to just open up that door and find her?

This is the moon shining down so close to the hills Chris thinks something's wrong with Earth's orbit or gravity, and the world is in danger of being struck by the moon. This is the picnic bench she sits on, listening to the filaments in the light buzz above the bathroom door. This is the deep breath she takes that's full of the cool night air and the smell of a dew-filled lawn that in the morning will probably be dotted with mushrooms. This is Chris getting sleepy, knowing that if she lies down on the picnic bench she will fall asleep, but then wake up cold and dew-covered and with her dress probably soiled by whatever wet film the rotting wooden tabletop seems to be coated with. This is Chris driving back down the highway, feeling good, feeling that this was a start in the right direction toward finding the killer or having him find her.

This is Chris imagining the killer. He has a thickly wrinkled forehead, as if the wrinkles were a flight of stairs a very small creature could climb up or down. He has eyes that are small and set wide apart. Their lashes are straight, and sometimes the top lashes stick right into the bottom lashes, or even go under his bottom eyelid, so that he has to open his eye wide and roll it to the side and insert the pad of his finger into his eye to free the top lashes. He has teeth that bits of food become easily caught in, and his breath often smells like the bits of food caught days ago in the spaces of his teeth. He has hangnails he bites off. He has sideburns as thick as Velcro. His straight hair is thick, not showing any signs of thinning even though he is approaching fifty. He is amazed by the thickness of his own hair and often puts his hand through it just to feel how much there is.

This is Chris back home in her bedroom, taking out the handgun from her pocket and putting it on the top shelf of her closet, and then taking off her clothes. Paul doesn't wake up. This is Chris, stepping into Cleo's room to make sure her daughter is covered, even though the night is warm. This is Chris seeing Cleo asleep with her arm stretched out to the side, and wanting to bring her arm back in close to Cleo's side, because her arm looks as though it could be grabbed so easily if someone were to walk into her room and take her away. So as not to wake her, though, Chris just tiptoes backward outside of the room, closing the door in front of her.

CHAPTER TWENTY-ONE

*I*n the morning, Thomas, while slurping his cereal and reading his science magazine, tells you that amnesia is actually caused by having too many memories and the brain not knowing what to do with all of that data. So you feel better. You know why you can't remember if you put honey in your tea or not. It's not because you're losing your mind, but because there's so much going on all of the time. The dog, for example, is barking to go out and then, a second later, barking to come back in. The hummingbirds are at the feeder all taking turns sipping at the homemade nectar Thomas made of boiled sugar and water. The goose is honking and flapping her wings in the front yard, ruffled by something you can't see, the dog, perhaps, or a low-flying hawk, or Alex up early searching for caterpillars in the milkweed as tall as she is to bring them in the house and put them in a jar. So, of course, who could remember if honey were in the tea or not with all of that taking place?

The brain can be trained. It is capable of doing much more than we think, Thomas says, reading from another article in his magazine. A child born with a weak eye can put a patch over the strong eye and train the weak eye to do what the strong eye already can. An aging person's failing vision can be corrected by having the person sit for hours of training in a darkly lit room trying to make out blurry lines and shapes. Sounds like torture, you think, because you have become as attached to your dime-store reading glasses as you have to sidling up to your children and having them read small print for you whenever you're confronted with it. The plasticity of the brain can be stretched by a person living in an active environment, with diversions and friends and plenty of time for exercise, Thomas reads. All of this just spells vacation to you, and you realize you are the kind of person who actually really does see the spelling of words when they're spoken, and not just in English. Once on vacation you heard a French man, who had lost his little dog, searching all along the beach for him calling "ici," and you kept seeing the letters spelled out as he repeated the word, so to you he was calling out "i-c-i, i-c-i, i-c-i," over and over again.

To you, even Paul's name is sometimes "P-a-u-l" when you think about him, which of course you have continued to do even though you've tried to stop thinking about him because you started to believe that the only reason he kissed you was to make you forget about him being with Bobby Chantal. Now you're not sure what to think. You just know you're afraid you'll say his name when asking at the table for the ketchup to be passed, because after all, you have just learned from Thomas's magazine that the brain is capable of anything, and you're afraid yours will rebel. That like the strong eye covered with a patch allowing the weak eye to grow strong, if you're constantly trying not to think of Paul, then a part of you will compensate and do it anyway. Maybe soon you will be saying his name when you want to say "soap" instead. "Pass the Paul, please," you're afraid of blurting out in front of your family at the dinner table instead of asking for the salt. You imagine that like some supernatural phenomenon, his name, because you are thinking of him so often, will burn through your skin and show up on your chest with smoke and the smell of your cooking flesh rising up from the burn.

What makes everything suddenly clear about your brother is Thomas reading to you that pain is addictive, that the same pathways that handle addiction handle chronic pain, so the body keeps wanting to feel the pain long after the trauma has occurred. Now, for example, you have been able to stop thinking about your brother by thinking about Paul instead. You've just transferred addictions instead of curing the first one. Until something else comes along and takes its place you'll be doing it indefinitely, and now Thomas is talking about taking the girls to swim practice this afternoon because he will be headed up that way anyway. "No," you blurt out, "I'll take them," thinking that if you don't go you'll miss seeing Paul, but then you remind yourself that Paul is an addiction, and that you shouldn't want to see Paul. Probably the best thing for you and for everybody is that you not see Paul, and so you say, "Yes, that's a good idea. You take them instead."

You know later that day when you're standing with Chris in her studio why you're really there. It's not to visit with Chris, or to see her latest artwork—paintings mostly of dark-colored flowers on dark canvasses that you know have already been bought by a wealthy collector/admirer in Connecticut even though they're not yet completed—but to be standing in Paul's house, touching the pen with the bank logo on it that he might have touched, and touching the door handle he touched and the window sash he might have opened on a hot, restless night after one of his nightmares woke him up. You should turn around and leave. You're ashamed to realize why you've really come. You stand to leave. I will get up and go home. I'm ridiculous, you say to yourself, but you don't go. You know Chris would be offended if you took off and left. Already she has put water on to boil for tea, and started talking again about how there still is no evidence against the killer. She shows you one of her latest paintings. You're surprised. It's not one of her usual dark ones of dark flowers painted on an even darker background. It's a portrait of what she thinks the killer looks like. He has a forehead that hangs across his eyes like a ledge and wrinkles on his forehead so pronounced they look like rolls of flab. "I don't get it. How do you know he looks like this?" you ask. Chris shrugs. She sips her tea and looks at her painting as if she were seeing it for the first time. "I don't know," she says. "I only feel that he looks like this, but it's such a strong feeling I think maybe I should show it to the police. What do you think?" You shake your head. "Yeah, I guess you're right," she says. "They'd think I was crazy. But it's the first time I've started painting anything in weeks. I was just so upset about Paul that I couldn't. Now, though, I can't stop painting this guy's face." She shows you multiple sketches she's done of the killer's face. She shows you his profile and she shows you him head on. Each time you wish you could turn away or push the sketches away, or better yet that she'd move the papers for you so you wouldn't have to put your hands near him. "I think somehow me painting his face over and over again will help the guy get caught," she says.

When the phone rings and Chris goes to answer it, you're relieved. She takes the sketches with her to the kitchen, where the phone is, and you don't have to look at them any longer. You wander around her house sipping your tea. You go into their bedroom. On the shelf is a picture of Paul and Chris on their wedding day in their wedding clothes holding hands and jumping off a dock and into a pond. Midflight, they are smiling, and the sun is shining so brightly the water looks white. You wish you had been at their wedding. You bet it was fun. You wonder which side of the bed Paul lies on. The right side looks just as rumpled as the left, the covers are peeled back on either side, and there's a glass of water on a table on one side, but of course there is no way to tell if it is Chris's, because you have never seen Chris wear lipstick, or any makeup for that matter. You wonder if you held the glass up and just saw the imprint of the lips on the glass if you could tell whose they were. Would you know by just having felt Paul's lips on your own what the shape of them could actually look like? The picture of them on their wedding day has a silver frame. One side of the frame looks smudged with fingerprints, as if Chris had picked it up time and time again just to stare at it, remembering how they once were.

You look out the window. Is this the view Paul sees every day? It's a windy day. The kind of day that makes you think that colder weather will come back for sure and that you shouldn't be fooled by the bright sunshine, because the wind brings down some dried leaves off a nearby gardenia bush, making you think of maples losing their leaves in the autumn. There is a hedge of

American Beauty and a small cherry tree that looks newly planted, with wood chips circling its base. There is a robin pecking at the ground. There is an old wooden playhouse that must have been Cleo's when she was younger. The shutters by the playhouse's window look as though they could fall off in the next breeze.

The tea has been served in mugs without handles that look like Japanese teacups. They are beautiful, like most of the things in Chris's house. Even the plate surrounding the wall switch is a beautiful scene of a mountainside with a pink sunset painted on ceramic. You think of your own house. You have barely decorated it. You believe the knots in the wood form enough pictures on their own, and you don't want to put up anything on the walls to detract from them. You haven't even planted flowers outside of the house. The layering of the rocks on the rounded stone wall that garden snakes sometimes slither out from is artistry enough for you. How nice it must be for Paul to come home to this house, where the photographs are framed in silver frames, and where the windows have curtains.

You take another sip of the tea. Holding the mug without handles is comforting. It warms your hands. After Chris gets off the phone, she shows you articles and a website she found that talk about the past murder victims of the rest-stop killer who probably killed Kim.

"I've read through all this information, and I can't find any link between them all," Chris says. "Some were very young, and some were just young. What they all had in common was the slit in their necks when they arrived at the morgue, and of course the fact that they were killed outside of a rest stop. All of them were women alone. Some lived in the state, some lived in a neighboring state and were just passing through. I don't think the cops had a thing to go on. There wasn't the science back then to figure out the identity of the guy, but now we can look at the DNA. We can see who did it. Hell, we can even dig up a body and look at the old DNA and get an identity match. I think the police should be asked to dig up the bodies. I've even talked to the families about it."

"You've what?"

"There's one who's all for it. It's the daughter of one of the victims. Her name is Pam Chantal. Her mother was a nurse named Bobby Chantal. At the time of the murder, Pam was only five. Her father was a Vietnam vet, but he never married Bobby Chantal, and he disappeared not long after Pam was born. Now Pam wants to know who killed her mother, the only relative she ever knew. I told her I'd help her talk to the police and tell them they have permission to exhume the body and test it for DNA samples. She seems to need someone to go through it with her."

"Chris, are you that obsessed by this case?" you say. "It sounds like quite a job to take on. Are you serious?"

"Yes, I am," Chris says. "This guy killed a girl on our team, Annie. It could have been one of our girls. It still could be."

This is you, sitting on either Paul's side of the bed or Chris's, not believing what you're hearing, and by accident letting tea from your cup pour off to one side and stain the foot of the bed. This is Chris coming up to you and taking the teacup from you, telling you with a small laugh that it's all right, that it's Paul's side of the bed and he'll never notice the stain. This is you saying out loud, "I think you made more sense when you were convinced Paul was cheating on you," and this is you wishing you hadn't said anything out loud and then immediately saying, "I'm sorry." This is the bed, the tea stain now shaped like a puffy cloud. This is the room getting darker, the sun going down behind the other side of the house. This is the way the bed feels to you, as though it's the floor beneath your chair at your kitchen table that threatens to suck you down to the center of the earth every time you think about your brother, but you are not thinking about your brother now. Maybe thinking about him would be better than thinking about Paul and Bobby Chantal. Maybe imagining your brother's chipped front tooth, and his long fingers, and the way it sounded almost silent when he laughed is better than thinking about Paul. This is you standing up from the bed and getting your purse, which you left on the table in the entryway. This is you saying you hadn't realized it was so late, saying there is dinner to get started before the girls come home. They always come home starving. Isn't it the same with Cleo after a practice? you ask.

"Yes, she's ravenous when she gets in the door," Chris says.

"What about the swim meet this weekend—will you be going?" you ask, standing in the doorway to be polite instead of just leaving right away as you'd like to.

Chris shakes her head. "I'm not. I'm just not cut out for those swim meets. I can't stand to watch them. Even if Cleo's winning a race, I'm nervous for her. I feel it like a knife in my stomach. Where does it say in the parent's handbook that swimming has anything to do with your gut? There are only pages about getting your kid to practice on time and feeding them a healthy meal, nothing about acute ulcers on race day afflicting the parents."

CHAPTER TWENTY-TWO

*T*his is you shaking your head while driving home, thinking of Chris, thinking you've got to hand it to her. How many women would bother to help find a serial killer? You realize you're almost jealous of her for being so involved.

When you get home and the telephone is ringing and the girls are practicing violin and the dog is barking and Thomas is standing on the log pile chainsawing, you think about the place you stayed in at the equator. At the equator, beaches stretched on for what could have been miles and there were no other people on them. There were a few caves you could walk into and hear your voice echo. At the bottom of the caves there were pools of water where small fish swam and sea urchins lay shored against rocks. In the water one day there were jellyfish. The sting of the jellyfish was not so bad, and you could pick up the jellyfish by holding your palm over their tops and then turning your hand over, and you could throw jellyfish at one another for fun. Your children liked this game, and Thomas liked to hold a jellyfish up to his eye and say, "Oh, darn, I lost my contact," or put the jellyfish on the top of his head and say, "I think the water's lovely today, don't you?" Thomas also liked putting two jellyfish over his chest and asking, "Do you like my new bikini?" You wish that you were back at the equator and swimming in the ocean and riding the waves. You wish you hadn't met Paul and didn't think about him every night right before falling asleep. You should be thinking about your girls instead. Sofia's been reading too many YA books that are poorly written. You want to go through your own books and find one that's a classic, one you know she'd like, but lately you haven't had the time or the energy, the wherewithal to get up from your chair and do it. You'd like to take Sofia for a haircut. It's getting so long now and she keeps hiding behind it. Some days she pulls it so far in front of her face it seems as if it's just the tip of her nose that peeks out. How can you make her feel good about herself and at the same time suggest that she's got to change the way she wears her hair? You remember how at her age your brother also hid behind his hair and wore it so long that a big swath of it covered his eyes. If he ever wanted to see something he had to spasmodically jerk his head to make it flap away from his eyes. If only your father would have stayed with the family and been there those years to watch your brother switch from playing trumpet to guitar, how easily your brother did it, how beautiful he sounded in no time at all, then maybe your brother wouldn't have killed himself, you think. This is you thinking how Alex's birthday is only a few days away and you haven't begun to think of what to get her. Does she really need new sneakers? Can't she just wear the old pair another few months? She keeps telling you she needs a new racing suit, but you refuse to believe it. You bought one only a few months ago, right before the summer swim season. Could she have possibly grown so much? Shouldn't there be some kind of balance between the rate of their growth and the rate of how much the suits stretch out each time they wear them to race? The suit she has now, you're sure, fits fine. It fits the way it's supposed to. It digs into her shoulders and leaves a raw-looking red mark as much as it ever did, but not any more so. It cuts into her thighs as much as it ever did. It makes it as hard for her to breathe as it ever did, and it hurts your fingers as much as it ever did, but not more than usual, to squeeze her into the suit when you're standing in a bathroom stall, banging your elbows against the metal wall every time you get a good grip on the sides of the suit and heave your arms up to try and lift it over her rear.

That night you watch a movie with Thomas and the girls. In the movie a man is about to kill himself by putting a pistol into his mouth. Your daughters know what your brother did to himself. They came with you to your brother's funeral just two years ago. You were so thankful they were there. You slept with them in the same bed at your sister's house, and held them to you in the night. It didn't matter that Thomas thought your brother was an asshole, and that he didn't come with you to the funeral. You didn't think he could have provided as much comfort as your two girls did at that time. Nothing was more comforting than feeling your girls in your arms, watching them in their sleep, and seeing the smoothness of their skin, the perfect arch of their eyebrows, their high cheekbones slightly colored from the summer sun. "What a jerk. Why does he want to do that?" Alex says, watching the man on the television with the gun in his mouth, but it is not a question she is looking for an answer to. You are glad your daughter can say that killing yourself is stupid. You are glad she will not end up like your brother, with her blood forming another head like the head of a cauliflower. You want to tell Thomas that genetics isn't everything, that maybe, just maybe, this idea of killing yourself doesn't run in the family the way he thinks it does.

It's fungus we should worry about, Thomas tells you at night while you're reading in bed. The bats, the corn, the frogs, they're all dying from it. We know much more about viruses and bacteria than we do fungus, and it's the one thing that we should really be worried about. Out the window, you see the moon, and the way it lights up the field by the pond as bright as a searchlight. You are more worried about the killer than you are about fungus.

You read the paper in bed. There is a picture of the same trooper with the battered nose who came to the pool to talk to the coach. The picture was taken on a rainy day. The trooper is wearing a plastic covering that fits with elastic over his hat to keep it from getting wet. The trooper says that the public should not be worried. They are working hard on the case. They will find this man. You feel confident when you look at the picture of the trooper. If he is the kind of man who cares enough about his hat to cover it with plastic so it will not get wet in the rain, then you are sure he will find this killer. There is no need, you think, to have Paul get involved in the case. He's right. It would just complicate the search. This man, this trooper with his hat encased in plastic and his strong, square shoulders, will find the killer. Even Chris, with her paintings, is helping to find the killer. The killer will surely be found.

You find yourself the next day at practice asking the water a question while you swim. Will the killer be found? You strain your ears to hear the answer, but all that you hear are swimmers splashing the water. It's someone's birthday, and so for fun the swimmers all sit on one side of the pool and the swimmer whose birthday it is has to swim the pool's length while it's being furiously kicked by thirty or so swimmers, who are churning the water so that it's white with froth.

 T he next day at practice you wish you had not fallen asleep so early the night before. You wish you had moved close to Thomas and reached out for him and stroked him the way he liked, your fingertips moving in an upward motion. You wish you were not seeing Paul walk into the facility right at this moment. You think he's smiling at you and then you realize he is actually smiling at Chris. You wish you were done with your laps already so you could stay and talk to Paul, but you have not swum yet. While swimming, and lifting your head to the side for a breath, you see Paul and Chris in the stands, sitting close to each other, watching their daughter. You see Paul put his arm around Chris while they watch Cleo, his fingers dangling close to one of her perfect breasts. You wish they did not look like such a perfect couple.

This is you at home trying on Sofia's racing john. The suit has legs that reach to just above your knees. The children are out playing in the stream and Thomas is at the lab. You try it on in front of your dresser mirror. Since Sofia is a few inches taller than you are, and the size is bigger than what you would order for yourself, you think it might possibly fit. You want to see if it sucks in all of your fat and makes you look as thin as Chris is. You wonder if one day Paul would somehow want to see you in it. You do one leg at a time. Just getting the legs on takes you a good two minutes, now comes the rear. You tug and pull to get it up. As you're struggling your rear gets compressed upward, and your cheeks rise up above your waist looking like two bubbles on your lower back, looking like two of those Styrofoam life preservers in the shape of an egg that mothers from your mother's generation put on their children when they were first learning to swim. You begin to sweat all over and at once, as if you were seriously ill and had a high fever and your fever just decided to break now. For a moment you think you might rip the suit by mistake, but then you remind yourself how much the suit cost, and how the seams are ultra-reinforced, and how there is no way it could rip. You think you might faint, but you take a deep breath, exhale it slowly, and then get back to work. You tug. You pull. You extend your buttocks forward and back, a rocking motion to help slide it up and over. Pop, you think you distinctly hear when the suit finally does go over your rear. Now for the body and the straps. With the body on, you feel your chest being compressed. You wonder if this is how the women hunted in the Salem witch hunts felt when they were stoned to death. You have to suck in your breaths so deeply just to get some air down in your lungs, and you have to work so hard at exhaling. You reach down to slide the straps over one shoulder. You have to bend over to the side with your whole body to provide enough counterforce to lift up on one strap and get it over your shoulder. The strap digs in hard the entire time you're sliding it across your skin. With just one strap on, your body is forced down on that side, and you are standing crooked, one shoulder higher than the other. You try to bring your shoulder down away from the overbearing pressure, just to relieve it. When you have the whole suit on and you can barely breathe, and your genitalia feel as though they've been pushed up inside you, you look at yourself in the mirror. You are a panoply of red marks and scratches. Your legs look as if the claws of a cat have raked them where you've dragged the bottoms of the suit up to the tops of your legs. Your arms, which you pulled the straps forcefully across, have the top layer of skin scraped off in intermittent sections. Your chest, neck, and face are all blotchy from the exertion and heat, and you still feel as though you're going to pass out because you're not getting enough air, but the way you look, ah, the way you look, you think. You are as thin as Chris now. Your breasts, which you once thought were too big, are now pleasantly rounded and squashed behind the black polyester fiber. Your rear sits tight and high. And most of all, you feel faster, even though you're just standing in a room. No wonder all the girls like these suits. You feel that if you dove into water and kept going, you'd go down as fast as a bullet. Then, if you touched pool bottom and turned around for the resurfacing, you'd shoot straight upward, coming up a few feet out of the water like a great white after it's grabbed its prey. You think of taking a picture of yourself. If you can't believe it's you standing there looking so thin and firm, then nobody else will either. What stops you is the location of the camera, all the way downstairs and in a hard-cased bag on the floor by the door, where you left it the last time you came back from a shoot. You're scared to bend down. Just bending over slightly you feel as if your organs are rolling one on top of the other and you're cutting off some blood and other necessary fluids from your tissues. You think how you might just buy a girdle, not a girdle like old ladies wore when you were a girl, but the new kind of girdles, the girlie girdles that all the brides you photograph are wearing these days, the girdles called body shapers that come in styles like corsets and bodysuits and waist shapers and are made of comfortable spandex guaranteed to firm what you've got and add cleavage to what you haven't got. You feel younger, it's true, and even though it takes you almost as long to get the suit off—your top layer of skin gets even more damaged and your rear swears it will never take the suit off and protests and protests and fights back every time it hears you grunt and groan to work the fabric off your hips—you love yourself in the suit. Paul would love me in that suit, you think. Once it's off, you put it back in Sofia's closet, where she dutifully hangs it up after each meet. It still has the shape of your rear inside it, and it's damp from all of the sweat you lost in your bathing suit battle. You avoid looking at your body free of its suit in the mirror. You don't want to see how badly your muffin top is drooping toward the floor. If you don't look in the mirror, then maybe you can keep the image in your mind of how you looked when you were in the suit. You can keep that image in your mind when you speak to Paul next, and you can feel okay about feeling sexy when he talks to you, because you know that anytime you want to, anytime you have, say, an hour free, you can squeeze yourself back into Sofia's suit, and you will fit the bill. You will really be that sexy.

CHAPTER TWENTY-THREE

*T*his is Dinah deciding to lose weight. She's tired of seeing her daughter grow as large as she is even though her daughter swims a two-hour practice every day. Dinah decides she'll set an example for her daughter. She learns of a new regimen to lose weight that requires human chorionic gonadotropin. She's not sure what that is, but thinks it has something to do with babies, and every day she pours drops of this stuff on her yogurt and she lifts the spoon to her mouth thinking she's eating failed pregnancies and intended abortions. The taste isn't so bad, especially since she mixes maple syrup on top of the yogurt as well. She starts losing weight, but the down side to that is her husband is becoming more attracted to her, and because he is losing his hearing, he talks to her loudly in the night, pleading with Dinah for love, while Jessie, who shares a bedroom wall with them, can probably hear what he's saying.

Dinah knits in the bleachers, the needles swishing together, as her daughter swims her practice. Dinah has, by accident, knit some of her hair into a pink-and-brown-striped scarf, but she leaves the hair in the scarf anyway, wishing she knew of a person who would want such a personalized gift from her. She can't think of anyone right now, except her husband of course. Right now she wouldn't want to give any gift to him. Dinah's husband blames his going deaf on one day—the day he shot a buck and the rifle report in his ear was much louder than usual, because at the exact same time another hunter shot the same buck. It was never decided who made the kill shot, and Dinah's husband didn't take up the other hunter's offer to split the buck, because he didn't want to partake in the venison anyway. "I just want the antlers," he told the other hunter, and so the rack of six points was given to him and it now hangs above his bed and Dinah tells him how the antlers drive her nuts because the board they are mounted on bangs against the wall, making a rattling sound every time her husband rolls over, and making her think the buck has come alive and is ready to trample her with its cloven hooves in her sleep. "I can't hear the rattling sound," Dinah's husband tells her. "I'm going deaf, remember?" Then he walks away, knowing that if she answers him he will not hear her anyway. Dinah's husband hates going deaf. He tells everyone that at least he won't have to hear his daughter's pop music and he won't have to hear all the loud, obnoxious mothers who cheer for their children from the bleachers during a race, but then he also tells everyone that what's terrible about going deaf is that not everything is tuned out, you still hear muffled sounds that make you think you're going insane because you're always trying to make sense of them, as if they're everyone's voices telling you secrets or telling you what to do, but you can't understand them.

This is Dinah, who has put down her knitting and is now looking through her opera glasses at her daughter swimming, or not swimming, really, she thinks. Her daughter is a cheater, as she can see through the lenses smeared with what must be her own oils, from her hands and her face. Her daughter pulls on the lane line to drag herself through the water when she's tired. Her daughter is not doing the entire set. Dinah can tell because she's been counting, she's even ticked off on a sheet of paper how many two-hundred IMs her daughter has done and she has only done seven and the coach told them to do eight. Dinah thinks she should go down there on deck and tell her daughter to knock it off, to finish the set like the rest of the girls or she'll never get faster. She'll threaten to take away her novels if she doesn't. Dinah then realizes she doesn't want to go down on deck. She doesn't want to burst through the double glass doors and have everyone notice her, even though she has lost weight, a lot of weight. She's still not sure she wants to be seen crouching by the end of the lane and admonishing her daughter while the other swimmers and the coach look at her. She doesn't want the coach to see her and then later call her into her office and give her a talking-to, because she has been called into the office a few times before, for various actions that the coach said were over the top, not necessarily against the rules the way Annie would go against the rules, but they were not how a swim-team parent was expected to behave. Once Dinah ran through crowds on deck before a race to get to her daughter and scream at her to get up to the blocks because her heat was about to begin, and she pushed her daughter from behind to get her up on the blocks, and she was wrong. It was not her daughter's heat. She has been called into the coach's office for calling the director of an away swim meet and entering her daughter into a meet that her daughter's team, as a whole, was not going to attend, and therefore her daughter wouldn't have the coaches there representing her. She didn't know it was against the rules. She just wanted her daughter to attend the meet because Jessie had a good chance of winning some of the events there. She has been called into the coach's office for sending too many e-mails telling the coaches what events she thinks her daughter should be swimming, which is not against the rules, but, she was informed, was uncalled for and meddlesome. She has been called into the coach's office after a swim meet at which she organized the concessions stand and then—when she felt there weren't enough people helping her sell the gooey mac and cheese, the brownies in baggies, and the cold tasteless pasta salads—she sent a mass e-mail to all of the parents telling them that they weren't pulling their fair share, that the proverbial scales had been tipped, and not in her favor, and that they had better volunteer more and harder next time or there would be no concessions stand. She wrote that it would be a devastating disappointment to their team as well as the other teams who came to the meet. Imagine, she said, arriving at a meet and having nothing to buy for your child. Imagine no Ring Pops, sodas, bagels, or oat granola bars to tide them over throughout the long grueling day. The e-mail was lengthy, at least a page. She did not check it first. She did not think the other parents deserved that much consideration. Let them be assaulted by bad grammar and typos, she thought while emphatically hitting the send key.

Of course, there are a few parents in particular she doesn't care for. No, that's wrong. There are a few parents she doesn't like at all. There's Annie, whose daughters often lead the practice lanes and are always ahead of her daughter. Annie, who doesn't entirely play by the rules. Annie, who went off with Paul and hung out in his hotel room while their kids watched TV together in another room. And what was that remark she made to her about her bathing suit being very Marilyn Monroe? On the surface, you'd think Annie was being nice, but Dinah wasn't fooled. Marilyn Monroe had killed herself. More likely Annie was hinting that the suit made Dinah look pale, and corpselike. She's probably sleeping with Paul, Dinah thinks to herself. I should tell her husband she's having an affair. People think it's not their business to tell other people things like that, but it is. If you see blatant injustice like that staring you in the face, it's your duty, your obligation to report it. She told her husband, Joseph, that she was going to tell Annie's husband, Thomas, that his wife was having an affair. Joseph rarely becomes angry, but when she told him she planned to tell Thomas about Annie's affair, he promised her that if she told him anything, he would tell Thomas not to pay any attention to her. He would tell Thomas, he said, that Dinah had finally come "undone, unhinged, in-fucking-sane." In that moment, Dinah felt that she could honestly say that she didn't love Joseph anymore, so she told him so and asked for a divorce in the same breath. She felt that telling the truth to those who least wanted to hear it was what she was probably best at. Even to herself, she was good at telling the truth. When she first got the idea to lose weight, she stood naked in front of the mirror. She made herself look at her reflection for a solid hour. She started with her feet, the flab on her ankles that hung over her ankle bones, that made her look like a doll made of nylon stockings and stuffed with pillow filling. She made her way up to her legs, which were riddled with varicose veins, and then to her waist, where the fat hung over her hips, and then up to her neck, with its three rolls. She held up her fingers to the mirror, and they were so swollen it looked as if her wedding ring would never come off. And it didn't with just her pulling on it, so then she went to the kitchen sink and squirted dish soap onto it and ran warm water over it, but even then the ring would not twist off. She would need a jeweler's saw for that task, or better yet she would need to lose weight. So she did. It was when she reached the twenty-five-pound goal after seven weeks that the ring fell off by itself while she was washing her hands in the restroom at the facility. She could hear it clink its way down the spiraling pipe for the first few seconds, and then she could hear nothing but the water running and the distant sound of children playing in the current of the lazy river and the coach on the main pool deck yelling, encouraging her swimmers in practice to "Pick it up, pick it up," and quicken their pace.

But that mother and the father of that poor girl Kim, who was murdered, Dinah liked them. At away meets, the mother, Gina, would always save seats on the bleachers for the other parents by putting down extra sweaters or jackets. Poor Gina. Dinah can't imagine what she's going through, having a daughter who was murdered. Dinah feels glad she doesn't know what Gina is going through. At the moment, it's hard enough to be going through what Dinah is going through herself, watching her daughter cheat in her workout. Her daughter is getting out of the water and heading toward the bathrooms, though she just visited them not even half an hour ago. This is another tactic Dinah knows her daughter uses to get out of doing the complete workout. Dinah, not having her daughter to look at through her binoculars, uses them to look at the other parents sitting in the bleachers. She doesn't see the usual suspects. Where are Paul and Annie? She thought for sure they'd be sitting together, their knees touching, Annie tossing her graying hair behind her shoulder like a teenager, and Paul the whole time not looking at anything else but Annie. They are not here tonight. Neither of them. Dinah is tempted to go out and see if they are together in the lobby, talking at one of the high café tables with the high chairs that once took such an effort for her to lift herself up onto. Or maybe they are sitting outside in one of their cars. Dinah has noticed how many parents do that. They sit in each other's cars with the lights on and chat with each other until their children are finished with practice. She can see them in the dark some nights, lit up by their overhead ceiling lights, eerily glowing from within, laughing, talking, sharing snacks that are meant for their children but that they can't resist partaking of themselves, the dinner they will eat still a long way off considering how far they live from the facility. Dinah is almost ready to go outside and check to see if Paul and Annie are in a car together, when her daughter comes back from the bathroom and dives into the pool to finish her workout. Dinah fixes her binoculars on her daughter now. The set is a breaststroke, her daughter's best. She is gaining on the girl who has already taken off from the wall and is ahead of her daughter in the next lane over. Dinah wants to call out her daughter's name, and then she wants to call out, "Go, Baby, go!" and she almost does, until she remembers that this is not a meet and this is not a race, but only a practice, on a rainy Monday night, just hours after she has told her husband, very loudly so that he could hear, that she is through with being married. "Done," she said. She wanted to add, "Up to here," and motion to her neck with a hand that looked as if it were slicing her head off, but really it is higher, where she is fed up. It is way past her neck. It is as high as the bit of stray hair that stands up from her head, and then some, that she is fed up. It is up to the rafters of the facility, where the ventilation ducts cross. It is through the sliding-glass roof that is opened on warm, stultifying days caustic with the smell of chlorine, and it is all the way up to where the glorious china-blue sky can be seen. Dinah puts down the binoculars now and slumps slightly in the bleachers. The practice isn't even halfway over, and she is so tired. She just wants to go home and sleep, but the first thing she will do before going to bed will be to take those antlers off the wall above her four-poster. Tonight, she swears, she will sleep for once without hearing deer trampling through her dreams.

This is Paul trying to decide what to do. He is sitting with his hands on the sides of his face looking at a painting of the man his wife calls the killer. It has been months since he has been in her studio, but he is in her studio now, wanting to ask about who is going to drive Cleo to the next meet coming up. No one told him when he was standing before the priest on his wedding day that someday he might have to consider whether or not she needed mental help. "This is insane," he says, and gestures toward the painting. He doesn't like how the eyes of the man in the painting stare at him. What has gotten into her? "It's him. I know it's him," she says. "Chris, what's gotten into you?" he says. It's so difficult talking to her these days. She doesn't seem to answer him when he asks simple questions. She almost imperceptibly inclines her head toward her shoulder, as if there's a small person perched there whom she's acknowledging, but she doesn't open her mouth to speak. If only it were Annie he was talking to instead. From her he knows he could get a straight answer, and Annie, at least, would be looking directly at him when he asked the question. He thinks of Annie as his muse. It was after he met her that he started writing the Bobby Chantal story in earnest. Before that he was just staying late at his office toying with a way to approach it. The actual writing of the story didn't start until after he met Annie. Annie's gray hair, almost white, framing a face that seems younger than the hair surrounding it, reminds him of his own mortality, reminds him he only has a finite time in this world to write fiction that matters before he too starts to turn gray and, eventually, dies. Annie is also so grounded and strong, so much the opposite of Chris, who right now is grabbing her car keys, saying she just needs to go for a drive.

When he walks back to the house from the studio, Cleo is standing in the doorway. "What was that all about?" she asks. Paul can only shake his head. "Your mother will be back later. It's time for you to go to bed," Paul says. He puts his arm around Cleo as they walk back into the house. He notices how strong and round her shoulder muscle feels beneath his hand. "My God, you're getting fit," he says. Cleo smiles. "Coach is working us harder than ever. She says it's her tribute to Kim. She says if we all swim harder then it's as if Kim didn't die in vain. And guess what? I'm leading my lane now." Paul says, "No, really? Well, that's great, Cleo."

This is Paul, alone in bed, remembering all too vividly that night he spent with Bobby Chantal and how they kissed and had sex on the picnic table that was up on the hill.

This is Paul's computer in his office. It holds the first few pages of the story he's writing about that night with Bobby Chantal. It is not a story he thinks he will ever try to publish. It is a story filled with too many personal details that would implicate him in the murder. First of all, it describes Bobby Chantal to a T. From the freckles on her nose, and her soft light-brown hair, down to her white-soled nurse's shoes, which she said she kept looking white by covering the smudges with Wite-Out. It also describes Paul, a first year college student, with hair that was so dark it almost looked black, hair tied behind his head in a ponytail. It details the rest stop, with its picnic table, and with its view that had the ability to send Vietnam vets back in time with flashes of recognition so striking that sometimes they were left staring into the darkness of a deep depression. The story is like a written confession by a man who cannot help embellishing the facts and turning them into a story. It was when he first started staying late at his office, trying to plan the story, that Chris started accusing him of cheating. Maybe, in a way, he is cheating on her. He comes to the office most evenings after dinner to work on it. He sometimes even wakens with an idea or a detail for the story he hadn't remembered, and rolls away from Chris's warm body and gets into his car and drives to his office to write it down. He knows that reading the news article about the serial killer in Colorado, who was finally caught after strangling his last victim, and the news of Kim being murdered are the reasons he has been thinking about Bobby Chantal so much again. He knows it is the reason his nightmares are more frequent, and why in them he keeps trying to bring Bobby Chantal back over and over again. In truth, his memory of Bobby Chantal and his writing the story have been consuming him. He is not concentrating well in his teaching. He is reading students' work without even leaving a constructive comment. He writes "Fine job" on the last page of their work, or something just as nondescript, when really their writing could use helpful criticism throughout. What do I really know about writing anyway? he thinks. He is doubting his own ability to tell the story. He feels that if he can get the story right, then somehow he'll be rid of the guilt. I'm not stupid enough to go to the police and tell them I was there the night of her murder, he tells himself. That could ruin my life, and the lives of Chris and Cleo as well. But writing the story in a way that exposes the humanity within him, that might help. It might redirect his thoughts, so that while he is eating dinner with his family he might have a conversation with them instead of staring at the salt shaker and thinking of how small leaves and blades of grass were mixed in with Bobby Chantal's blood on her face and the front of her dress when he turned her over and saw the slit in her neck that ran from ear to ear, like the proverbial second smile that so many other victims murdered by having their throats cut are described as having. And best of all, getting past writing the Bobby Chantal story might just get him back to writing work that can be published again. There are stories inside him he wants to tell, only right now it's as if Bobby Chantal isn't going to let him write them unless he writes her story first.

CHAPTER TWENTY-FOUR

Y ou swim in a lane next to your daughters' lane, where they are practicing reverse dolphin kicks on their backs. Waves from their undulations buoy you from side to side as you swim a slow free, your kick barely fluttering, your turnover rate high since you're not pulling hard enough when you extend your arm below the surface of the water. You think it's a good thing you're not in the ocean, as the movements from the kids on the team would probably buoy you far away from the shore and out into the open sea where you'd . . . drown? Be lost forever? Swallowed? Saved by Japanese fishermen? You picture yourself lying on the deck of a trawler beside dolphins whose eyes are clouded over and whose skin is dull gray. Maybe the fishermen would give you salty broth made from soy and you would say *arigato*, and they would nod their heads up and down and smile, pleased you acknowledged them in their own tongue. Would you have the heart, then, to denounce them for the treatment of the dolphins?

This is you in the water swimming slowly, thinking of being saved by Japanese fishermen. Your stroke weak, your hair gray, coming out from under your cap in wisps, your hips on your backstroke sunk low. If you'd only tilt your head back more in the water, those hips of yours would rise up. Ah, there, you tilt your head back now. Good job, Annie, you think you hear the water say. You are not thinking of your brother now, how his wife, after he shot himself, found bits of his blood and skull on the dial for the volume control of the stereo system, and how she threw out all of his toothpaste and there were so many tubes. He must have stocked up one day, a day before he knew, of course, that he would choose to end his days. You are not thinking of Paul or the killer. This is you now laughing in the water, watching Alex being silly in the water as she swims beside you, coming up from underneath the lane line and crossing her eyes and blowing up her cheeks with air when she sees you. This is Alex being told by the coach to get back over into her lane and finish her set. Alex gives you one last funny look before she goes. This is you hearing the water again. You were wrong, you realize. It is not saying, Good job, Annie. It is saying, Do the job, Annie. Do the job, and you don't know what it means.

We the parents agree not to interfere with the coaching of the swimmers and agree to let the coaches coach. We have to sign forms to that effect every year. We the swim parents, we think we are good swim parents. We the swim-team parents drive our children sometimes almost an hour just to get to practice, and we the swim-team parents hang out for two hours at practice while our children swim, then we drive almost an hour back. We the swim-team parents wake up at five a.m. some mornings to drive our children two hours away to a meet where they may only swim a few races, their actual time swimming in the water not totaling more than three minutes and thirty seconds. We the swim-team parents work at the swim meets, to help the team, for no pay. We the swim-team parents make sure our children are rested the night before, and that they have eaten pasta, because every good swim-team parent knows that pasta will carry them through the next day so they can drive home the finish and motor into the wall. We the swim-team parents buy our children the swimmer's backpacks for exorbitant prices because they have mesh pockets to keep the wet swimsuits in for the car ride home, and we the swim-team parents buy the swimmer's parkas with the swimmer's name embroidered above the breast that the swimmers wear during swim meets to keep themselves warm in between races. We buy them the skintight racing suits that take two adults to get one child into. We the swim-team parents, some of us tell our children we saw how hard they tried when they raced but didn't win or shave off time. Some of us tell our children to swim faster, to build up an oxygen debt. We want to see them panting for breath after a race, so tired they can't pull themselves out of the water. Some of us, the swim-team parents, tell our children nothing and just let them sit on our laps after they've raced, even though they are too old for sitting on our laps and they are taller than we are, and we place a hand on their backs as they sit on us and the two of us just look at the people around us and the pool below, in constant motion with the movement of swimmers' bodies. Some of us work at timing, holding stopwatches in our hands, or at admissions collecting fees for programs and heat sheets, or at the concession selling the ziplock baggies of brownies and paper plates of the gooey mac and cheese, or at the timing console making sure the touchpads are reset for the next race, or as officials faulting swimmers for single-hand touches or for wiggling before a dive off the blocks. Some of us don't tell our children good job at the meet. We save our praise for later. We tell them in long car rides home when they're tired and hungry and don't want to hear it, and just want to read their books (all swim-team children are good readers in the car and rarely get carsick because they are so used to the long rides). We tell them how amazingly they swam and how proud we are and how we think all the hard work they've done all those evenings at practices in the pool have paid off, and we the swim-team parents can't believe how much better we feel now that we're out of that pool and that facility, and we the swim-team parents think that even the stale air of the car—we can smell where the wet dog has sat on the upholstery, and where there are bits of stale chips under the seats, and where there might even be a blackened, shriveled banana peel—is a much better smell than the smell of the hot, chlorinated pool deck we've been standing on for so long.

Your house, you think, is just a bigger version of your car. Inside there are also stale bits of food and the smell of the wet dog, and there are clothes scattered here and there, and wet towels no one bothered to hang up, and plastic containers that once held snacks for swim meets, such as fresh diced fruit (a swim-team parent doesn't bring chips for their children to eat at a meet—each chip, a Frito, for example, acting like a small anchor inside the child's belly). Some of the swim-team parents buy their children only organic milk, and some of the swim-team parents would like to buy only organic milk for their children, but like you, they have more than one child, and a husband like Thomas who drinks so much milk that buying organic milk would cost too much, and then where would the money come for the vacation you and your family took close to the equator, where Thomas held your arm as you walked on the beach and you saw the panther bounding toward the edge of the forest, and the ocelot crossing the road, and the puffer fish in two feet of water so blue it was the color of someone's eyes you once dated, but never trusted, because with those eyes you couldn't tell if he was sincere or not. What was his name again? you think. And then you don't try to remember, it doesn't matter. He has another life somewhere with some wife whose purse contents he knows forward and back, or doesn't. Maybe he couldn't recognize her purse even if it were stuck up under his nose and he were inhaling the leather smell, and would swear it wasn't hers even when the contents revealed photos of him on their honeymoon.

CHAPTER TWENTY-FIVE

*T*his is the water, still remembering the way Kim felt moving through it, how her body broke the surface with both her arms being brought forward over the water and pulling back at the same time displaced the water, how it's not just the molecules and atoms of past forms that compose it, but the memory of how bodies once moved through it. The other girls, although they can't name the sensation, can feel the water remembering, and it gives the girls a better sense of how the butterfly is to be swum. The simultaneous up and down movement of the legs and feet. Each turn at the wall on the breast. Each finish double-handed at the wall. This is the coach nodding her head while watching her team swim, noticing how they are better than they were before at the fly, how at least this is something to be grateful for since there has been such a pallor cast over the team since the shocking news of their star flyer's death.

This is Adam, the father of the boys who would rather be playing

in the adjacent water park than swimming on the team. He is telling his boys in a voice that never rises, that stays the same, as if
he were talking to them in a quiet room rather than a noisy facility with a rushing waterslide and continuous air-exchange vents
pumping air, and fifty other small children screaming and splashing, to get out of the lazy river and get on over to the competition
pool where their coach is starting practice. His boys don't listen.
They continue running up the stairs to the slide and coming down
yelling, their feet flexed to increase the surface area when they hit
the water and to make as much of a wake as possible cascade over
the side of the plastic slide and swoosh onto the cement floor and
disappear into the drains. This is Adam shaking his head, wondering how angry he has to become, or wants to become right
now. He realizes he could become very angry now, something he
never likes to do, so he walks away from his boys and looks out
through the glass doors and windows that lead to the foyer, where
the tall café tables are set up with their tall chairs, where the drink
machines line the wall, and where the snack bar and the front
desk are located. What he notices, though not right away, is a man
in his midfifties with thick, dark hair and prominent wrinkles on
his forehead. Adam has never seen the man before. He seems too
old to be a parent who has a young child on the swim team. He
doesn't seem like a member of the facility. Members of the facility all look as though they have enough money to afford it. The
women wear pricey, casual athletic clothing, and the men wear
shiny athletic shoes. Perhaps he's a new janitor, Adam thinks, and
he's just changed out of his work clothes and is waiting for a ride.
Where the man sits he has a perfect view through the glass windows of the pool, where the swim-team girls and boys are coming

onto deck. The girls are adjusting their swimsuit bottoms to cover their rears, and they're piling their hair on top of their heads and then leaning over, asking their friends to help scoop their swim caps over their heads. Adam notices the man watching the girls. For a moment he's glad he just has boys, and no girls to worry about, but then a feeling of protectiveness over the girls on the team comes over him, even though they're not his. He decides that later, after he gets his boys out of the lazy river and onto the competition pool deck where practice is about to begin, he's going to point the man out to the head coach.

But Adam's boys are not cooperating. The youngest starts splashing Adam while Adam's on deck. The warm, chlorine-smelling water drenches Adam's shorts and tee shirt. "Enough now, boys. It's time to get out," he says. The boys swim away from him, back to where they can get out of the pool and climb up the stairs again to the slide. Adam makes his way to the slide, where his boys will shoot out. He is lucky this time. They have slid down together in the manner of a train, and all he has to do is grab them both up under an arm and drag them to the other pool. He practically holds them off the ground as he walks with them, their small toes suspended in the air, only grazing the wet cement now and then. His boys start howling as he drags them. "I'm going to call social services and report you!" his older boy yells. Adam can feel the other parents on the team trying not to embarrass him, looking away from him and his boys. He's thankful, but still, he's embarrassed. When the assistant coach sees his boys, Adam sighs with relief. She's all smiles and gives them high-fives. "So glad you made it!" she says, and the boys high-five her back as hard as they can. "That's all you've got? Let's see how hard you can really do it."

She has them high-five her again, and now Adam's boys are diving in for their coach, who whoops and hollers for them as they're in midair.

Adam just wants to disappear from the pool deck as quickly as possible, so he goes out to his car and sits with his head back against the headrest listening to the radio. It isn't until later at night when he's in bed, and his boys are asleep after countless requests for glasses of water and hugs, and his wife is asleep beside him, that the image of the man at the pool comes back to him, and Adam remembers now that he forgot to tell the coach about the man. He wishes he hadn't forgotten, because the way the man looked at the girls, Adam thinks, wasn't good. It wasn't good at all.

This is Sofia doing no-breathers during practice. Since Kim's death, Coach has been having them do a lot. She has them do six in a row, swimming the length of the pool and back in freestyle without taking a breath. This is Sofia thinking she has enough time left to do a seventh, even though the coach hasn't asked them to do it, because Sofia thinks the more she does them, then the more she can do them during her one-hundred-free race, at least for the first fifty, and that will definitely make her faster. This is Sofia climbing out of the pool after her seventh no-breather and standing on the deck and beginning to black out. This is Sofia sitting down on deck against the wall made of glass and putting her head between her legs and her hands on her knees and staring at the tiles on deck and thinking how the voices of her teammates sound so far away, as if they were outside even, close to the hillside where the granite rocks, so shear, stick out like chunks of black ice.

CHAPTER TWENTY-SIX

On the equator trip you left the air conditioner off and the doors wide open at night, wanting to hear the waves rolling in, not even minding the din of the howler monkeys in the nearby trees that sounded like your front-loading washing machine at home after you have crammed too many towels and jeans into it and it is complaining at a high pitch. If you had bought only organic milk, you wouldn't have been able to afford the trip, but on the trip you felt pangs of guilt when you looked at Alex, your nine-year-old, whose breasts you could see budding through her swimsuit. Maybe, just maybe, all that highly processed milk was making her hormones kick in prematurely, and what have I done, you think, and now, with all this about the killer, you feel even more often that the earth is sucking you in from below, and if it weren't for being able to think about Paul instead or the handles on the chair you are sitting in while eating your raisin bran, you'd be all the way sucked in, the image of your brother with his blood running out of his head feeding the vortex, providing the extra whoosh that would make your journey to the center of the earth entirely possible.

Driving to practice, the road is gleaming from an overnight shower, but the sun is lighting up the blacktop in a promising warm glow as you pass by a man who opens his mailbox and hands his newspaper to his collie, who takes the newspaper gingerly in his mouth, and with his tail high trots back toward the house. On the car radio you hear a report from the same trooper with the battered nose who was at the pool and who was pictured in the paper. In a voice that is sonorous and clear and can be heard even through the static you're encountering because you're traveling between mountains, he says that unfortunately there are no leads, no leads at all in the murder case, but he knows that in time, a shred of evidence will appear, and when it does, he will act on it. The killer will be caught.

What's that in the water? you think while swimming your workout. There are stretches of silt at the bottom that cover the tiles like dark scarves settling down to the ground after blowing in a breeze. The filter on the blink again, you think, and wonder if you or your daughters should even be swimming in the water today. Isn't it bad enough that you're not protecting them from a killer and that you're not feeding them organic milk and their breasts are rearing their small heads? Now, on top of everything else, your girls have to swim in dirty water? What if they inhale those bits of silt? What if they have an open cut and the dirt gives them an infection that will never heal?

You swim anyway. The cool water wakes you up. You are always tired as you drive to the pool. You yawn huge yawns, one after the other, that make your eyes close up because your jaw is stretching so wide and you're afraid your yawning will affect your view of the road. But when you're actually swimming you're always impressed that yawning is the farthest thing from your mind. You look down at the silt at the bottom and wonder why everything you see you interpret like a Rorschach, why the silt looks like scarves to you and why your daughter's menstrual blood on a pad looks like an hourglass and why even the grain of the wood in your bedroom walls looks like a smiling face, and clouds, oh my god, you have seen more shapes of animals in clouds than you've seen on the sides of the roads while driving, more cottontail rabbits up in the air than you've ever seen in a summer field, more whales and dolphins than you've ever seen in your life, and more horses rearing, their manes flying behind them, than you've ever seen before on the many farms you drive by every day on your way to practice. Even in people's faces you have seen things—the shape of the lines around Thomas's mouth look like the hats the Japanese wore while working in the rice fields long ago, and in your own face you have seen scars on your forehead from cuts you received as a child, and it looks as if someone created a scene of a rural landscape on your forehead. Slightly wavy lines representing the lay of the rolling land, and other stray marks representing random birds in flight.

You even see things in things you haven't seen. For example, your brother's blood pooling on the carpeted floor was, in your mind, in the shape of a head of cauliflower.

You hear the water soothing you, telling you it's okay. Shush. There now, the water says. There, there.

You sit on the topmost bleacher after your swim and lean back against the wall. You were practicing your fly in the water, trying to get more glide in your stroke and also trying to bring up your arms faster instead of letting them drag behind you and slow you down, but you don't think it worked at all. Your fly was as slow as ever, and did not resemble at all the fly the swim-team girls do where they look like sea serpents moving through the water. You see your daughter Sofia sitting against the wall of the facility. You wonder if she's tired. You tell yourself to remember to feed her a better snack before practice next time. You've heard of the other swimmers eating bananas before practice and even yams because they keep you going for so long. Yams. When was the last time you even bought a yam? You see Thomas in the facility. He has come with you and he has used the treadmill and the weights and now he is walking to the water fountain, holding his fingertips to the inside of his wrist. He likes to check his pulse when he feels his heart flutter strangely or skip a beat. You think that whenever you feel your heart trip and stumble, you don't want to stop what you're doing to see if it will pass. Instead you keep doing what you're doing, even if sometimes that's swimming. You think dying will probably hurt as much as the time you and Thomas were stacking the woodpile and he threw a log on top of your thumb by mistake. You wanted to puke, it hurt so badly, but you lived through it. After your fingernail turned the purple color of the inside of a mussel's shell and fell off, you got out your pink nail polish and painted all your fingernails pink, as well as the skin on the thumb where your nail used to be. If anyone noticed the bumpy coat of polish on your thumb that looked as if a child had painted it for you, they didn't say so. You admire how people can be so polite sometimes, not even mentioning if there's food hanging off your lip, or if your underwear is showing above the waistline of your pants in the back.

You want to get back to reading *Anna Karenina*. Karenin is thinking of divorcing her, and he's demanding she hand over the love letters that Vronsky wrote to her. It's taking you forever to finish the book, months even. You've only been able to concentrate long enough to read a few pages a night, and Thomas keeps interrupting you. Thomas tells you about nicotine, how years ago people drank it. He wants to create a new alcoholic beverage, one that has caffeine in it as well as nicotine. Think how it would sell! he says. You, of course, think how bad the drink would be for people's health, but then you start thinking there may be a profit in it. You think of all the people you see in your town who smoke cigarettes and drink coffee and drink alcohol and you are sure they would try the beverage, and just as soon as you start imagining the possibilities, the people you know who could help promote the product (Larry, the liquor distributor, for example, whose daughter is on the swim team and who often has his daughter help stack the displays of bottles in the grocery stores after hours), and the fortune to be made, Thomas tells you it's probably not possible, what with all the tobacco regulations the government has, and the control the tobacco companies have over their own product, you probably couldn't do it. You, deflated, look out the window on the drive back from practice and listen to the conversation of Sofia and Alex in the backseat. They are talking about cheaters. Swimmers in their lanes who don't do the full workout. Swimmers who when the coach isn't looking don't bother to kick when they're on a kick set, or who don't bother touching the wall to complete the set, and turn around early, going back down the lane, or who say they did the whole set, but end early, or who reach a hand out and grab on to the lane line, giving themselves a little extra propulsion. Thomas tells your girls how those cheaters will suffer come race day. Come race day they won't be as fit as the others, and it will show in their times. You can't hide poor training, he says. What's worse is not bothering to study, say on a math test, he says. What's the point of even taking the test if you haven't bothered to learn the material? And you see Alex in the backseat shrink down, and you wonder if Alex is one of those swim-team cheaters or not, or maybe she hasn't shrunk down in her seat at all for feeling guilty, but has merely shrunk down in her seat because she's tired, because she has swum her heart out for the past two hours and every fiber of her adolescent muscles is saying I'm tired, and feed me. How did I expect them, you think, to be satisfied with just one apple a piece on the ride home? I should have brought granola bars and bananas too. You reach out behind you in the car to touch one of your daughter's hands, to more than pat it, to hold it up in your own hand and squeeze it, to somehow parlay some energy back into her. If only I had the energy to give, you think, and then you feel a warmth course through your body, and as if on cue, your body seems to have found the extra reserves to share with your daughter, the endless supply of mother energy that all mothers have, even when their children are full-grown.

CHAPTER TWENTY-SEVEN

Some of the time Mr. Floyd Arneson, aka the killer, likes to show up at work on time, and sometimes he shows up early, but he never shows up late, because he does not want to have to be called into the principal's office. This is Floyd Arneson thinking, I know perfectly well there is a pretty blond woman who is trying to bait me into killing her. I can see the outline of the handgun sitting in her oversized pocket. She is careless, though, and turns her back to the woods too often, where I could come out quickly and be on her in no time. Floyd Arneson likes thinking about this woman rather than having to think about work. He is so often annoyed with the teachers when they want to order supplies and say they need them right away and need him to type up a purchase order for them right away and then, when he orders them right away, even cutting his lunchtime short to get it done, the package arrives and they leave it in their mailboxes for days. So it was no hurry, really, at all. He is tired of the way they come into his office without knocking, while he is working, asking for substitution forms to fill out, asking where the principal is, or asking how to work the new phone system, which they should have learned by now since he has put a copy of the manual in each one of their mailboxes. He is tired of the way they open up his desk drawer while he is out, searching for postage stamps or scissors or tape or pens when, of course, if they weren't so lazy, they could just go down to the supply room and get most of those items themselves.

Floyd Arneson likes the children. He likes hearing their small hands rap on the sliding glass window when they come up to deliver the attendance list. He likes opening the sliding glass window and peering down to where they are standing up on tiptoes trying to see him and pass him the list. He likes how yellow like corn silk the little girls' hair can be, and he likes how long the boys' lashes can be. He doesn't like how at recess he can always hear the teachers telling the children to stop climbing the trees and to stop playing with sticks and to stop playing by the stream where the poison ivy grows. He wishes the teachers would just let the children have fun.

He knows that if he wanted to, he could easily kill the blond woman he sees at the rest stops, but he doesn't want to stop seeing her when he goes and parks his car on a dirt logging road on the other side of a rest stop and walks through the woods to get to the rest stop. He likes how she keeps patting the pocket where her handgun is located right before she walks into the restroom. He likes how a few times he has looked through the door and seen how she stands at the mirror and washes her hands, hardly looking up at her reflection, when you would think a woman that attractive would be drawn to looking at herself all of the time.

CHAPTER TWENTY-EIGHT

*T*his is you at home hanging up your suit after your workout, noticing how it's stretching out, how it now looks as if it could fit one of the dancing hippos. This is you listening to rain falling on the copper roof and Thomas going around the house shutting the windows, the rubber stripping in the windows making a sucking sound as they're closed, sounding vacuum-packed, as though the house is being sealed in for good. This is you thinking maybe it's for the best, that you shouldn't be let out of the house again anyway. Locked inside, you won't be talking to swim-team husbands you shouldn't be talking to. Locked inside, maybe you will finally clean out the pantry, arrange the myriad of spice containers and sponge off the shelves, wiping away the overlapping circular stains the bottoms of the containers have left on the wood and making it look as if your pantry were some kind of an official Olympic item, sporting the signature interlocking rings. This is you in the evening looking out your office window at a lilac bush

getting its leaves battered by the heavy rain. This is you hearing
your girls fighting over something in the other part of the house.
Sofia is shaking the carpet from her loft bedroom down to the lev-
el below where Alex has her bed. Alex is shrieking about the dust
and dirt falling on top of her covers and Sofia is telling her she's
imagining things, nothing is really falling from her carpet. This is
you debating whether to go and mediate and tell Sofia to knock it
off, or whether it's best if you stay out of this one. Your girls can't
always expect you to be there when they fight. They will have to
learn how to stand up for themselves and be strong. This is you
thinking you have to be strong too. You have to keep away from
the facility for a few days. The facility is no longer safe, not with
Paul there, or Chris there to remind you of Paul. Not with the both
of them reminding you of Kim and Bobby Chantal. You could
always visit with another friend at the facility, one who could make
you laugh, one who could talk to you about the swim team and
get your mind off whatever that feeling is that grabs you from the
bottom of your chair at the breakfast table and wants to drag you
down, but now you have to stay away and lay low. This is you lying
in bed with Thomas, and the rain outside is still coming down,
and the wind is shaking the treetops back and forth as if it is trying
its hardest to uproot them. This is you listening to Thomas asking
you how Foucault made his pendulum, and how he accounted for
the movement of the earth when he did. This is you not under-
standing what Thomas's question means in the least, but knowing
he doesn't really expect you to have an answer anyway, he just
asked the question in order to say it aloud and help himself answer
it. This is Thomas falling asleep. Snoring when he's just drifted
off. This is you taking the pillow and laying it on top of his face

so that he stops. This is Thomas rolling over, showing his back to you. How many moles and spots are there on Thomas's back? Too many to count, you think. These are the calls of the coyotes down by the hollow near the stream—they are short and overlapping, and then there is one last long call that sounds as if it were a wolf's instead. This is the smell in the air, the rain smelling like a pond. This is you thinking that even if you don't have any wife energy, and you search inside yourself and find there is none, that you will have to start finding some wife energy pronto, because it seems so much hinges on this wife energy. Even if Thomas didn't respond to this energy before, you have to try again. This is you waking Thomas up with your touching, having found some shred of wife energy somewhere in the marrow of you. This is Thomas turning away from you and toward the closet where your clothes hang. You dislike all of them. They are so unflattering, the blouses that make you look pregnant. The jeans that are too tight and have been for a couple of years now, but that you refuse to get rid of because you think it's a waste to toss a perfectly good pair of jeans. This is Thomas falling asleep again, facing all the clothes that hold the shape of you that you don't like.

This is the next week. This is you seeing Paul in a knot in the wood in the hallway. You stand there with the laundry in your arms staring at the wall, not believing your endless ability to see shapes in everything, and how the knots in the wood remind you of his eyes. They're small knots, and what would seem to be the outside parts of the eyes are tapering upward, as if they were smiling. You try not to stare for too long at the knots in the wood, especially since Sofia is walking behind you wanting to go downstairs as well. "Speed the plow," she says, passing you, and you think how you never would have used certain expressions around your children when they were young if you had known they were going to start using the same ones with you when they got older.

You have not seen Paul in a few days, almost a week. To avoid seeing him, you have not taken the girls to practice, but let Thomas take them instead. For the best, you told yourself. But you aren't feeling the better for it. You are sullen and don't feel like doing anything. You can't even bring yourself to brush the dog, and you have been looking at the dog every day for the past few weeks thinking, I really must brush you, what a mess of matted hair you have become! Twigs are wound up in her sweeping tail hair, and she licks and chews her hind legs to free the sticky nettles clinging to them. You wonder if Chris has told Paul that she has met Bobby Chantal's daughter. If he does know, you are sure Paul will stop Chris from trying to exhume Bobby Chantal's body. His DNA would be on her. But what does it matter? The police don't have Paul as a suspect. No one would even approach Paul for a sample to match the DNA because no one ever saw Paul and Bobby Chantal together. Unless, of course, someone from the coffee shop or the restaurant they went to recognized Paul because he was a regular, and recognized Bobby Chantal's face in the newspaper the next day. But if that were the case, then Paul would have been questioned long ago. So no one remembers seeing them together. Paul is safe, and you are relieved you have come to this conclusion. It's as if you've been carrying the weight of his possible implication in the murder on your shoulders ever since you visited Chris and learned she knew Bobby Chantal's daughter. You go upstairs and begin to pack for you and the girls. The next morning you are leaving for a big swim meet and Paul will be there. The weather will be warm, so you pack short skirts and tank tops to wear. As you put them into your bag, you wonder if the skirts are too short. Do they show off too much of your legs, which, at your age, might be better off covered? Do the sleeveless tops reveal too much of your arms, which you call bingo arms, because when you lift them up in the air the wings of fat that have started to hang from them remind you of the flabby arms of old women playing bingo in unair-conditioned halls and raising their cards and shouting out "Bingo!" when they win.

You check your girls' swim bags, making sure they have towels and swimsuits and goggles and water bottles, the water bottles being important because the coach, this coach with many all-star athlete commendations under her belt, has told the swimmers that they cannot swim without a water bottle positioned at the end of their lane to drink from now and then during a two-hour practice. You agree with the coach on the drinking of water during practice. You have seen how red in the face your own girls get during a strenuous workout. You have seen other girls, paler girls, get red down their necks and their shoulders and their chests as well, after swimming, for example, ten one-hundred frees on a 1:10 with only a ten-second interval. You do not agree, though, with the swimmers drinking electrolyte drinks during practice. You think all they need is water, even though you have sat in on those parent education meetings the swim team sometimes provides in the spinning room where it smells like sweat, and you have learned that your daughters need more than just water during practice, and that your daughters need to eat right away after they swim, and that the best thing for them after practice is chocolate milk. You just cannot bring yourself to give your daughters sugar water during practice, even if it does have electrolytes, and you cannot bring yourself to give your daughters chocolate milk after practice, because as a girl you yourself never got chocolate milk except on special occasions, and since when did it become okay to have chocolate milk every day?

At the meet, after the anthem is sung by three girls who sound like cats in heat, the meet director asks for a moment of silence for Kim Hood, the swimmer who recently died. You want to yell out, "Murdered! She was murdered!" because to you there are such big differences between just dying, and having been robbed of your life, and even taking your own life. When your brother killed himself, there was no crime committed, and you could not understand why so much taxpayer money had to be spent on cordoning the property off with crime scene tape and starting an investigation. Wasn't it obvious to everyone around that the cauliflower stain of blood forming by his head, and the gun in his own hand, was not the scene of a crime, but the scene of a jerk, an asshole, a complete idiot who thought only of himself and who was so narrow-minded and devoid of willpower that killing himself was the only solution he could come up with to provide himself with some relief? If only he was one to exercise, then he might not have done it, you think, and you wonder really if that's true, if there's some study that's been done where those who exercise regularly have lower suicide rates, and if so, think of the decline in need for shrinks and pills. Wouldn't some kind of a mandatory facility membership be just as effective? Or is that just narrow-minded thinking, not taking into consideration chemical imbalances in the brain and genetic predispositions. You close your eyes and, along with everyone else, you remember Kim. You do not want to remember the way she was in the newspaper, out of the water. You remember her in the water, the way she moved up and down, a perfect body moving in perfect fluid rhythm in the shape of a sine curve, a motion that looked as if it could last forever, a motion that seemed more like the real girl than the girl herself did when she was just standing on deck or in the foyer after practice. There are sniffles heard while everyone's head is lowered and remembering. There are also the hard choking sounds of people trying to keep from sobbing. The head coach makes the sound too, and then the meet announcer announces the first race of the day with a long whistle, and the swimmers in the first heat stand up on the blocks with a weak morning sun breaking over them that makes you think all of what you are seeing you're seeing through a tropical haze.

CHAPTER TWENTY-NINE

It's a break-even day. Your girls gain time in some events, and shave time in others. Sofia does well in the first fifty of her two-hundred free, though, going faster than she ever has. Her coach high-fives her on the deck, telling her the no-breathers really paid off. At the end of the day, after the girls have drunk numerous drinks promising to replenish all the electrolytes they lost throughout the day (of which a total of four minutes was spent racing. The rest of the time they were sitting on blankets under tents with their noses in books, or they were racing around on the grassy grounds of the facility, playing tag and ninja with their teammates), you pack up their things and get ready to head back to the hotel. You and Paul had been timers for most of the day, but timing for different lanes, so you didn't get much of a chance to talk to him except to say hello and to wish Cleo good luck. Now, on the walk back to the parking lot, Paul and Cleo catch up to you. "Can we order pizza again and watch TV in the hotel with Cleo?" your girls plead. You look at Paul to see what he thinks. "It's okay by me," he says, and you tell your daughters, "Okay, but we're not staying up as late this time. You girls still have to race tomorrow."

It's funny, really, how you were hoping the girls would request to repeat what they did the last time they stayed in a hotel together. You are the one who, when the door closes behind you and you're inside Paul's room, wishes you had all night to be together, because not much time passes before he goes over to you and you start kissing again, and you think, Oh, good, we can finish the kiss that we started in his office. We can finish all of this and I can go back to Thomas and he can go back to Chris. I can lie beside Thomas in bed and listen to him talk about a fifty-thousand-year-old girl whose remains they found and who, they can tell from her DNA, already carried the gene for a speech disorder. I can listen to him tell me about how submarines are really just cylinders welded together at the seam. I can listen to him tell me that feed laced with antibiotics increases growth in farm animals by 15 to 20 percent. When Paul goes back to Chris, he can sit on his tea-stained bed and look at his silver-framed picture of them jumping into the pond on their wedding day. He can watch her in bed on bright nights when the clouds are gone and the moon is high and he can admire her beautiful face and breathe in deeply, smelling something like mint.

But the more you kiss Paul—the more you feel his mouth inside of yours and his hands on your back, pulling you close—the more you know that the kiss is a kiss that can never be finished, and at the same time it is a kiss that never should have been started. When you pull back from him, you immediately wish you hadn't. The warmth of him, the way he smells of his leather jacket, is something you want to step inside of again. You reach out and hold on to the wall for a moment, and know that the coldness of the hotel room wall is good, even though it feels anything but good, it feels hard and shocking, but at least it is going to wake you up. You won't have to go up to Paul again and start kissing him as long as the wall is there to hold on to.

"You're right. You're right," he says, and shakes his head at the same time, making you think you were anything but right. Why doesn't he come back to you? Why doesn't he take your hand from the wall and start kissing you again? "Ah, we should eat," he says. He opens a pizza box that is on the desk. He tears off a slice for you and puts it on a paper plate and hands it to you. You don't want to take a bite. You want to remember the taste of him in your mouth. But neither do you want to hand back the plate, because by holding it you look as if you are in his room for a reason. If another swim-team parent or your girls come knocking on the door, at least you can say you are just there to enjoy a slice topped with mushrooms and sausage.

Now he's telling you about Cleo's race day. How she hit the lane lines on backstroke because, he is sure, the sun was in her eyes. He is looking forward, almost, to the fall season, when the indoor meets will start up again and true backstroke times can be counted. He says that in the middle of the day he finally wised up and bought Cleo some tinted goggles at the facility's front desk. They helped, but still, Cleo didn't do as well as she usually does in the back. The front-facing strokes were a different story. Cleo shaved off time in every one of those.

You take a few bites of the pizza. Paul isn't even eating himself. He is sitting on the end of the other bed. How can we keep from

touching each other again? you think. "Can we watch TV?" you
say. In a second Paul is grabbing the remote to turn it on.

You don't have a television at home because where you live
there is no service to receive the major stations. You are amazed
by how many cuts to commercials there are and how loud they
are. The pace of the images and the loud, fast music accompa-
nying them makes you eat more quickly, and before you know it
Paul has placed another slice on your plate. You pick up the remote and change the channel. When you find the news, you stop
and watch. Kim Hood's face takes up the screen. They still have
no leads, no clues as to who killed her, but they have established
through measurements taken of the other victims' throat wounds
that he could be the same man who killed other women at other
rest stops around this part of the country. The same state trooper
with the battered nose is now being interviewed live. "Yes, that's
right," he says. "We've had a request from Bobby Chantal's daughter to exhume the body of her mother. If we think it will aid in the
investigation, we will certainly comply, but there was a thorough
examination of the body at the time of the murder." The news
program then cuts to a beautiful blond-haired woman. It takes you
a moment to realize it's Chris. You are so surprised you can't say
anything, and just watch the TV with your mouth open. The reporter puts the mike in front of Chris, so close to her lips it's as
if she wants her to eat it. "Is it true that your client has agreed to
exhuming her mother's body? How does she feel about that after
all these years?"

"First of all, I'm not her lawyer. She's not my client. I'm just
someone who supports her. Exhuming her mother will be emotionally difficult, of course, but she's prepared to go forward and

do that if it means putting a stop to the murders. The examination, twenty-eight years ago, can't be considered a thorough one by today's standards, not when scientific testing has advanced so much. Take for instance DNA testing, which wasn't even used in criminal investigations back—"

Paul grabs the remote and shuts off the television. "I can't believe this. What does she think she's doing? Who does she think she is?" He's standing now, staring at you, waiting for some kind of an answer, when there's a knock at the door. Paul doesn't even look as though he's heard it. The knock comes again. It doesn't sound like one of your girls knocking. If your girls were on the other side of the door, they would knock about thirty times in a row and kick the bottom of the door and call out your name, or call you a name even, and demand to be let inside the room. This was an adult knock. "I'll get it," you say.

Dinah doesn't wait to be asked in. She marches into the room, taking everything in—the condition of the beds, the pizza on the desk, the clothes that are still on the backs of you and Paul.

"Well, what do we have here?" she asks. "A romantic dinner for two? I came by to let you know a bunch of us other swim parents on the floor are ordering in from the nearby Chinese place, but I can see you two have already taken care of your needs."

"Get out, Dinah," Paul says, and as he does, he pushes her backward out of the room.

"Hey, hey, didn't mean to interrupt your wild night with Thomas's wife!" Dinah yells, but you can hear she's not yelling it into the room at you or Paul. She is yelling it so that it carries up and down the hotel floor, so that all of the other swim-team parents can hear. You stand up to leave.

"I'd better go," you say.

"No. No, please don't go. I need you," Paul says. You play back in your head what Paul just said. They are words Thomas has never spoken to you. He may have told you he needed you for something utilitarian—to help stack the wood, for example—but he has never told you he needed you for anything emotional. Then again, you have never asked Thomas for anything emotional either. When you received the phone call telling you your brother had shot himself, and you stood leaning over the counter, feeling as if your legs would not hold you up any longer, and you started to cry, it was the dog who came to you first, whining beside you, wanting to jump up and lick your face, to see what was the matter. Thomas stood off to the side and watched you, and later that night when you questioned aloud why your brother had done it, why he had shot himself, Thomas told you it was because he was an asshole, and there was no need to waste any more energy discussing it. "Why is he an asshole?" you asked Thomas, and he answered that anyone who leaves three kids without a father is a jerk. You wondered if Thomas was right about your brother being an asshole. You didn't sleep that night, crying intermittently while Thomas slept beside you. You were surprised that grief could cause such insomnia. In the past it had always been worries or anticipation that had made you stay awake.

Now, in this hotel room, Paul is reaching out to you. "It's all right, I'm not going anywhere," you say, taking him in your arms as you rub his back and stroke his hair. You stay that way until he leads you to the bed, and still in bed you hold him, and you can hear his breathing in your ear. It is sending up the hairs on the back of your neck, and you want him to start kissing you again.

You feel ashamed by the desire. The man is obviously devastated. He has just seen his wife on television declaring that she is intent on getting involved in the biggest drama of his entire life, one that he has been trying to keep secret for so many years.

"What if they connect me to the murder?" he whispers in your ear.

"They won't," you say. "They can't. They don't have your DNA on file. It's not like you're a criminal with a record."

"I can't believe this is happening. Maybe it wouldn't have happened if I hadn't started spending all that time working in my office on a story about the whole thing. Maybe in a way writing those words down put it out there again, as if the killer himself sensed the words were written and it prompted him to strike again."

This is you thinking how sometimes you feel as if you're living in a world not where things aren't what they seem, but where things are real that you never knew were real, and every day you're discovering something new—like the possibility of the mere writing down of words making something happen. Even the idea your younger daughter had that the image of a murderer could still be seen on the victim's eyelids seemed possible to you. Maybe when they exhume the body they should pull back what's left of Bobby Chantal's eyelids and see if the image of the killer is still there.

This is you going back into your hotel room after a little while because it's getting late and your girls need to go to bed and Cleo needs to go to bed. These are the girls all under the covers of one bed watching a movie in the dark and asking for just five more minutes and this is you saying, "No, tomorrow's a big day. Off to bed."

This is you at night trying to sleep in the hotel, hearing the elevator reach your floor occasionally and ding when its doors open, hearing the ice machine down the hall clunk while perpetually making ice. This is you thinking how Paul's head is probably on the other side of the wall from your head. When you hear a faint ringing of a cell phone coming from his room, and then hear his voice, you imagine he's talking to Chris, though you aren't able to hear exactly what he's saying. Maybe there is a rise in the volume of his voice, you think, and he is angry with her for taking on the plight of Bobby Chantal's daughter, for getting involved in something she has no business getting involved in. You think you can hear quiet then, coming from Paul's room, so he must have hung up. Suddenly your phone rings, and you grab it quickly from the bedside table so as not to wake up the girls. You take the phone to the bathroom and shut the door before saying hello. It's Chris. She's excited and talking so loudly you think her voice carries through the phone and could wake up the girls, who need their sleep, who have to wake up early and eat the hotel's lousy breakfast bagels, and pack their bags, and then ride to the meet and squeeze into their cold swimsuits that are still not dry from the day before, and then dive into the cold water and do warm-ups in a pool that only a short time ago reflected the moon through a chilly morning mist that clung close to its surface. "Did you watch the news?" Chris is saying, her voice high and breathy and loud. You can picture Chris's cheeks flushed over her tan, smooth skin. "I did," you say, but so quietly that Chris says, "What? Speak up. I can't hear you. Annie, are you there? Are you there?" and this is you not wanting to be there for Chris at all. This is you closing the phone, because you have an old-style phone that disconnects when it closes, and you like how quietly you can close it. This is you turning your phone off, thinking if there's really an emergency at home that Thomas needs to call you for, then it will have to be an emergency he can handle by himself, and you know he will, because really even when sometimes he says he needs you to stack wood, or help with some project, he doesn't really need your help at all. You know that if something happens, if he hurts himself or gets sick, he will either tough it out or drive himself to the hospital, and so really, there is no need to keep the phone on ever. You think of how much battery you would save then with your old-style phone if you only ever used it to call out and never left it on for people to call in. Maybe a phone, in its metal and plastic lifetime, is not capable of transmitting bad news more than once. The news of your brother's suicide, for instance. Maybe a phone only gets so many tragedies it can pass on, and then its phone personality, its karma, its existential self, blocks or keeps at bay all other tragedies from ever being received.

CHAPTER THIRTY

*T*his is the water the next afternoon at the pool looking cloudier, partly because it is mirroring the overcast sky of a hot late summer's day gathering storm clouds, and partly because it's dirtier from so many hundreds of kids swimming in it and having unknowingly taken into the water with them bits of grass that clung to the sides of their feet, and bits of dirt, and traces of sports energy drinks, and traces of body lotion used without success to moisturize skin that stews for hours every day in water treated with chlorine. This is Paul cheering Cleo on. He watches her race a one-hundred IM in the next lane even as he's timing for another swimmer in his own lane. When she hits the wall he stops his stopwatch instead of stopping it when the swimmer in his own lane touches two-tenths of a second later. Paul writes in a time he thinks the kid in his lane might have gotten, but is not worrying about it too much, because after all the kid didn't come in first or second or even third, but maybe second-to-last.

Driving home, Paul keeps telling Cleo how proud he is of her for winning her heat. He tells her so many times that she says, "Dad, can we just listen to the radio now?" and he turns it on to some popular station where she knows all the words to all the songs and he wants to know how she knows them all when he hardly lets her listen to that station in the car. The songs are all songs he listened to growing up, only now, after a few lines, the poetic lyrics are rudely stopped, interrupted by riffs of rapping and the disjointed telltale mechanized bass beats of dubstep.

This is Paul passing by rest stops along the way, unable to keep from craning his neck back to watch them a little longer as he wonders if the rest-stop killer is there, sitting in his red Corvair, or probably some newer car by now, thinking about who his next victim will be.

This is Paul entering his driveway, seeing that Chris's car isn't there, thinking how she's probably off with Bobby Chantal's daughter, Chris putting her hand on the daughter's shoulder, helping her deal with the upheaval of having to exhume her mother. He doesn't feel there's any stopping Chris now. He could have done something before, maybe, if he'd known this is what she'd be up to. Maybe he could have called Chris's parents and asked them to come for a visit and try to talk to Chris and explain to her how she was getting caught up in a world that wasn't her own, but now it is too late. Bobby Chantal's body is on its way to seeing the light of day once again after so many years, and Paul is on his way to facing months and maybe years of a legal nightmare that he can only hope turns out in his favor.

When Chris comes home later he is in bed, but not asleep. He reaches out to her when she comes into the bed, and he can feel her tense up immediately. She quickly turns to face him, as if she thinks he is going to hurt her, or that she wants to hurt him. "Hey, it's okay. It's just me, your husband," he says. But he does not feel her breathing relax and her body still seems tense and her skin is cold, as if she has been outside for a while without a jacket or sweater.

"Can we talk?" he says. She shakes her head. He can hear her hair rasping on the pillowcase she shakes it so firmly. "But I've got to tell you something," he says.

"Can it wait until tomorrow? I'm tired," she says.

"No, it can't wait. It's a story I think you'll want to hear," he says. He leaves the bed and goes and gets his briefcase. He printed out the story the last time he was in his office, and now he sits beside her on the bed and reads it to her. The light from the moon is strong enough that he doesn't even have to turn the light on, and he likes reading his words better that way, without even a pen in his hand to stop and make corrections to the writing. When he is finished Chris says, "That was you, in the story?" He nods. "You could have told me," she says. "You had so many years to tell me."

"I didn't want to upset you," he says. "It wasn't like I could make Bobby Chantal come back. It wasn't like I took her away. I wasn't part of the equation."

"How could you say that? You were! You saw the car. You saw the license plate. You knew what Bobby Chantal was doing up until minutes before her throat was slit."

"If I had gone to the police they would have focused on me, Chris. They would have spent time, everyone's time, trying to figure out if I was the killer or not. It was better that I didn't come forth. Don't you realize that when this happened we had just decided to start seriously seeing each other again? It's not exactly information I was going to share with you to get you to date me."

"No, you're right. If I had known how you were just watching out for your own self, I wouldn't have dated you at all. How do I even know you aren't really the killer?"

Paul knew this was coming, but still, to hear it from Chris at that moment makes him so angry.

"I am not the fucking killer!" he yells, and of course he realizes at the moment he yells it that he yelled too loud, his voice too high, even the moonlight seems to cringe from how loud he was and seems to dim, or is it just a passing cloud in front of the moon that makes it look as though Chris's face is darkening?

Cleo opens their door then. "What's going on? Why's Dad yelling?" she says. Paul steers her back to her room, to where the mobile of the planets swings and glows. "It's nothing. I'll tell you in the morning," he says. "You and Mom are fighting, aren't you?" she says. "Yes, we are having an argument," he says. "Are you going to get a divorce?" Cleo asks as he brings the blankets up to her chin and smoothes her hair away from her forehead. He shakes his head in the dark.

CHAPTER THIRTY-ONE

Only a few weeks have passed and it feels already like fall. Typical of New England, you think. One moment you're complaining of the bugs and the heat, the next morning you're waking up to a lawn covered with gold and red leaves. Even outside the facility leaves blow across the grass lawn next to the entrance. The sound of a bicyclist fitting and locking his bike into the bike rack, the metal hitting against metal, sounds sharper now than in summer, the cold somehow changing how things reach the ear. Decorative gourds on the facility's Moroccan blue check-in deck sit in a wooden bowl.

This is you inside the facility, where you watch a man who has come from the weight room walking toward the water fountain. He walks strangely, lifting each foot high off the ground as if the soles of his sneakers are covered in gluey wads of chewed gum, or as if he were walking on Jupiter and the gravity is so high it's a labor to lift up each foot and walk across its surface. And who knows, you think, maybe it's possible I went to sleep on Earth and woke up on Jupiter, and everything is the same as it is on Earth when I walk outside, though there will be many moons to keep me awake at night instead of just one. You know there are sixty-seven moons of Jupiter because Thomas once read you an article about Jupiter's moons and you were surprised that many of them have names. You had known about Europa and Io: Io is caught in a tug-of-war between Jupiter and the other moons. The tension between the two has made it very hot, and Io is the second-hottest object in the solar system; only the sun is hotter. But you had never known about all the other moons, which have beautiful names like Amalthea and Ananke. Why, you want to know, didn't our moon get a beautiful name? Why is our moon just the moon? Why didn't we bother giving it just one name, when we have bothered to name moons of Jupiter so far away they are invisible to the naked eye?

You jump in the water and start your workout. While you're swimming breaststroke, you hear the susurration of the water sounding as if it were a wind that talks to you every time you put your head down and your hands out in front of you for the glide. You think you hear the water telling you to move over. You look in front of you. Why would the water tell you to move over? There is no one else swimming down your lane. There is no coach at the end of the lane telling you to move over because they need that lane for the swim team kids. Then you remember that when you walked into the pool you saw a workman hanging from the pipe in the ceiling in a safety harness. He was right above the lane you dove into. He was up high fixing an air vent whose seal had come undone. You dive under the lane line and enter the other lane, and just as you do, you hear the splash of a large metal cuff that wrapped around the air vent, holding it in place, as it comes crashing down into the water. If it had hit you, you would have been seriously hurt. After everyone asks if you are all right, you dive down to retrieve the metal cuff for the workman. Its edges are sharp and it weighs a good ten pounds. The workman didn't even know it was about to fall. The lifeguards and the coaches keep telling you how lucky you are you decided to change lanes when you did.

On the drive home from the facility, you ask your daughters what you should call the moon. Sofia doesn't want to join in the fun, she reads her book without looking up, but Alex wants to call the moon Fred. "Okay, agreed," you say. "Fred, don't be so bright tonight. Let me get some sleep at least."

Thomas and Sofia work on algebra when you and the girls get home. While you cook dinner you hear the numbers being rattled off by Thomas as he dictates to Sofia, who writes them on a whiteboard. It has been years since you have had to think about algebra and doing equations with negative numbers. In school your teachers said you would need algebra and that it would come in handy as an adult, but algebra is never something you need to know. "Isolate the terms," "Subtract the negative," "A negative times a negative is a positive," you hear Thomas saying, and then you think that maybe your teachers were right. Learning algebra is important. Learning algebra is one of life's greatest lessons. Who else taught you such lessons?

"What you do to one side, you have to do to the other side," Thomas says.

And such fairness! you think to yourself.

"Again, a negative times a negative is a positive," Thomas says. And such optimism! You want to stop cooking and go over to Sofia and Thomas. You want to learn algebra all over again, but there are the onions you're sautéing that you have to stir or else they will burn. There is the water you want to come to a boil, but you haven't yet found the lid that fits the pot to quicken the process. There is Alex asking how do you say coins in Spanish, and you can't remember even though you studied Spanish, and there is the dog, who is lying down in the kitchen beside you and following your every move with her eyes, asking, in her own way, to be fed her dinner of kibble soon. The goose outside is pecking at the door. Tick, tick, tick, tick, she is saying with her beak, wanting to come in because dark is falling and the coyotes might be out, and the days are shorter now, and the colder temperatures might cause a frost to fall over night.

This is the fall night, freezing the grass on the lawn, freezing the petals on the tomato plants already picked of their fruit, edging them in white, freezing the topmost surface of a bowl of water left out for the goose. This is the goose in her crate, put in for the night, her eyes closed for short periods of time, and then open again, listening for the sound of the coyote or the fox or the fisher cat. This is you awake, but with your eyes closed, thinking how Fred must not have gotten the memo. Either that or Fred just didn't bother to heed your request, because Fred's shining in through the windows as brightly as the sun, and you wonder if Fred, like Io, is caught in its own tug-of-war, one between itself and Earth that is causing volcanoes to form and its temperature to rise.

CHAPTER THIRTY-TWO

*T*his is the body of Chris. Contrary to your beliefs, she's not perfect. This is her neck. There's a scar there from when she went to the beach and stayed too long and got a second-degree burn from the sun. This is her right foot. There's a callus on her pinky toe that every once in a while she shaves down with a razor blade. This is her vagina. Between her labia there's a brown beauty mark the size of a dime. She has had to explain the dime-sized brown beauty mark to all of the four men she has slept with in her life. This is her left breast. It's smaller than her right. This is her left earlobe. There's an indentation in it as if she were born with her ear half-pierced. This is her right knee. There's a scar on it from having fallen off a high-powered moped on a rocky road on a Mediterranean island. Make that three men she has slept with that she had to explain the dime-sized brown beauty mark to. One was a one-night stand and they never turned the lights on and she left his house before daybreak.

This is her house. Nearby is a small town with a gas station and a convenience store that sells all the usual drinks and chips and gum, but also homemade chocolate cream pie by the slice. The house is on a main road twenty minutes away from the facility, but behind the house there is a winding trail where Chris and Cleo sometimes cross-country ski in the winter, and in the summer they ride their bikes on it or they run down it, chasing each other for fun, their bodies brushing up against the leaves and branches of the gooseberry bushes as they go. This is what they have seen on the trail—garter snakes, baby chipmunks in a group of three, a snowshoe rabbit who looked too skinny to survive winter, a deer with twin fawns, and a black bear with his nose to the ground.

This is her childhood. A mother and father who owned a general store up north. She did homework behind the counter, and whenever she was stuck for an answer to a question, she'd ask a customer rather than her parents, who never seemed to know the answer or who were too busy slicing cold cuts or restocking beer onto shelves. This is where she learned how to skip stones, in a wide stream where after she swam she would lie down on flat rocks warmed by the sun. This is the owl she heard every night from her bedroom window. It's a barn owl with a white face that she liked to think of as being the ghost of her grandfather, who had a white beard and mustache. This is the length of her hair when she cut it for women who had cancer. Halfway down her back. This is her back. The shoulders are square and flat. She could rest a book on one of her shoulders and the book would not fall off. She has many muscles that can be seen on her back, even small ones that show up distinctly when she just raises her hair up to put it in a hair tie. This is her mouth. She has never had a cavity. This is the story you already know, the one of her babysitter named Beatrice and how she was raped. This is how Chris sometimes sleeps, with one arm rising in the air, and staying there as if she's holding it up for someone to come and grab it and bring her up from the deep. This is her in her studio, painting over and over again the face of the killer she has never even seen, while thinking of Beatrice. If only those rapists had been stopped beforehand, then Beatrice would have been spared, she thinks.

This is the lawyer Paul knows he has to hire eventually, but cannot bring himself to meet because he knows it means a huge chunk of his life will be destroyed. Paul passes by the lawyer's office, which looks like a bed and breakfast, and probably was at some point, and Paul thinks how could a lawyer who practices out of an office with lace curtains and window boxes be the lawyer who stands up in front of a jury and explains that even though Paul's semen was inside the exhumed body of Bobby Chantal, and Paul never came forth in all these years to tell the police that he had been with her the night of the murder, he is still innocent? Paul stops in his tracks and sits on the rock wall outside the office with his back facing the lace curtains and the window boxes. He doesn't believe in God, but he wants one to know, if one exists, that he prays it will never come to him sitting in a courtroom facing a jury. He prays that there's no way to find out it's his DNA. He prays that Chris doesn't decide to report him to the police and tell them he was with Bobby Chantal the day she was murdered. He prays she understands how it would derail their lives forever.

CHAPTER THIRTY-THREE

*T*his is Mandy at the facility, scowling. Cold rain is coming down hard outside, and the floor at the entrance is quickly becoming wet from water dripping off the clothes of everyone who comes through the doors. She mops the puddles up and then goes on to start cleaning the restrooms, but the minute she gets her cleaning cart to the ladies' room door, the director comes up to her and asks her to mop the entrance floor again, saying it's a hazard, a child or an old person may slip and fall. She already knows she'll have to stay at the facility later than her usual quitting time if she's going to get the restrooms clean. She starts mopping up the floor again when a man she's never seen before walks in. Mandy thinks she knows just about everybody who's a regular. She knows the overweight mother and the overweight daughter who always work out on the elliptical machines together and always seem to have matching sweat stains appear at the same time on their shirts, under the arms and below their breasts. She knows the man who lifts his legs strangely and walks as though he's walking on the moon. She knows the young man who has a muscled chest but legs like matchsticks, which to Mandy look so out of place, as if the man were one of those drawings where one person drew the top half and then folded over the paper and had someone else draw the bottom half. She knows the swimmers, of course. There's Joy, who always smiles at her. There's Maya, whose pale complexion reminds Mandy of the inside of a just-cut potato. There's the big kid named Carl, who moves his arms like windmills through the water but doesn't seem to go faster than anyone else. But this new guy, who is he? Mandy moves the mop near the check-in desk even though there's not much water there, just to see if the receptionist says his name when she scans his card. The receptionist doesn't say his name, though, and just says hello. The man, who wears slacks and a button-up-the-front shirt and tennis shoes, and is carrying a gym bag, doesn't head for the locker rooms first. Instead he heads for the tall tables located in front of the big windows that look onto the pool. He sits on a tall stool and watches the swimmers on the team swimming. Mandy can see that when the swimmers are asked to dive in, sprint, get out at the other end, and then walk the perimeter of the pool with their arms extended and their hands together in a streamline, the man watches intently, every once in a while running his hand through his thick black hair. While mopping the entrance, Mandy keeps an eye on the man. Why isn't he changing out of his clothes and working out? she thinks. It isn't until the swim practice is over, and the girls have pulled off their caps and let their wet hair fall darkly to their shoulders, that the man gets up and finally goes into the locker room. When he comes out he's ready for swimming. Mandy can see him through the glass window wearing baggy swim trunks and goggles that hang around his neck. Unlike most lap-swimmers, who dive right in, he holds onto the edge of the pool and lowers himself in. Once he's in, and sliding down under the water, he's smiling as if he were lowering himself into a warm Jacuzzi instead of a bracing competition pool that is regulated at a precise temperature of seventy degrees so the swimmers don't warm up too quickly and become overheated. The man, Mandy thinks, has a strange smile, as if he's not smiling at all, but ready to start crying. "Mandy," the director says over her shoulder. "The mop. We need the mop again in the foyer."

In cyberspace, Sofia is heading home, rounding Florida and coming up past the Keys, she has estimated, after she tallies up the miles she has swum since she last tallied them up and she was in Saint Kitts. In the facility's foyer she shows you an avatar of herself in the water on the screen. The first thing you think is that it's a poor avatar. Sofia is prettier, and Sofia in real life does not sport such ridiculously huge breasts and such a narrow, pinched-looking waist.

This is you wishing you were in the Keys or, better yet, back at the equator. The water warm, not smelling of chlorine, and the waves rolling in. This is you seeing Paul outside the facility standing under the awning to stay out of the rain while talking on his phone. He is turned away from the doors, he is turned away from other people, the phone call obviously not one he wants others to hear. This is you trying to read Paul's lips, even though you have never been able to read lips before and know you will probably never be able to. Still, you think that maybe because you have kissed these lips of Paul's, you will somehow read them more easily, and then you look at your thirteen-year-old daughter and think how she probably has more mature thoughts than you have. And oh, crap, I hope she has more mature thoughts than I have, you think, because really, lately your thoughts have been so childish. Daydreams of Paul leaving Chris to be with you have begun to crop up throughout the day. You have had them while rinsing your hair in the shower, while feeding the goose a bit of banana on the porch, while heating burrito shells in a pan. You think how when you were a teenager you probably didn't even daydream as much as you've been daydreaming lately. When you were a teenager you were more like your daughter is now—reading books whenever you could, especially seeking them out when your brother was upset for days because his girlfriend had left him. He was busy smashing his guitar, and a few days after that sending every one of the dining room chairs down the staircase. From the bathroom where you were hiding, and reading, you could hear them tumbling, striking the steps as they fell, the slats of the cherrywood backs and the cross rails and spindles on the legs breaking, sounding wood-on-wood. "Come on, girls, let's go home," you say to your daughters, and going out the door, they pass by Paul, who does not see you because he is facing the other direction, facing the grounds of the facility where there is a sheer face of granite exposed in a cliff.

Just as well, you think on the drive home about not having talked to Paul. It's for the best, really. You start thinking about a man too much, you can't get anything else done, and there is much to be done now that it's September. There are the September weddings you have to shoot, and you have to have final meetings with the clients. The clients of the September weddings are always perfectionists, because they've had all summer long to plan exactly what they want. They tell you the shots they want, down to small details. One year a bride wanted one shot of her hand resting on her fiancé's shoulder taken with just the diamond engagement ring, and then, after the vows were said, another shot that was to be exactly the same, but taken with her wedding ring now on her finger alongside her engagement ring. The only problem was that the sun, unaware of its role in the shot, was farther down after the vows were said, and the shots did not look the same. In the first shot, the diamond ring sparkled, sending rays of light all around it. In the second shot, the sun didn't cooperate. There were no rays of light, just the diamond ring looking opaque, almost like rock candy, and the wedding ring looking too tight, too close to the knuckle of the woman's finger and accentuating the thickness of the knuckle and its wrinkles. There was the woman afterward, complaining to you about the disparity between the two shots after you had sent her the bill for the shoot. You offered to retake the photo at the same time of day, but she had said the moment was lost now. It was irretrievable. You assured her the sun would shine again and those rays cast from the diamond ring would be there again. No, you misunderstand, the woman said. You made a mistake you can't fix. That moment is forever gone, she said. You tell yourself that next time you meet with a client you will have to explain the rotation of the sun, the changes in daylight, the simple passage of time, and that even though they want a picture to look just so, it may not look that way at all. There is still more to do now that school has started up. You have to bake pies for a bake sale to raise money for playground equipment. You have to meet with teachers who will tell you things about your children you already know. You have to remember to give Alex five dollars for the empanada festival. You have to sign the forms for the school pictures and choose a colored background and choose whether you want, for extra money, the blemishes on your children's faces airbrushed so that they're invisible, or whether you want to leave them, a reminder of how they really look—not a bad thing, but a thing more real. You want to stop the car. Your brain is working faster than your body. If you could just pull over and not have to do so many things at once, like hand your daughters their snack of apples and cheese where they sit in the backseat, and remember this is the stretch of road where the cop always sits and you better slow down, and this is where the bump in the road is that always scrapes your undercarriage if you drive over it too quickly, and this is where there always seems to be a deer crossing the road, and the leaves, my God, are already starting to turn from green to bits of orange, gold, and red, and how can this be, you think, when I'm still in my summer shorts and a faded tee?

You stop the car, just for a moment. You pull over, hearing newly fallen leaves crunching under your tires, and Sofia wants to know right away what's going on, why are we stopping? You just shake your head. You don't think you can begin to describe that you just needed your brain to slow down. Your practical daughter would want a real reason. "I need to pee," you say. "Oh, brother!" your daughters say. "Can't you wait until we get home?" You open up the door and go to the side of the road, pulling down your pants, not worried that anyone will see you, because so few cars are ever on this stretch, there are just rows of corn, the stalks tall, the tops brown, soon to be threshed. When you're done you walk a little down the road. "Where are you going?" Sofia yells. "Just moving my legs," you say. "Can we get home already? I have homework to do," Alex yells out the window. And you think: These swim team girls, do they all have to be such good students? Such achievers?

I will tell Thomas about Paul and me, you think, or is it Paul and I? Or is it just I because Paul is not walking around all the time thinking of our kiss while in the shower, while feeding the goose, while turning burritos in a pan. Paul is only thinking of himself appearing as a would-be, could-be kind of a murderer in a jury's tired, hotel-slept eyes. This is you staring at dried brown stalks of corn taller than yourself whose leaves make a scratching sound in the wind. You get back in the car and drive home.

"Thomas," you say at night before bed while he's brushing his teeth. "Ah-ha?" he says while still brushing, his wrist moving energetically up and down and toothpaste lather dripping out of his open mouth and into the sink. "Can I talk to you?" you say. You imagine yourself saying a sentence whose first words begin "Paul and I." He spits out the toothpaste and lifts handfuls of water into his mouth, rinsing, and then he dries himself with the corner of a towel that has your last name written on its bumpy terry in Sharpie. The towel has been to overnight camp with one of your children. It has sat rolled up in the corner in a bunk, molding and wet. It has been down to grassy shores and spread out on the ground beside canoes and kayaks. It has heard the shrill whistle of a counselor. A summer wind off a mountain has blown back its edges. "You know, I read we're losing our polar ice cap faster than they could have ever imagined," Thomas says. "The melting water absorbs more heat than the ice ever radiated. It's changing the jet stream. Where we live now may become a desert in ten years' time." He doesn't say, "What do you want to talk about?"

When you're both in bed your daughters come running into the room and jump on Thomas. It has been a while since they've frolicked this way, and you love that they're doing it now. They pretend to give him CPR, and hammer at his chest with their fists. He coughs and yells and he laughs while they do it. "Oh, maybe, just maybe, he's got appendicitis too. Let's check!" Sofia says and pokes at Thomas's side so that he's laughing and kicking. It's not until someone gets hurt, of course—Alex kicked by accident in the mouth so that her lip is bleeding and the bedcover spattered in small blood drops—that they finally leave the room and go to bed. By that time, Thomas has forgotten that you wanted to talk to him. He falls asleep quickly beside you, not even patting your hand before falling asleep. You look up at Fred, the moon that is a perfect half-circle and that scares you because even just half full it's so bright that looking down on the lawn, if there were an animal there walking by, you would be able to see it clearly, and you wonder what you will be able to see when it's really full, in just a couple weeks.

Part Three

Part Three

CHAPTER THIRTY-FOUR

Winter State Championships is months away, six months to be exact, but already the coaches of all the teams are considering where it should be hosted. Some like the facility near the seashore, where if families only have children swimming in one session a day, they can go to the beach and brave the winds, and breathe in the salt air, and maybe even run barefoot in the sand, letting the water creep up between toes still sporting sock lint. Some like the home facility for the meets—the travel is easy, and the facility is one of the best around. The water never too chlorinated, the blocks not slippery, and the timing board so new it even shows videos in addition to the names of the swimmers and their heats and lanes. You like the away facility. You like the Mexican restaurant in the town. You like it when your family can make it to the beach and watch the waves. Your daughters don't like the away facility's freezing cold water, or the way the start horn is hard to hear because there's only one speaker by the starter instead of a speaker under each one of the blocks, as there is at the home facility.

Mandy, who of course doesn't even go to the meets, likes the away facility too, since it means she doesn't have to clean up after hundreds of people who come for the home meet and stop up the toilets with their constant flushing and get the locker room floor sopping wet. Dinah has already compared the two pools, and has learned from her research that the away pool is a slower pool than the home pool. The away pool's gutters are deeper, making more turbulence, creating more resistance against the swimmers' bodies, and slowing down their times. The home pool also keeps its lane lines tighter so that it's less likely a lane line will float into swimmers and cause them to jam their hands into one of the hard plastic cuffs. At practice, Dinah lets everyone know what she's learned. She suggests all the parents sign a petition so that the coaches know they all want to swim at the home pool. You don't want to sign it. You figure the coaches have their own reasons for voting where States should be swam, and you don't want to get involved. "You just like staying at the hotels and staying up late talking to other women's husbands—that's why you want it to be away," Dinah says to you in front of some of the other parents, trying to sound as if she's joking. Thankfully Chris isn't at this practice.

We kill because we hear voices that tell us to kill. We kill because we feel we are on a mission to rid the world of a certain type of person. We kill for lust, for sexual motivation. We kill for the thrill of killing. We kill for power and to have total control over someone else's fate. We kill to gain money. (The killer, our killer, laughs. He has checked the wallets and the pockets of the women he's killed, and there has been hardly enough money to replace the clothes he was wearing at the scene of the crime.) Once we kill, we can keep killing, or we can stop killing. We can kill again after years of not having killed. We can go on a spree. We can do all of our killing in two weeks or less. We can kill all of our lives. We can have had parents who were divorced, or parents who pecked each other on the cheek every time one walked in the door, and said "I love you" multiple times throughout the day.

You never know how many we really killed. You can blame us for three or four, but you never really know.

Our killer minimizes the screen on the computer. A teacher has come into his office to use his fax machine. "Hey, Floyd," the teacher says while she's feeding in the document. "I came in early this morning and heard coyotes howling at the edge of the woods near the playground. I think we'd better let the other teachers know not to let kids play too close to the woods during recess."

"Coyotes?" Floyd says. "Do you know how many coyotes actually attack people throughout the year? It's about one person, in the entire United States, every ten years. I think the poison ivy by the stream is more of a hazard than the coyotes."

"You didn't hear? We're getting sheep to eat the poison ivy," the teacher says.

"Sheep?"

"They love it. We pen them in and they eat it. The only thing is, the kids can't pet the sheep, or they may get the poison ivy."

Floyd laughs. "I wouldn't have thought of sheep."

After the teacher leaves the room, Floyd doesn't have time to go back and read the rest of his article. He has lunchroom duty and has to sit with the kids while they eat. We the killers, Floyd thinks as he descends the stairs to the lunchroom, past walls lined with children's depictions of human organs. A roll of toilet paper, cut in half lengthwise and with Cheerios stuck inside it, clings to a poster board, held by smears of glue stick. It is meant to be the esophagus, and the Cheerios are what the person just ate. Floyd makes a slicing motion against the toilet paper roll with his forefinger. If only a real neck were as easy to slit, he thinks, but no, we the killers have to make sure our knives are extremely sharp. We the killers have to stay in shape to overtake our victims. We the killers do push-ups at night, our sweat beading at our nose tips and falling to our carpeted floors. We the killers even have to join gyms. We exercise to keep limber and strong, because it would be a mistake to let your body grow too weak to fight a woman who fights back. It would be a mistake to pull a muscle, a tendon, while in the middle of killing someone, because then you could be caught, and we the killers, contrary to popular belief, have no desire to be caught. We just want to keep killing.

When the sheep come, and are fenced in with electric fencing, Floyd watches them from the window. Up on the fencing there are hand-painted signs the children made that read, "Poison Ivy Sheep, Do not Touch!!" The paint they used was bright red, and very watery, so it dried with drip marks extending down each letter. While typing up the school newsletter, Floyd hears the sheep call to one another. Baaaa-baaaa. A photographer from the town's newspaper rings the school doorbell. Floyd can see him on the screen that projects the images from the video camera situated right outside the front door. From the reporter's neck, a long strap

hangs with a camera attached. The principal told Floyd the photographer would be coming. "He'll come to shoot the sheep," the
principal said. The photographer wants Floyd to take him to the
fenced-in area where the sheep and the poison ivy are. He wants
Floyd to be in the picture. He wants Floyd standing by the dripping sign painted in red. He wants Floyd to smile. Floyd asks not
to be in the picture. He says he will gladly find a student from a
classroom who could be in the picture instead, but the photographer does not have time for Floyd to pull a student from a classroom. The photographer is on his way to shoot a small circus that
has come to a neighboring town, and so the photographer must
work fast, before the evening takes its toll, and the clown's makeup
washes away, and the color of the coats of the dancing horses turns
from white to smoke with their sweat. "Perfect," the photographer
says after taking a picture of Floyd in front of the sheep. "It will
be in the next issue of the paper. They'll probably give the article
some catchy title, something like, 'Sheep Save School!'"

Before the photographer leaves, Floyd points at the red marks
forming around the photographer's neck from the strap that holds
the weight of the camera. "It's cutting into your neck. You should
do something about that," Floyd tells him. "You could fasten a
foam pad to it. That might help. Unless you like walking around
looking like someone tried to strangle you."

"Yes, that's exactly how I want to look when I show up to shoot
a circus where children are in the audience," the photographer
says as he gets into his car to drive out. "Thanks for the advice."

Floyd doesn't go right back up to his office. Instead he goes
back to the sheep. He wonders if they're really eating the poison
ivy, or if it just looks as though they are. He feels sorry for them

when they near the electric fence, thinking he has food for them, and they receive a shock. Baaa-baaa, they say plaintively. To Floyd, they don't seem happy to be fenced in and living on a diet of poison ivy. He imagines they would much rather be roaming the field and feeding on sweet grass.

CHAPTER THIRTY-FIVE

When you and the girls get to the facility for evening practice, Paul is waiting for you. "Hi, Annie. Can I talk to you for a minute?"

Your girls go on ahead of you into the locker room and change into their practice suits made of polyester. The practice suits, after a few swims, start to hang and bag and balloon. The practice suits lose thread at the seams from the stitching starting to unravel. The practice suits fade and the chlorine from the pool deteriorates the material in a line at the sternum and in a line up through the rear, so that the practice suits become sheer after time. After the practice suits start to fall apart, the swimmers wear them over other swimsuits they have that are also falling apart, to give them that drag. This is how you feel, at the moment, like you are wearing two practice suits instead of one, as you walk over to Paul. You wish you did not have to talk to him, because you know that once you start a conversation, it will be that much harder to walk away from him.

"Let's go for a walk," he says. Not far from the facility is a reservoir with trails connecting all around it. The roots of trees cross over the trails, filling the walk with stumbles now and then. Paul grabs your arm to hold you up when you falter over a slick root hidden by the first few fallen leaves of autumn. The day is cloud-covered, and a light mist seems to cover you both like a spray from a perfume bottle you've walked yourselves into. No one else is on the trails, only the occasional chipmunk rustling the leaves. "I've missed you," Paul says, on a part of the trail where you cannot see the sky through the thick canopy formed by the dense tops of pine trees. He turns to you and starts to kiss you. You feel as if the trail just came out from under your feet, and you're falling through an airshaft, only you're not alone. Paul is falling with you. He's bolder with you than he's ever been before. He reaches up under your fleece pullover and your tee shirt. He slides his thumb up under your bra, touching your nipple, just slightly, while he kisses you. Between your legs you're aware of how quickly you're becoming wet, so quickly you're almost embarrassed and hope his wandering hands don't find themselves down there.

It was Dinah's promise to herself to lose weight and at the same time exercise. She didn't want to be one of those women who has lost a lot of weight and looks as though she has wings of skin hanging from her arms. She tried, at the facility, to do the weights, but she didn't like the grunting the men beside her made when they lifted the barbells. She tried doing the treadmill, but she didn't like how she was constantly staring at the same scenery out the window while she jogged. She considered doing the stationary bicycle, but was annoyed by seeing women on the bicycles able to pedal and flip through pages of a magazine at the same time. It made Dinah think that the bicycling wasn't going to tone her muscles in the least if it looked that easy to do. For these reasons, she started walking the trails by the reservoir. She liked how she hardly saw anyone else on the trails, except for the occasional lone person walking a dog. She liked how, when the wind was right, she couldn't even tell there was a major four-lane highway nearby, and she could only hear the sound her feet made stepping on the newly fallen leaves. She even liked looking into the reservoir, where in places it was choked with some kind of underwater menace of a weed. It was almost a frightening scene to look at, reminding her how dark and twisted things in real life could be, a good reminder, she thought, of how the mind could be dark and twisted as well. Not all things were as nice and paved over and smooth and predictable as our civilized world made them out to be. There weren't going to be fast-food restaurants at every exit with molded plastic seating and bright lights. There weren't going to be predictable people either. Some were just plain evil, like the man who killed Kim. Dinah felt lucky she could recognize this. She didn't think many people could. There were some people out there who thought everyone had a grain of goodness within them, when it just wasn't true. Dinah knew better than that.

Dinah would usually take the trail that first looped around the reservoir, and then went up to the top of a steep hill and came down again. By the time she was done, she was sweating, and slightly out of breath. It was a much more satisfying workout than she could get at the facility.

Today, just for variety's sake, she decides to go up the hill first, and then do the loop around the reservoir. There is a lot on her mind, of course. Now that she has told her husband she wants a divorce, she wants it right away. She doesn't want to spend another night in the same house with him. She and her daughter will be the ones to move out, she has already decided that. She even looks forward to finding another house in another town. Of course, there is the question of which school district her . . . Is that Paul and Annie? Dinah almost says out loud, interrupting her thoughts. She stops in her tracks as she spies on them through a stand of thin maples on a connecting path that is a few hundred feet below the path she is on. Paul has his hands up Annie's shirt and they are kissing. What Dinah first notices is how much thinner Annie is than her. She can see the vague outline of Annie's stomach muscles as the shirt is lifted off her skin. Will I ever look like that? Dinah thinks to herself. And then she thinks of taking a picture with her cell phone. A picture, after all, is proof. She will show it to Thomas the next time she sees him. He will have to see for himself what he is up against. Her mind races. If need be, when the time comes, she can help Thomas file for divorce. She has a lawyer who is decent. She can help Thomas look for property in the area, because, of course, if a swim-team parent has to relocate, they will relocate closer to the facility. Everyone is tired of the long commute. Wouldn't it be nice just to be within fifteen minutes of the place, get home at a decent hour, cook dinner, and have time for your child to get their homework done, instead of driving almost an hour in the car each way, having your child do homework on the road, and quizzing your child for tests while you hold one hand on the wheel and the other on their textbook? She will mention to Thomas how the area near the facility isn't bad. The town nearby has a lovely coffee shop, neighbors are in walking distance, and there is a movie theater for the occasional night out. Dinah tries to think of women she knows whom she could fix Thomas up with. There is Marianne from the office, who is fit, runs triathlons, and reads books. She wears pretty lace camisoles under her blazers. Dinah bets that Thomas would find Marianne attractive, or maybe, if she loses enough weight, she will consider going with Thomas to the movies herself. After she takes the photo, and puts the phone back in her pocket, she feels that the cell phone, a pricey one already, is now even more valuable. She is worried she'll lose it, so she holds her hand against her pocket as she walks back to the facility.

If Dinah had stayed a few minutes longer at the scene, she might have taken a photo of you pushing Paul away, and saying to him, "Let's just walk for now," despite the fact that your whole body seems to be leaning in toward Paul's and wanting you both to keep kissing and touching. On the walk up to the top of the hill, Paul tells you that he has finally contacted a lawyer. He hasn't hired him yet, but has run the facts by him. "The lawyer wants me to convince Chris to convince Bobby Chantal's daughter to stop the exhumation. But what if Pam Chantal won't do it?"

All around, you can see how fall is on its way. Orange and gold maple and oak leaves are covering up the blades of green grass that were on the ground only a week ago. Every once in a while, a bright leaf from a tree falls slowly beside you, sometimes softly touching you, landing on your shoulder for a moment before falling to the ground. They fall slowly enough for you to even reach out and catch them. Now that the leaves are thinning on the trees, the sun is weaker than it was where it shines through the larger spaces between branches. In the distance you can hear what sounds like tour buses traveling on the highway. The leaf peepers are on the roads now, stopping at country stores to take pictures of pumpkins piled on porches and Indian corn hanging from the eaves. You want to tell Paul how you don't want to hear any of it anymore. You don't want to know how crazy Chris has become.

You wish you were at the facility now. If only you hadn't listened to Paul and gone on a walk with him. If you hadn't you'd be in the water now, maybe working on improving your scapular plane of motion in the free by making sure you rotate a little on each side before lifting out your arm, and making sure your elbow is pointed high into the air before you dive your fingertips back into the water to start your reentry.

Paul moves closer to you now and takes you in his arms and starts kissing you again. The sun's gone lower in the sky, and you think that because it's darker now, maybe you're letting Paul kiss you harder, his fingertips more than just brushing your breasts, his body pressing into yours so that you can feel the concentration of the warmth of the blood that's making him hard. It's the sound of crying that pulls you apart. Not a child's cry, but a woman's. She's calling for help. When you and Paul get to Dinah, she's on the ground, grabbing on to her ankle. "I can't stand up," she says.

Paul pulls off her shoe to get a closer look. Her ankle, with her skin so white, looks like a large puffball mushroom, the kind that have been cropping up every morning on your front field because the weather's been damp. "What happened? Did you just trip?" you ask her.

"Yes, stupid me. This never would have happened if I hadn't been walking with my hands in my pockets. Oh, my phone. Is my phone all right?" Dinah moves her body so she can reach into her pocket, but when she does, her ankle moves, and she sucks in her breath.

"I'll get it for you," you say.

"No!" Dinah says. But you have already reached into Dinah's pocket for her, and slid the phone out. When you turn it on for her, to see if it's still working, the photo of you and Paul kissing is on the screen.

"The picture doesn't matter," Dinah says. "Even if you erase it. I'll just tell Thomas and Chris I saw the two of you together."

"What? Let me see that," Paul says, and grabs Dinah's phone.

"You're spying on us?" you say.

"You always think everything's about you, don't you Annie? Well, wrap your brain around this. I didn't come out here to spy on you. I came out here to get some exercise, and then I saw the two of you swapping saliva like some teenagers."

Paul deletes the photo.

"Come on, Annie, let's go," he says, grabbing your hand.

"We can't just leave her here," you say. Paul tosses Dinah's phone next to her hand on the ground.

"She's got her phone," Paul says. "She can call whomever she wants to come help her."

Walking back to the facility, you can't even answer Paul's question when he asks you if you're all right. You're feeling the familiar feeling all over again. The glistening road, wet from the misty weather, threatening to crack open and suck you down into an abyss you'd never be able to crawl your way out of. But you're with

Paul, and thinking about your brother isn't supposed to happen when you're with Paul or thinking about Paul. How is this happening?

Thomas, you think, would not listen to Dinah even if she did approach him with the news. You even think how at first he would probably tell you that Dinah started babbling away at him about you and Paul, and that he didn't believe her, thought the pressures of being a swim-team mom were becoming too much for her, especially now that her daughter is not winning any more of her races. Thomas would tell you that he felt sorry for Dinah, having to make up such low stories about you and Paul. Thomas, if you don't say anything to ruin it, might never even believe Dinah, and you could carry on as usual, no matter what absurd stories she may tell him. Because that's what it is, absurd—a grown married woman kissing her friend's husband in the woods.

This is the facility, the light coming in from the tall windows above the entrance now a little darker, the sun close to setting. This is you going up to the front desk, telling them there's a woman on the upper trail at the reservoir who probably sprained her ankle so seriously she will need medical treatment, a clinic, a doctor, some X-rays to make sure nothing's broken. These are your daughters coming out of the showers after practice. Their hair dripping wet at the ends, creating water stains on their shirts above their small breasts. These are the girls saying almost immediately when they see you, "We're hungry, what's for dinner?" This is Sofia saying, "Sounds god-awful," when you tell her falafel with tahini dressing. This is you not feeling up to driving home just yet and seeing Thomas. "I've changed my mind. Let's order pizza," you say. These are the girls, cheering in the parking lot as they're walking to the car. "Saved by pizza!" Alex yells.

This is you pulling into a nearby pizzeria you have seen many times before but have never gone to. These are the girls fighting over pepperoni or sausage. This is you, with a window-seat view of the hillside you and Paul were just standing on. This is you looking at the hillside, scanning it for signs of Dinah, even though you know you wouldn't be able to see Dinah from so far away and through the gold and red leaves. This is you wishing your girls wouldn't eat the pizza so quickly. You don't want to have to go home any time soon and face Thomas. Maybe Dinah has already called him and told him the news about you and Paul. This is the pizza, mostly eaten, mostly, Alex says, because your daughter has just seen the movie *Aliens* and likes to repeat the line about the aliens that goes, "They mostly come out at night, mostly." Now your daughter expresses everything this way. She says, "I mostly feel sick, mostly," and she says, "I mostly feel like not doing my homework, mostly." And you think to yourself, I mostly feel like not going home, mostly.

This is Chris driving to Bobby Chantal's daughter's house. It has glass on the front door that looks as if cold weather has frosted it, as if it were already winter instead of the start of fall. When Pam Chantal opens the door she's eating a yogurt cup with a plastic spoon. Chris tells her she's come to the house to tell Pam something amazing, and after Chris tells Pam Chantal that her husband, Paul, was once her mother's lover, the yogurt cup Pam Chantal is holding falls, spoon and all, to the carpeted floor. Chris tells her what she knows about that night, how the picnic table was their bed for only a short time before Bobby Chantal went to the ladies' room and was killed. Chris tells Pam how sorry she is. Chris, wanting to protect Cleo from a scandal, asks Pam Chantal to think twice about exhuming her mother's body, saying that if the body is exhumed, it may actually keep the case from being solved, because so much time would be spent on finding a DNA match for Paul, and he is not the killer.

This is Pam Chantal shaking her head. "I'm not stopping now. You're the one who gave me the strength to do it. I've already made the arrangements. Someone killed my mother, Chris. Someone's still out there thinking he's gotten away with it." When Chris leaves Pam Chantal's house she's thinking only of Cleo and how to protect her from being swept up in the biggest crime story in their area's history, something that could happen simply because her husband slept with a murder victim on a rest-stop picnic table twenty-eight years ago.

CHAPTER THIRTY-SIX

 T his is the fall night. A coyote's call quick to pierce the darkness with such a high pitch you startle under the covers. Then a hemlock beam in your timber-frame home cracks. The man who built your house told you the house would do that. He called it "checking," but you did not know at the time how loud it would sound. It is as if the house were being ripped apart, and you can hear the ringing sound of it in your ears for a moment afterward. But you like the word "checking." You like to think the house was always making sure of itself, recalibrating, stepping back, getting a perspective so that it could go on, continue being the house it should be. Thomas breathes next to you and you are struck by the thought of all of your family in the house, how each is dreaming a different dream and how even though the house seems still and quiet, each is dreaming of doing things and going places—maybe Alex is flying, maybe Thomas is surfing, maybe Sofia is walking the hallways of her school looking for a classroom she cannot find.

You find it surprising that even during the day, when everyone is so close together in the house, in the kitchen for instance, they can't hear each other's thoughts. You are floored by how many people there are in the world, and how many different thoughts are taking place at one time. Surely there must be a scientist in some science article Thomas has read who addresses this thought, who has studied it, quantified it, or even just guessed at it, the way they have figured the grains of sand to equal the number of stars in the universe. The moon on the grass makes it look as if your lawn is lit by stage lights, and you would not be surprised if actors came out onto the lawn and held out their arms, gesturing and emoting beneath your window. Who would the actors be? You imagine you and Paul and Thomas and Chris, all standing out there. Thomas set off in the corner of the stage closest to the woods where the coyote calls, alone and quiet, reading his science magazine. Paul at the feet of Chris, pleading with her. And your own likeness, your own Annie actress standing behind Paul, tapping his shoulder the whole time, trying to get his attention, but Paul never turns to her.

This is Kim's mother at a home meet, watching Kim's younger sister race. She cannot bear to watch this daughter, though; it reminds her too much of watching Kim race. Kim's sister will grow up to look like Kim. Kim's sister has the same wispy blond hair that looks almost white. Kim's sister's butterfly stroke even seems to have the same rhythm. This is Kim's mother leaving the bleachers, walking out to her car and sitting in the driver's seat with her hands draped over the wheel and her head down, hating herself for not being in the bleachers to cheer for her younger daughter, the one who still lives.

This is Sofia at the same home meet looking around her at all the other swimmers. Before races, some swimmers are goggle-adjusters and some are heat-sheet freaks and some are bathroom-goers and some are visualizers. The goggle-adjusters can't stop adjusting their goggles while they're up on the blocks waiting for the start whistle. They pull their goggles away from their eyes and put them back on again, and then they tighten their straps and tighten them again. The heat-sheet freaks, before their race, check the sheets taped on the wall, making sure they know their correct heat and lane, even though they have checked it ten times before. The bathroom-goers do just that. The visualizers, Sofia thinks, look the most foolish. She sees one now behind the block. She's a girl about Sofia's height and build. She's waiting for her event with her eyes closed and moving her hands in the air as if the air were the water and she were already swimming her race. Sofia knows that the girl is visualizing her entry, she knows she is visualizing how many strokes she will take until she gets to the wall, she knows she is feeling the wall under her feet at the turn and seeing herself winning the heat. Either the girl read about using visualizing as a technique or her coach encouraged her to do it. Either way, Sofia thinks, it looks ridiculous. I will not be a visualizer, Sofia says to herself. No matter how much I want to win for the team, to win for Kim, to win for myself, I will be a no-breather, a goggle-adjuster, a heat-sheet freak, a bathroom-goer, but never a visualizer. I just can't do that. She dives in at the start of her one-hundred free, feeling good and knowing that she didn't visualize the race at all. She has no idea how it will end. She has no idea if she'll win or not. She's just going to try her best, and enjoy it. When she's finished and out of breath, taking her goggles off at the wall, she looks up at the board. Whoever the girl was in lane four came in first, she thinks, and then she remembers, Oh, I was in lane four. She smiles and says thank you after she pulls herself up out of the pool and the timer in her lane says, "Great race!" In the warm-down pool she hears the shouts of children playing, going down the slide in the water park that connects to the warm-down lane. Out the windows, clouds are passing quickly in front of the sun, and she is enjoying watching herself underwater, the light at play, turning her arms from dark to brightly lit with each stroke.

CHAPTER THIRTY-SEVEN

*F*loyd can still do as many chin-ups as he did thirty years ago. He stays in shape. He has a metal bar in his doorway that he bought at a sporting goods store and attached to the doorframe. When he first put the bar up, and tried his first chin-up, he fell. He had made the mistake of screwing it into what he thought was solid wood, but was really a composite wood the previous owner had used to fix the rotting doorframe. When he fell he hit his head, and blood poured from where he had cut it on the sharp corner of the base molding. He was surprised at the blood that poured down his forehead and into his eye. He thought it strange that with all the blood he had seen pour from his victims' throats before, the sight of his own blood still made him queasy. He immediately began to take off his bloodied tee shirt and went to reach for a plastic bag, ready to dispose of it the way he did his other bloodied clothes. He would weight it down with a rock and throw it into a nearby lake, or burn it in a campfire, far out in woods that were not near his house, such as the wooded land owned by the state, where the occasional black bears lived, and where hunters baited them by dumping feed corn in piles on the ground near wild blackberry bushes or near the occasional wizened apple tree that no longer bore sweet fruit, but had been left unpruned for so long its fruit was sour and worm-holed. He sat back down and laughed at himself. There was no reason to hide traces of his own blood from a cut he had received from a fall in his own house.

He has been asked by the principal to look in on the sheep this weekend. Everyone who works at the school is taking turns on weekends watering them and tossing them a flake of hay over the electric fence. He wants to tell the principal no, because he has chosen this weekend to do what he has really wanted to do lately. He wants to kill again. It has been weeks since the last time, and this is how it goes for him usually, when he has a killing spree, a word he likes because it reminds him of "free," which is exactly how he feels afterward, free for some reason that he doesn't care to explore or explain. There are some things, he believes, that should not be questioned. He doesn't know how he will have time to water and feed the sheep, when he will be busy, of course, cleaning up after having just killed. "Floyd, please, could you do it?" the principal asks, and Floyd, not wanting to be asked why he can't do it, says, "Yes."

So this killing weekend will have a slight twist to it, Floyd thinks. There will be a shadow of something hanging over him because it will be something he will have to do for the school, and usually when he has a killing weekend he does not have to think about anything except the killing, and in this way it is like a vacation for him. He does not even cook for himself on a killing weekend. He likes to go to restaurants. He sometimes goes to a movie. He does not behave like his usual self on those weekends. He will not shave. He will wear clothes he would never wear otherwise—polo shirts and khakis. He will even buy a bottle of cologne on those weekends and put it on outside of the drugstore where he bought it, and then he will throw the bottle away so it cannot be traced to him. He feels different on those weekends. He feels younger and stronger. If he catches sight of his reflection in a restaurant window, he can see how the short sleeve hem of the polo shirt he's wearing clings to his bicep muscle, which is firm and defined from his labors at his chin-up bar in his doorway at home.

He can't wait to do it another weekend, when he would not be asked to feed and water the sheep, because his spree is on. The time is now. Because it is a weekend, he knows that no one else will be at the school, and it will be dark, and no one will see that he is dressed in a polo shirt and khakis. Stopping at the school and taking care of the sheep will be on his way to the roads he will take whose woods border the back of a rest stop he has been planning on going to. Contrary to popular belief, Floyd is not predatory, as most people think serial killers are. He does not need to select a woman to follow for weeks beforehand. Kim was an exception. He is content to just wait in the woods until a lone woman drives up into the parking lot of the rest stop to use the bathrooms. He likes the young women, he must confess, because they seem the most surprised when they realize they are going to die. The older women, in the space of a second, seem to come to terms with their death, and tell themselves that at least they have lived the best years of their lives. He hopes he will encounter another young woman like Kim. One who has just begun driving, who has listened to the advice to stop every now and then when you're driving at night so that you don't fall asleep at the wheel. It is in a woman's eyes this young that he seems to see the injustice so acutely. Floyd wishes, at times, that he could capture that look with a camera.

This is Chris working on a painting in her studio. It is a painting of the killer. She makes his earlobes thicker. She is sure he has thick earlobes. Possibly, they're the size of the pads of her thumbs. She holds up her thumb to the portrait to use as a model for his earlobe, and when she closes one of her eye's, she sees she can wipe out the killer's entire face.

This is the water. The temperature warm for some reason, even though the days have become colder and the winds have started blowing, carrying yellow and gold leaves off trees in great gusts that remind you of swirling drifts of snow. The pool water, though, is warm, and you think after swimming only a few hundred yards you are already so warm and relaxed you might be able to fall asleep in the water, if only you didn't have so much to think about. Alongside you the team is having an intrasquad mock meet, and every now and then you feel a surge of water from a swimmer who has just dived into the pool. It gives you a crooked stroke, eventually disturbing your path to the point that you reach in for the pull and hit your hand on the plastic lane line. It jams your fingers so hard that in turn you kick harder, responding to the pain. When the swimmers on the deck first start to cheer one another on, you think something's the matter, and that people are shouting because there's an emergency. Maybe they've noticed that the stands with the bleachers are about to come crashing down, and everyone's yelling, trying to get out of the way. You stop midstroke to tread water for a moment and look up to see what's going on. When you realize it's just the team cheering, you go back to swimming, but you can feel your heart beating faster now, pounding really, and you imagine your heart is creating small wave pulses that radiate from your chest, and that the pool is just one large body of water with pulses pushing up against one another. You hear the heart of the water now. You didn't know it even had one. But of course it has one. It can talk to you so naturally it's alive. It isn't speaking now, though. It's allowing you to hear its heart more distinctly. You hear the throbbing, the *voom, voom, voom* sound of its soft pulses. The pulses seem to push all of the swimmers closer to one another to form one heart, to form one beat. You know you're jumpy because in the morning Thomas told you that Dinah had called him. He thought the phone call was for you. "For a moment, I couldn't even remember who she was," he said. "She wants to meet with me. What do you think that's all about?" You shrugged and shook your head. "No idea," you said. "Well, I'm not going to meet with her," he said. "I told her you'd see her at practice probably later, and she could relay whatever information she wanted to you. If it's about conscripting volunteers to work extra meets that my kids aren't even going to be in, I'm not doing that. You can tell her that right off." In front of Thomas was a science magazine.

"Anything good in that issue?" you said, pointing to it.

Thomas picked it up. "Oh, yes, listen to this," he started saying, but you didn't listen. You couldn't listen. All that you heard was a roaring in your ears, the sound of your blood rushing to your head, the fear and embarrassment of what could happen if Dinah told Thomas about you and Paul.

CHAPTER THIRTY-EIGHT

*T*his is you, standing in the shower after a workout. In the next shower stall are the woman and the boy in the wheelchair. The boy who says, "Water, water, water." It is the same conversation they have had many times before. The boy saying, "Water, water, water," and the woman saying, "Yes, that's right. This is the water." This is the boy being wheeled out of the shower, his head at an odd angle to the side, his eyes slanted and almost shut, as if he's on the verge of falling asleep. This is you undressing in the locker room with the boy in his wheelchair, wondering if he is looking at you, because it looks as if through his half-closed eyes he is looking your way. He is not a small boy. He is probably a teenage boy, and you dress as quickly as possible, not wanting to be stared at. When Chris walks into the locker room to change her clothes and work out, you don't recognize her. Is it the harsh light, or does her hair look less blond? Less like bright yellow corn silk? She's also thinner, her perfect rear not so perfect anymore. The skin on her tailbone looks pronounced and red, as if just sitting on it hurts. "Hey, Chris," you say. "How have you been?" "Good," she says. "Would you help me put Cleo's new suit on? This is her second one. You were right, they deteriorate so quickly. The first one only lasted a few meets before it became see-through in the rear."

This is Chris and Annie helping Cleo try on her new racing john. This is Chris in the bathroom stall in the locker room, lifting it up over Cleo's rear. This is Cleo asking if it will help if she holds her breath, and this is Chris saying that it just might. This is Mandy, the cleaning lady with the crooked teeth, pushing water into the drain with a mop, listening to Chris and Annie grunt while trying to get the racing john over Cleo's rear. This is Mandy thinking they would have better luck with lard, if they spread it over Cleo so that the suit would glide over her rear. This is Mandy shaking her head at how ridiculous it is that the parents let their daughters try to fit into such tight suits just to swim. Mandy herself doesn't swim, not wanting to fit her body into even a loose suit, a suit for old women with a flouncy skirt to hide thunder thighs and with extra support in the bra cups. She cannot imagine trying to wear the fast skin suits these girls wear. To Mandy, even the girls look strange when they walk in the suits, and she swears when she looks at the wet footprints she mops up from the tiled locker room floor that the girls are walking only on their toes, it being too painful to walk flat-footed in a suit so tight. She often hears the girls after they've raced cry out in pain when they try to pull the straps down off their red and raw shoulders in the shower. This is Mandy shaking her head, wanting to think about something else, wondering if the pickup truck she drives will make it to the lake this weekend. Her husband likes to fish and she goes with him, although she doesn't fish herself. She likes to sit in the boat and hear the call of the loons while her husband lifts and lowers the oars, rowing toward his sweet spot near a far bank.

This is Chris after the suit goes up and over Cleo's rear, slightly panting, and saying, "Come out with me tonight. Just the two of us. We'll see a movie. How about it?"

"Of course," you say. Things will get better now. Maybe you won't think about Paul. Paul will stop kissing you. He will stop putting his hand up your shirt. Thomas will get better. He will talk to you about you. He will put down the science magazines. He will stop worrying about the lab. He will kiss your lips. Dinah, even Dinah will get better. She will stop spying on you. You will not feel as though the kitchen chair where you sit to eat your breakfast is sucking you down and the only thing stopping you are the armrests you're holding on to. You will not feel that the drain in the shower can sweep you away. You will not feel that the floorboards beneath you will split open and take you down into the ground. You will not feel that the space between your bed and the wall is really a chasm you will never climb back out of once you fall in.

"It fits you perfectly," you say to Cleo about her suit, and it does. Her breasts are flattened by the tight fit, the straps at the shoulders have no give, and she says already the circulation around her thighs is beginning to feel cut off.

The boy in the locker room who says "water" over and over again now starts yelling. What he's saying is indecipherable. He kicks his legs in his wheelchair, making a loud banging sound. He flails his arms, and when his helper tries to stop him, he hits her in the face. "Shhh, it's all right," she says to him, but it just makes him yell louder.

This is Mandy driving home in her pickup, turning the radio low, then lower, then finally off, trying to hear if the engine is acting up the way it has in the past, when it has sounded as if some miniature mechanic were already at work on the pipes beneath the hood and clanking them with tools, making a plink, plink, plink sound. This is the loon on the lake where Mandy likes to go with her husband, calling to her mate over the mist covering the water in the morning.

CHAPTER THIRTY-NINE

T his is you being picked up by Chris later that night. This is you thinking the boy who says "water" all the time was trying to warn you. The road is slick with a fine coat of rain, and when Chris pushes the car above seventy, she says it feels as if it's hydroplaning.

When you told Thomas that Chris was coming to pick you up to go to a movie he said, "Be careful driving, the roads are slick," before you left. "A movie! I want to go," your girls said, but you told them it was not a movie for young girls.

The movie ends late. The two of you talk about it on the ride home, and you do not talk about Paul or the killer. Then Chris stops at a rest stop. It's the same one Bobby Chantal and Kim were killed at.

"Maybe we shouldn't stop here," you say.

"I'll just be a minute," Chris says, and walks into the bathroom.

She parks far down the lot, away from the lights that are probably always turned on for safety reasons, and she leaves the keys on in the car so you can still have the heat on. You wonder why she's parked so far away. Why does she want to walk so far? But you don't have time to ask her because she is already opening the door and walking into the restroom. While she's gone you peer out through the side window. You look to see if you can find the place in the woods where, if you were a killer, you would come from to surprise a woman. The woods are dark, though. There is nothing to see close to the restroom but some newly planted trees whose trunks are no thicker than your bare arms and whose leaves in the fluorescent light look pale, and closer to yellow than green. You can feel a strong wind buffeting Chris's car from side to side as if someone were shaking it. You can hear the leaves rustling in the tops of the trees and deep inside the woods, probably skittering along and blowing up from the forest floor. Chris is gone so long you wonder if she really had to go to the bathroom. You wonder if there's a way for the killer to enter the bathroom from behind the rest stop. You wonder if he was already in the rest stop bathroom, waiting for her to come. You look at the wall and door of the rest stop. You try to tell yourself that if something terrible were taking place right now inside of the bathrooms, then the walls and the door and the grass just outside the rest stop would let you know. You would sense it from them, even though they are inanimate. The horror taking place would allow them some kind of a voice.

You jump, of course, when the driver's door swings open. For a second, you can't believe the door was left open and the wind so strong it blew it open wider. But then you see a man get into the car, and you realize that the car door was not left open and it was not the wind at all. The man, with his deeply creased forehead, looks just like the man Chris has painted so many portraits of.

He looks so much like his paintings, like he has lifted himself off the canvas, that you expect to smell the smell of the oil paint. You think to scream when the killer slams his door and pushes the button that locks all the doors, but just as you open your mouth he turns around with a knife in his hand. The blade shines, a knife with a blade so big it catches light from all the way across the parking lot where a single lamp is turned on. "Don't," he says, and you stop, a creaking sound coming out of your mouth now because you can't stop wanting to scream that quickly. He starts the car and you look toward the restrooms. Chris must still be inside them. You call to her, of course. It's raining harder now and the wind must be roaring because the tops of even the sturdy pine trees are bent over, and some maples look as though they could snap.

"Where are we going?" you ask, your voice not sounding like your voice to yourself, but tighter, wound up, as if let loose it would spiral out of control and turn into something almost visible as it shot out of your mouth. This man will not kill me, you think. I will end up killing myself from the inside out. I will die from my fear. You don't receive a reply from the killer. And why would you? Thomas has read to you from his science magazines of studies showing how animals are so different from humans that even if a lion, for example, could speak your language, you would not know what it was saying. You picture the killer as a lion. You think how you shouldn't ask him anything else again. It would be pointless. Maybe this is easier, not talking or begging for your life, because he would not understand anyway. You see you are driving on a back road made of dirt. The killer drives in the center to avoid the sides of the road that are washed out and riddled with holes and bedded with fallen dry pine needles. You think maybe he should

drive toward the right side of the road instead, because what if
there is an oncoming car? But of course, there will not be an oncoming car. The killer has chosen a road so untraveled he does not
worry about which side of the road he is traveling on. The road is
all his. There will be no headlights from the other direction. You
wonder if there is someone else in the car with you and the killer.
You keep hearing panting. You wish the person would stop. After
a while, you realize it is you doing the panting. You are so thirsty.
Would the killer understand? Surely, even a lion, if a lion could
talk, would understand water. Wouldn't it? Thomas, you are sure,
would disagree. Thomas would tell you about mind-mapping, how
an animal wouldn't have a name for water but might have a visual
map in its head of how to get to a watering hole, or it might have a
name for how it feels after it drinks water, when it could be ready
to chase and bring down an animal in a kill.

You remember how the killer is not one of those killers who
does away with the bodies. He does not bother to cut them or bag
them or burn them or bury them or sink them or hide them deep
in the woods. He leaves them where he kills them, not afraid of
leaving fingerprints on them because he is so careful not to leave
fingerprints on them. You notice his gloves. They are leather and
have stitches on their backs. They are like driving gloves and you
are on a drive in the country. You try to see what there is near you
in Chris's car. Maybe there is a hammer you can use to protect
yourself. Maybe there is an ice scraper, even though it has not
been cold enough yet for windshields to completely freeze over
in the mornings. You feel with your hands between the seats. You
feel what feels like a file folder. You feel papers inside and pick
them up. You reach up and turn the light on in Chris's car. "Turn

it off," the killer says, without looking at you. You see how the collar on the back of his polo shirt looks new and stiff. This killer is wearing all new clothes, you think.

"Listen to this," you say. You have no idea what's written on the papers. You start reading anyway. You read the first line: "I can tell you what she wasn't." The killer does not ask you again to turn the overhead light off. You keep reading now. It is Paul's story of Bobby Chantal. You wonder if it was between the seats all along, or if it just materialized, or maybe you even conjured it to appear. Whatever the case, you keep reading, and the killer keeps driving.

She wasn't my girl. She was just a girl I met at a coffee shop. She didn't wear shorts and a tee shirt, or jeans, or slacks. She wore a nurse's uniform and nurse's shoes and she smelled, ever so slightly, of rubbing alcohol. Her fingertips were dry and her nails clipped short to protect herself, because some patients she had known had gripped her hand so hard and pressed it into a fist so tight that her own nails cut her. She showed me some half-moon scars on the palm of her hand, proving it was true.

When I asked, she said she would go on a ride with me because it was such a nice day. I didn't know then that it would be the last ride she'd ever take. She suggested the place, a rest stop up north, a good drive from where we were.

It sounds strange to say that our first and only date was at a rest stop. It was one she said Vietnam veterans came to because the view from the hill above the rest stop looked just like the hills and lush valleys of the jungle, and they were sent back in time when they saw it. They were happy to go back, she said. Being back, they didn't feel the guilt, because it was as if no time had passed and there hadn't been time to let the guilt soak in. Being back, they had to think about protecting themselves again, and for so long they had been bent on destroying themselves. She made me close my eyes and listen. I heard an owl whose screech sounded like a woman's voice. I smelled what I thought was rice cooking. When I opened my eyes she was kissing me. We were sitting on a picnic table with names carved into the top, and I laid her across those names. She wasn't shy. She guided me into her and up from her body came a smell different from the rubbing alcohol. It was more like the smell of wood smoke mixed with steam. When we were done, she smiled. "Wait for me. I've got to use the restroom," she said.

I watched her walk down the hill easily. Those nurse's shoes have to be good for walking back and forth across those endless hospital hallways, I thought. She turned around once while she was on the path, and waved up to me. I waved back and then I looked to the hillsides. The sun was going down and the hills looked blue. The air was still warm and hot, though. A fly was intent on buzzing close to my head even though I waved it away several times, so I gave up and imagined I was one of those vets back in Nam. The owl screech this time really did sound like a woman's scream, and when I opened my eyes I expected to see some scene unfolding in front of me where I was with other soldiers in a village, and before us was a woman begging for her life.

You would keep on reading, but the killer stops the car. You look around and realize that there is nothing but trees lining the dirt road. The trees are close together, with no fields or open spaces in sight, and certainly no houses. The killer looks at you. You try not to think of all the women he has killed, but when you look at him you see the face of Bobby Chantal, the same face that you once saw in the paper after Kim's death. You also see Kim's face. "Please, let me go," you say in a voice that is a whisper. You are so scared.

"Why, when you read so well?" he says. "You must have children. They must have loved the sound of you reading to them when they were little." He is not looking at you any longer, he is looking down at his knife. "Did you and that friend of yours really think she could catch me?"

"No, no, I had no intention of catching you. I don't want to catch you," you say, your voice higher now than before. What can you say to make him believe you?

"The story you are reading," he says. "Who wrote it? Someone you know? You must answer me. I have the knife." He puts the tip of the knife on your knee, moving it as if he's spelling out small letters or drawing short lines. He is not pressing hard enough to break the cloth of your jeans. He is pressing as if what he is doing he is doing absentmindedly.

"I know him," you manage to say.

He nods. "Tell me more," he says.

You are suddenly very cold. With the engine off, you can hear the wind rustle the leaves outside and whip around the car, making it move from side to side.

"There's not much to tell," you say. "This man, it's the husband of the woman who, who owns this car. The woman who went into the bathroom at the rest stop."

The killer nods. "I'd like for you to finish the story for me," he says.

"You can have the story. Take the story. Just let me go. Let me get back to my children." You hold the papers out toward him. He doesn't take them. He doesn't even look at them.

"It wouldn't be the same," he says. "Go on reading." He's been using the tip of his knife on your knee the whole time he's been talking.

You wonder if you could say, No, not unless you throw the knife out the window and keep driving. You want out of the woods. Even if he did let you out of the car, you'd be miles from a major road. He could probably run you down. You are a poor runner. Your legs are not long, your stride is short, your feet always sore from bunions that are red and swollen at night when you take off your shoes and socks, causing Thomas to shake his head and say how awful they look. "You know the rest of the story," you say. "You were there."

When he jabs the blade of his knife through the top of your leg you draw your leg up into yourself. The pain is so strong it makes you see colors. You see white and then red and then black. You hope you have blacked out, but you are still feeling the pain. You still hear his voice. It's excited now. "Read it to me," he says. Then you see his face, sweat beginning to form, showing up first as just a shiny layer of water on his skin, and then pooling in the creases of his forehead. You try to stop the blood with your hand. Everything's running down now—tears running down your face from the pain, the blood running down the sides of your leg and soaking into your jeans, his sweat starting to drip from his temples. "Please, don't kill me," you say, and you are reminded again of how silly it must sound, as if you were talking to a lion. You think how running now is very much out of the question. You cannot even bend your knee without the colors of pain flashing again before your eyes.

The rest of the story strikes you as not so good. The rest of the story is about Paul finding Bobby Chantal's body and turning her over and seeing her head hanging far over backward, which reminds Paul of an open Pez dispenser, the toy he had as a kid ready to spit out its candy. You bet that if Paul's own students saw that metaphor in workshop, they'd be all over it, pointing out how it was incongruous. How was anything having to do with candy supposed to be compared with the atrocity of Bobby Chantal being murdered so horribly, with so much blood on her body and on her face that in the dark it looked as if she had been burned in a fire, her skin and clothes now char? The story, you realize, cannot save your life at all. The killer doesn't like the story either. He shakes his head. "Who is this guy?" he asks when you're done reading. "Bigwig writing professor," you say, breathy, because your leg is now throbbing and you're considering ripping your jeans to take the pressure off the wound that's swelling. "Not so good a writer, is he?" says the killer. "He must be good-looking. That's why your friend married him. Just for looks." You shake your head. You really don't know. "Well, is he good-looking?" the killer asks. You nod.

"Yeah," you say.

"I've never killed a man," he says. You don't have a response for that one. Are you supposed to say, "Hey, let's try killing one now?" so that the killer forgets about you and moves on? If you said, "I know you only kill women who are weaker than you," then would he kill you for saying it?

The killer scratches the inside of his arm. He scratches it hard. His nails make red raised lines up and down his skin.

He sees you looking at him scratching. "Did you know sheep eat poison ivy?" he asks. You don't answer this either. You think he is the lion talking to you now. He is talking about something so strange it is not anything you can begin to understand. You try to move your leg a little, just to see how badly it hurts when you do. You suck in your breath. There is as much pain as before, but it's not worse. You think you might be able to walk on it, but you would not be able to run.

Your phone rings. It is probably Chris or the police. Chris has told them about you being driven away, stolen in her car. What would you say to Chris anyway if the killer did let you pick up the phone? Hi, I'm somewhere on a dirt road miles into the woods. I'll give you a reference point—a thousand trees blowing in the wind. I'm fine, except I'm bleeding all over your seat. I'm fine, and by the way, your husband's story isn't that good. The killer says he's glad you didn't answer that because he didn't think you wanted the tip of his knife in your other leg as well. You think he is beginning to sound more like a killer now. That is something you think a killer might say. You try to think of books and movies in which someone was in the same position as you are. You try to remember how they escaped, but nothing comes to mind. All you can think of is how your brother escaped by putting a gun in his mouth. You don't even have a gun to grab from the killer and turn on yourself. If you tried to grab his knife, the tip would land in your other knee and you would not be free, you would be miles from free, as far away from free as you are far away from another person out here in the thick woods where the tree limbs creak and the wind whooshes around the frame of the car.

CHAPTER FORTY

You can't believe you are hungry. Aren't you supposed to feel nauseous instead? Locked in a car with a throat-slasher? Bleeding? It must be nerves emptying acid into your stomach and making you think you are hungry. Where does it say in those books and movies that the victim felt hungry while they were in grave danger? You'd like to complain. Letters should be sent to writers of thrillers everywhere. You never mention hunger, the letters should say. You are wrong. You haven't done your research. You yourselves haven't let yourself be victims so that you know exactly what's going on inside the head of one. Go out and be victims, the letter would say. Real ones, you'd add. The killer shakes his head. "What's the matter?" you say.

"You're too old," he says, and he stops the car. You've been feeling this way anyway, lately. Your daughter keeps laughing, telling you that you are on the doorstep of fifty. You wonder what that doorstep looks like. Is it a large sheet of granite like the doorstep to your home that continually has green splats of goose poop on it from the goose who likes to stand on the granite and peck at your glass door, wanting in? The flesh around your face has been feeling looser. You were hoping while kissing Paul the last time that he didn't notice. You think you even tried to think of kissing "firmly" last time, so that he would not notice. You used to tell yourself that your hair, with its gray, sometimes made you look blond in certain light or from a distance, but now it really looks as gray as a sad cloudy day, as bleak as crows calling in a fallow field on a sad cloudy day, as miserable as cold rain beginning to fall on that sad cloudy day in that fallow field with the crows wheeling overhead, calling their faraway call that reaches into your heart and splays it open.

Too old for what? you think to ask, but don't. There's no point in hearing an answer you wouldn't understand. He answers you anyway, even though you never voiced the question. "For killing you. When I kill people too old, they are more ready for it and the energy doesn't come out from their eyes." You don't say anything. You hold your breath. If he isn't going to kill you, then what is he going to do with you? Is he telling you to get out of the car on your own? That now is your chance? You begin to reach for the door handle, and think maybe when you try to open it he will press the button that unlocks it.

You are so amazed when he does unlock it that for a second you don't pull the handle to open the door. You look at him out of the corner of your eye. He is scratching both his arms again. He is shaking his head. You get out of the car. You step out on the side of the road onto fallen pine needles. You start heading down the road. The road, of course, must lead to somewhere. You will come to a house. You will come to a bigger road. Your leg with the wound wants to stay behind. Your leg with the wound wants to stay seated in the car without weight on it and without the cold wind touching it. Your leg with the wound doesn't care about the killer seated in the car with you. Your leg could stand that killer a little longer. You grab your leg from behind, lifting up on it to help it take the steps it needs to take in order for you to get away. Up ahead, it is so dark that you imagine you could walk off the road and into the forest and not even know it.

Then the sound you are dreading to hear you hear. It is the killer opening the car door. It is the killer's footsteps coming up behind you. You imagine he is going to grab you from behind and kill you here, instead of in the car, where it would be too hard to extract your body once you were dead. You start to run, of course, but your leg, the one that would rather be sitting back in the car, doesn't let you run. You hobble forward. You scream for help. You can hear your voice getting carried off by the wind, traveling behind you. He catches up to you and grabs you by the arm. "This way," he says, and he pushes you into the forest holding a flashlight in front of him, lighting up the fallen red and gold leaves. He puts you up against a tree. "Sit down," he says.

Great, it's about time, your wounded leg says. Your other leg, your good leg, could kick your wounded leg for being so stupid.

"You must be about fifty," he says, pointing the flashlight in your face. "Do you have daughters? Is one a teenager?" The face of your oldest girl flashes before your eyes. You see her long hair and her perfect eyebrows and her pointy elbows that seem to jut out all the time. "Is she?" he says. He kicks your wounded leg now with the heel of his shoe. You scream, and roll forward, then you nod.

It is your bad leg making you nod, not wanting the pain to happen again. "If you tell anyone what happened, or what I look like, I will find your daughter. I will cut her throat," he says. You think about your brother. His death was enough. Enough, enough, you want to say. This many members of my family can't kill themselves or be killed. There has to be a limit, you want to say. Isn't there some kind of limit? Isn't one tragic death per lifetime enough? Oh, no, you think. you can't kill her. She doesn't want to die. And realizing this you are relieved. You know now that Sofia, despite her sagging shoulders, despite her hair hanging in front of her face, is not like your brother at all. She wants to live. You see it in how she fights to regain her speed in that last twenty-five of her one-hundred free, how her shoulders power through the water, how she slowly, steadily gains on the field as if she imagines her former slow self is there in another lane and she will beat it. You make a deal, with God of course, because the killer is an animal and won't listen anyway. You tell God you'll remember to compliment Sofia from now on. You won't make the same mistake your father did with your brother. You'll stop yourself from saying, "Fix your hair," or "Keep your back straight," and instead you'll say things like, "Your first twenty-five was so fast!" "That swimsuit looks good on you!" "You got an A in English? That's terrific." Just let her live, you think. Deal?

"I read your identification in your wallet," the killer says. He recites your name, your address. He recites your driver's license number, which you haven't even memorized yourself, but it sounds right, as if he has memorized it. He throws your purse at you, and it hits you in the chest. You did not think your purse was so heavy. You did not think there was that much in there that could cause so much pain. Does your hairbrush with your hair and your daughters' hair in it really weigh so much? Does your ChapStick you never use weigh that much? Do your coins? And suddenly you remember how to say coins in Spanish, *monedas*, and you wonder why you couldn't remember that before when you were helping Alex with her homework and she asked you what the word meant. How is it that you remember this word when a killer is standing over you holding a long-bladed knife, and his arms, up and down, are covered in scratch marks, and your leg is throbbing and your mouth is so dry? Is this another thing to write and tell these writers of thrillers about, that even when you are faced with possibly losing life, with the lives of your family being lost, you remember stupid things you could not remember before? *Monedas* sounds heavier than coins, and now you are not surprised that for a moment you cannot breathe when your purse is thrown at your chest. All the *monedas* in Spain seems to have been thrown at your ribcage at once. The killer turns and leaves. He is not going to kill you. You will live. He is off to kill someone else. Someone young. You are too old to be killed. What good fortune, you think. But it is not something you want to tell others. I was spared because of wrinkles like rakes beside my eyes, and loose skin at my neck. You hear Chris's car drive off, and when it's gone you look up. A thin sliver of a moon in the shape of a curved sewing needle hangs up there, providing a bit of light, though not really enough to see much more than the leaves, which no longer appear warm red and gold, as they did under the beam of the flashlight, but look frosted, as if suddenly the temperature's dropped and everything's become white and crisp to the touch. You feel inside your purse, but your phone is not there. You do not have a way of letting anyone else know where you are. You think about what Thomas told you, that there is a zoo in Miami that uses iPads so that orangutans can order food by pointing at their choices on a screen. They have all the intelligence they need to speak, but their vocal cords aren't developed like ours. And here you are, you think, a human in the woods without your old-model flip phone to call for help. You use your vocal cords, but your voice just gets thrown around like a loser in a wrestling match landing hard on a gym mat. You can hear the wind take your scream and slam it back down when another crosscurrent of wind intersects it, and your cries for help end up by your feet.

You start walking toward where you think the road is. At least there you won't get as lost as you would deeper in between the pines and maples and bushes with thorns that embed themselves in your pants and continue to prick you long after you've left the place where they've grown up in tangles and thickets. You think how you will probably never remember where this spot off the road in the woods is, and how if you were in the woods by your house, or anywhere else, it would seem like the same woods. You would never be able to bring anyone back here to show them the blood that dripped from your leg and onto the leaf-covered ground. You would never be able to show them where the killer stood over you and threatened to kill your teenage daughter if you turned him in. Only the woods can talk for you now. The tree you leaned up against remembers the feel of the warmth of your back on its deeply lined bark. The sapling you grabbed onto so you wouldn't fall as the killer pushed you forward on your wounded leg remembers your weak grasp. Only those things know, and like the orangutan without the right vocal cords, they really can't speak.

The moon lights up the flat expanse of the road more brightly than the woods. You feel something shore up against your leg in the wind and reach down to find a page of Paul's story. The killer must have thrown it out the window before he left, unimpressed by the metaphors, the inexact images, the turn the writing took at the end. You can hear more pages fluttering around you, but you only keep this one page, because it happens to be the first page, and so much possibility lies in the first page when the final pages aren't there to end it. Bobby Chantal, for example, could still be alive. And you could end up not being here on this dark road, walking for what seems like forever, wishing you had never met Paul or Chris, wishing your bad leg would just remove itself from your hip and try walking on its own, because it's slowing you down. You don't look forward to not telling the story of the killer you cannot identify because he knows about your teenage daughter.

This is the tree in the woods cooling off after you lean up against it. This is the wind taking the warmth and sending it over the deer sleeping in a small valley on tall grass bent by their bodies now bedded down. These are the other pages of Paul's story mixing with leaves, acting like leaves, blowing up in currents, sailing down and wafting side to side. This is rain coming days later, dropping on the printed words, magnifying briefly the B for blood Paul wrote when describing the first moments he found Bobby Chantal with her throat slit.

This is more rain, sopping the page, and this is even harder rain, able to tear the paper because of its force. This is the paper, not even as hardy as the thin fallen leaves it's mixed with, crumbling, losing its whiteness, and becoming unrecognizable after the season's first snow.

CHAPTER FORTY-ONE

*T*his is days later when you open the paper and see the picture of your killer standing in front of a fence at a school where sheep are penned to keep down the growth of poison ivy. He is not wearing the polo shirt and khakis. He is wearing blue jeans and a button-up-the-front shirt. He is smiling, and so for a moment you're not sure if it's really him, but then you notice the unmistakable wrinkles on his forehead that are so deep and look like steps you could actually climb. The newspaper headline reads, "Even School Secretary Pitches In to Stop the Itch," and the article describes how faculty, staff, and students alike all take turns on weekdays and weekends watering the sheep named Cindy, Happy, and Iris, who eat the hardy poison weed with gusto in addition to occasional flakes of hay. Under the killer's picture is his name, Floyd Arneson. This is the other headline on the same page of the newspaper: "College Student Mindy Reynolds Missing for Five Days Straight—Last Seen at a Gas Station on I-91 on Her Way to Her

Parent's Home for a Visit." This is the picture of Mindy Reynolds smiling, holding up her fingers in a peace sign to whoever is behind the camera.

This is Thomas walking toward you with a cup of tea while you're reading the article, and this is you quickly folding the paper over so he can't see. This is the fireplace door being opened and you stuffing the paper inside, watching the smoke rise, and this is Thomas telling you to sit and have your tea before it gets cold. This is Thomas taking the cup from you when you're done and telling you to go upstairs and sleep. You look tired, and your leg, which you told him was pierced by a stick when you took a nasty fall in the woods, will never heal. This is your dream where the killer comes to your house and starts asking for your teenage daughter, and this is you screaming in your sleep for the killer to get out, and this is Thomas coming into the room smelling like chainsaw oil, shaking your shoulder, telling you it's okay, it's just a dream. This is Sofia at the dinner table, feeling your mother eyes all over her, feeling you staring at the way she brings the fork to her mouth and lifts her head back to drink from a glass. "Mom, what?" Sofia says, and you lower your eyes and say, "Your hair looks so pretty. The chlorine must be giving it highlights." And this is Sofia ignoring your remark and then complaining about how she ages up and has her birthday right before age group championships this year, and she'll never make the new cut times, and why couldn't you have had her a week later? she asks, and you answer, "You were premature. You were the one who wanted to come out early," you say, and your daughter says, "Right, it's always my fault." "No, it was probably mine. I did too much that day. I washed the windows in the house. I took too long a walk with the dog. It wasn't your fault."

This is the phone ringing and Chris wanting to come visit, and you knowing she's suspicious and doesn't believe the story you told her, how at the rest stop you got restless and stretched your legs and went for a walk in the woods and got lost, and while you were gone, someone saw the keys in the ignition and took off, probably a teenager on a joyride with his friends (the car was found the next day on a side road near the rest stop, the keys still in the ignition), and how, while on that walk in the woods, you fell on a stick and that's how your leg got such a deep cut. You tell Thomas to tell her you're just too tired right now to talk. Thomas comes up to check on you later. When he sees you're awake he tells you that Earth is made from the sun, and they've done measurements. They have checked our sun and what makes up our sun isn't what makes up other stars in our universe. "In other words, they don't know where we come from," he says. "Pretty cool," he says. It makes sense to you then that we have people like killers, because where we're from isn't like anywhere else. "Yes, pretty cool," you say to Thomas, and you smile because you want him to know you are all right and that soon you will be able to get out of the bed and drive the car and go back to taking the girls to swim practice, and you will not have to think about the killer. You will be caught up in the next big meet. You will talk to the other mothers about the latest racing suits. You will talk to the other mothers about aging up. You will be told the birthdays of kids who are not your own. You will remember Phoebe is younger than Alex by three months. You will remember Ellen's birthday is three days after Alex's birthday. You will remember that Dana, who even though she ages up a month before age groups, is such a fast swimmer that she already qualifies for the next cuts. You know that Michele has the best birthday, the week after state championships, the week after winter practice ends and meets don't resume until summer.

Already the parents are planning the next away meet. You lie back on the pillows, sighing. If only you could think about swimming and the swim team, about all their associated mundane details, which you call the "nothingness," and not about the killer whom you see every time you close your eyes. It's as if he's taken over the insides of your eyelids, and there's no such thing as darkness anymore. It's worse than darkness. It's his face.

This is the killer at school looking down at his forearms, which are huge and oozing and puffy from his reaction to the poison ivy. The students are calling him the Incredible Hulk, because his swelling looks like muscle mass. The puss from his arms leaks onto the newsletter he's printed and forms a ring of yellow crust on the heading's picture of the school logo—a happy little red schoolhouse with cartoon children standing out front holding hands. At least he won't have to take care of the sheep again. The teachers and the principal at the school feel terrible that he came down with such a bad case, and the principal went to the store himself to buy him a bottle of calamine lotion and cotton balls. The killer thinks about how he'll go swimming later, and how the cool water might relieve the burning itch. He can't tell if the sensation to scratch his arms and the adrenaline rush that comes with it are what's been keeping him up at night or if it's him reliving how he killed Mindy Reynolds. Killing her was more satisfying than killing all the others, for some reason. He can still hear her pleading for help when he cut her throat and felt the breath of her words forming against his face through the newly made slit. This time he was able to make the cut while facing his victim, and he could see her eyes shoot forth that light of wanting to live mixed with terror, and he thought he could feel that feeling too and that his eyes somehow absorbed it and he was now walking around with it inside himself—the light of Mindy Reynolds as he read over the school newsletter typos he'd have to fix, the light of Mindy Reynolds as he watched through the window the children on the geodesic play structure hanging by their knees, the girls' hair hanging like upside-down flames, almost licking the ground. Thank goodness I didn't bother killing that fifty-year-old woman, he thinks. If he had he wouldn't have been at the rest stop at the right time to come upon Mindy Reynolds as she walked out of her car, and to hear her singing a pop song and hear her charm bracelet jangling as she headed toward the bathrooms.

CHAPTER FORTY-TWO

*T*his is Thomas coming into the room while you are sleeping, your eyes probably moving back and forth in a dream. He thinks he should wake you. The dream seems disturbing. It's no wonder, of course, that you're in turmoil. When he picked you up from the hospital a few nights ago you were almost catatonic, only telling him in a monotone voice how you fell in the woods on a stick after you and Chris stopped at a rest stop, and you ended up with a hole in your leg that required ten stitches. You probably passed out for a minute, you said, and that's when Chris's car was stolen. The doctors wanted you to stay in the hospital longer, but you refused. You said you wanted to get home and be with your children. This is you turning your head left and right on the pillow, and it sounds as though you're trying to talk in your sleep but can't make the words come out. Thomas lies down next to you and puts his hand on your shoulder. "Annie?" he says, and you wake up so suddenly he thinks it's impossible that you were just sound asleep. You turn to him and hold on to him and he holds you back. It's been a long time since you've turned to him and wanted to be in his arms. He kisses you on the top of your head and smoothes your hair away from your face. "Bad dream?" he asks. "I didn't talk in my sleep, did I?" you ask. "You tried to, but nothing came out. What are you afraid of saying?" Thomas asks, and you notice how he's been looking at you the whole time, not turning away as he usually does or picking up a magazine to read at the same time you talk to him. "Keep waking me up if you think I'm about to talk in my sleep, okay?" you ask. "Sure," Thomas says. He begins to rub your back, and it feels good, a little of the tension you've been feeling is worked out with his hands. You've always liked Thomas's hands. They're strong and big and when he holds your hand, his hand nearly covers all of yours. Maybe this is all you have wanted for so long now, just to have Thomas hold you and run his hands on your back and look at you. You think of Paul, and how you have not thought of him for a few days, ever since the killer. You do not feel yourself wanting to be with Paul or have him kiss you. You want to be as far away from Paul now as you can be.

In the periods during which you half-slept and dozed and dreamed fitfully, you considered moving from your home. You and your family would move to another state, another country. The killer would not travel to find your daughter thousands of miles away, would he? You picture living down by the equator. Your children could go to the local school. They would become fluent in Spanish. They would become dark from the daily sun. They would become unrecognizable to people they once knew. They could surf in the waves every day. They could eat fresh fruit and fish. What was the point, really, of living here? Things were hard here. The summers were bug-ridden. If you spent any time outdoors, your skin would raise in welts from deerflies. From time to time you would find your fingers at your scalp, feeling crusted blood from insect bites. In winter the roads, muddy from fall rains, dried in rigid ruts that grabbed your tires and made your car drive in hard frozen tracks other vehicles had left, and you had no choice but to follow them. You could see your children living down there by the ocean. Everyone so heavy on land, taking to the water and racing down the clear faces of waves. Your daughters learning to be ocean-brave, paddling far out, ignoring days of jellyfish tides, and jumping from cliffs to the blue depths far down below. Thomas and you sleeping with the French doors open and a breeze skimming over you both as you slept naked and still in a white-sheeted bed.

Your leg is still sore, but you can walk on it now, almost run. There was a point, after the killer left you and after you walked on it for what must have been a mile, that you could not even feel your leg. The man who stopped for you looked more like a killer than the killer. He wore dirty striped overalls and no socks. You could see the hairs at his sharply boned ankles. He asked what in the world you were doing walking so far off the main road at night. You just asked him to take you to the hospital, and he nodded and drove. The glove box slammed open every time the tires hit a bump, and he repeatedly reached his arm over your wounded leg to close the compartment.

After Thomas leaves the room to go start some dinner, you wish you had gone with the girls to practice, to experience the nothingness of the swim team again. What would be better right now than entering the facility and sitting with the other parents

in the bleachers and watching your daughters swim and talking
to the other parents about swimming, schooling, and food? You
would even be glad to see the dancing hippos. You would wave to
them as they jogged in the lane with their foam belts attached to
their huge waists. You get up to help Thomas. At first you are light-
headed and afraid of blacking out and seeing the killer's face when
you do, but when you regain your balance you go downstairs and
help cook the dinner. The girls are at the table doing homework,
and you would like to turn off the lights, because anyone from the
outside standing by your house in the night could see your girls
plain as day, considering you don't have curtains in the windows
to obstruct the view. You shepherd them away from the table. You
send them to study in the back of the house, where they cannot
be seen from the road. They object. They want to know why. You
tell them you need the table to set out plates and forks and knives.
"Take these books, take your calculators, and go," you say. They
complain about your orders, they make nasty faces, they imitate
the words you used in a singsong disrespectful tone, not caring
about your leg. That night, when it's time for bed, Thomas turns
to you and hugs you again, holding you the way he did earlier in
the day. You hug and hold him back. If it were only this, you think.
How easy it is just to hold him. If this were all you had to do and
nothing else, not worry about the killer, not worry about the throat
of your daughter meeting the blade of that same knife that was
thrust into your leg. Why was it so hard just to make the effort to
turn and hold Thomas before? You feel as if you could hold him
forever now. You do not want to turn your head away from his
chest.

CHAPTER FORTY-THREE

*B*ecause you can drive now, and you are finally feeling better, you can take the girls back to practice. You arrive early, eager to wave to the cleaning lady, who knows you by name. Eager to feel the blast of warmth when you enter the pool area, the air laden with the smell of chlorine. Eager to talk to the other parents and watch how the swimmers swim. You and the other parents know the injuries, the aches and pains the swimmers have. You notice how Emily does breast instead of fly during a fly set, and you and the other parents decide that her shoulder must still be bothering her. You notice how during a fly set, Hannah's downward stroke smashed Candace in the nose. Candace had sinus surgery only a few months ago, and you hope she's all right. You notice how India's wearing a waterproof ankle brace made of rubber, and that her season of track that overlaps with the first few months of swim team made her sprain her ankle again. From up above in the bleachers, you notice even the health of the coaches.

You see the head coach looks thinner after a bout with the flu. The juniors' coach is thinner too, but that's because she's in training for a triathlon. Either Chris or Paul must have dropped Cleo off at the pool and then left to run errands. It's just you and the other parents and the sense of quiet calm you feel when you watch the team swim, as relaxing, if not more so, than watching the flames of a wood fire burning. You and the other parents compliment one another on your clothes, on your hair, on the way your children swim. You notice how Ben's daughter has really refined her fly. Her body profile is flatter over the water, and she's not coming up as high as she used to. You notice Eliot has straightened out his breaststroke legs. They kick on the same plane now, and not one and then the other as they did before, which would get him DQ'ed. Kendra can breathe free on both sides now, instead of only on the right. Phoebe's head is now down in her dives, giving her a better streamline on entry. Sofia's extra wiggle in her fly, though, still looks like a problem, and you wonder if she'll ever be able to learn fly the right way so that it looks as though she's moving forward and not backward with every pull of her arms. Somewhere in the middle of the next-to-last strenuous set, when all of the swimmers are swimming their hardest, you realize it's going to be all right. You don't have to uproot the family and move to the equator. You can stay where you are. You can stay like this, coming to practice every day, sitting on the metal bleachers, talking with the other parents, talking about cut times, talking about the best hotels to stay at during a meet, and which pools have the best places for viewing the races, and which have the best concession stands, and which have easy parking, and which are easy to find off the highway. You can keep going on like this as long as you don't ever tell anyone who the killer is. And that doesn't have to be so hard, does it? You can keep a secret. You can forget his terrible face with his forehead like steps. You can forget the gleam of his long knife blade. You can forget so much here because it is safe here. It is not a place your brother would have ever gone to, for example. You could never picture him here in the stands. He would never be on deck in a swimsuit. He would never be sitting with the parents you sit with, who at the moment are talking about the perfect food to bring to swim meets to feed to their swimmers.

You have a conversation, in the stands, about the new racing suits. You've heard the technology is even more advanced, providing turbo compression for a tighter core and better body positioning while reducing lactic acid build-up with a lightweight hydrophobic micro-filament textile that repels water and reduces drag. There's also a suit that uses zoned compression and a body stability web, which provides targeted support with a network of seams that are bonded with high-frequency welding instead of being sewn. You have just learned that another advance is the creation of a unified system in which the suit, cap, and goggles all work together to improve water flow around the head and body. Hundreds of heads of athletes were analyzed to come up with the design and to see how water could flow faster over that part of the body. The cap needs to come all the way down to the goggles for seamless transition.

After practice you stand in the foyer with the other parents waiting for your swimmers to come out of the locker room. They are slow because they are talking in the showers, trying out each other's shampoos and singing songs together that play on the radio. Your leg, you feel, is almost all the way healed. The tip of that killer's blade did not meet the bone in your leg. You take a poll, who is cooking what for their swimmers for dinner tonight? Stuffed shells, pizza, mac and cheese, they answer. Oh that's good, you say, the carbs are what they need for the upcoming meet. You feel hungry yourself, when you have not felt hungry in days, not since, of course, you came home that night with a hole in your leg. You tell yourself you will have to remember getting that hole a different way, a way that did not involve the killer. That will be easier. Remember instead that you decided to take a walk in the woods and you fell on what you thought at first was a stick but turned out to be a stake, maybe something farmers in this area long ago used to tie their sheep to in the fields when they needed to be kept apart from the rest of the flock.

Paul and Chris walk in together, and they make a beautiful pair. Paul with his hair pulled back in his ponytail, wearing his leather jacket, and Chris wearing an oversized sweater the color of light-green sea glass. They are smiling at everyone as they enter, as if they've just arrived at an awards ceremony and not the foyer of the facility. They look at you and smile and wave, and you do the same back, and isn't this wonderful, you think. None of what's been happening has ever happened and here the king and queen of the swim team have arrived, arm in arm, happy again. When Chris does catch you alone for a moment while you're in the ladies' room before your long drive home, she puts her hands squarely on your shoulders. She wants you to look at her. "Tell me you're all right?" she says. You nod. "I know you'll never tell me what happened that night, but I have a feeling it almost got you killed. You sure you're all right?" she says. "Yes," you say and then, even louder, "Yes." You are all right. The nothingness is back. Chris is relieved, you can tell. She looks more beautiful than ever. You can't believe she doesn't catch sight of herself in the bathroom mirror and stop to stare. The mintiness of her is so strong you expect to see mint on her body somewhere, pinned to her breast or adorning her hair. "Just so you know," she says, "things are better now between Paul and me. Even though Pam Chantal's going through with the exhumation, it's going to be all right. Paul's lawyer is going to be involved every step of the way, and who knows, it might not even come to that. Maybe the killer will strike again and be caught this time, and Paul's DNA won't matter."

"What's he going to tell the police?" you say. Suddenly you feel the fear rising up inside you like blood rising in your face because what if somehow the killer thinks that because you know Paul you are working with him to have the killer caught.

"Whatever he knows, that's all," Chris says. When she turns to leave you want to reach out and grab on to her. Don't let him, you want to say, but you know it won't work. Paul has to save himself and his family first.

This is the killer on the pool deck, standing in his swimsuit. This is the killer lowering himself in. This is the water wanting to part when he turns and enters the water, wishing it didn't have to let him in, but it can't do anything to stop him. This is the water sighing, having to close up around the killer, having to enter and sit in his ear as he swims a poor sidestroke crooked down the lane, having to meet the burn of the rash on his arms with its coolness and its chlorine.

This is the drive home. Your arms itching and you trying to scratch them with one hand on the wheel. You see the red streaks up and down your forearms the way you saw them on the killer's arms, and now you also feel small bumps on them, and you know what they are because you have had poison ivy before. This is strange, of course, because you haven't been near poison ivy recently, unless of course the killer walked you through it in the woods. You do know that you can get it from clothes that have the rash-producing oil on them, and you guess that when the killer grabbed you and pushed you, the oil rubbed off on you. Your body's always been slow to react to poison ivy, sometimes taking a week before it appears. You've even gotten it weeks later from clothes you wore while walking through it, the oil rubbing off onto the material of your pants, for instance. It's horrible, thinking that something of the killer's has physically transferred to you. You scratch even harder, thinking you don't care if you scar your skin. You already will have the scar on your leg. "Mom, stop scratching," Sofia says without looking up from the book she's reading. You grip the steering wheel with both hands, holding on tight so you don't scratch. When you get to the house, you wish you could take the steering wheel inside with you, because holding on to it helps.

That evening Thomas takes out the rifles and fits one against Alex's shoulder and says, "It fits fine." He shows her the safety, how to load, how to use the German Zeiss scope that he says is such a strong lens, and how to eject the bullets. Tomorrow is the first day of youth hunting season, and Alex wants to go up high on the ridge at the back of the house and hunt deer. You know how to use the rifle yourself. You have hunted before with Thomas, but now is a good time to listen to him give Alex the lesson, because you may need to refresh your memory. Thomas has Alex focus on the hillside out your living room window, adjusting the scope on what must be one of the few remaining leaves left on the trees. "Don't worry about the kick," he says, and you know that the kick of the rifle is not anything to think about at first. It never hurts at first. It's later, when you are walking into the house that seems so warm compared to the tree you were leaning up against for hours waiting for a buck to walk through the woods, that you feel the ache in your arm. You wish Sofia wanted to hunt also. Anything that might help to protect her. She does not know how to hold the rifle. She doesn't want to learn. Thomas tells her that even if she doesn't want to hunt, she should know how to use a gun, since we have guns in the house, but every time he tries to teach her she goes up to her room and reads a book, and he can't talk her into coming back down.

What startles you isn't the explosive sound of the shot Alex takes, but the ringing phone. You see that it's a call from Paul's cell phone, and you stare at the number on the small screen, but you don't answer it. Avoiding him is best, especially for the safety of your family. You're afraid you may tell Paul something about the killer if you talk to him again.

That night you think you've been talking in your sleep, and you wake up sweating with fear, thinking you have given away details about the killer and Thomas has heard them and will tell the police. You look over, and Thomas is sleeping, so maybe you're still safe. Maybe you haven't said anything. Maybe Sofia is still safe and the killer won't ever touch her. After all, you have been holding up your end of the deal. Haven't you? Even when Sofia was being mean to Alex, grabbing a book she was reading out of her hands, you didn't tell Sofia she was being mean. Instead you told Sofia that you were pleased to know the two of them had an interest in the same reading material, that you thought it was sweet that Sofia wanted to read what her sister, three years younger, was reading. Very big-sisterly of you, you said to Sofia, and Sofia groaned, handing the book back to Alex—it was more like she threw it back at her, but at least it was you keeping up your end of the deal. It was the new positive you, and you were seeing what you thought were results. Sofia seems to be standing straighter these days. She isn't as shy. She even asked a salesperson for help when she was buying a battery for her watch the other day, not expecting you to ask for her. When you go to the bathroom and then go back into bed, the sweat in your sheets has already turned cold. The coyotes outside seem as if they're sitting strategically around your house in a circle. Their calls coming from all sides, and you and Thomas and the children at the center. Wide awake now, you scratch at your arms.

You read that some use gasoline on poison ivy rashes and some use juniper leaves. Some use a paste made from aspirin and some use bleach. Some slide into bathwater sprinkled with raw oats. Some use nail-polish remover, some use aloe, some use motor oil. Some get a shot from the doctor. Some use extremely hot water, some use extremely cold. Some swear by toothpaste, some by roll-on deodorant. You swear by the knife. You do not mind the cuts you have made up and down your arm. Anything to gouge out the rash. When Thomas sees you he yells, "What have you done?" and he gets the gauze and the Betadine and leans close to you and you realize the season of the wood is over and that hunting season has begun. He does not smell like the chainsaw oil any-more, instead he smells like the gun oil he uses to clean the rifles. This is a good smell, you think to yourself. Makes you think of the refreshing cold air of fall. He leans so close you can see how his hair is graying at the temples and thinning at the top, where you can see he has a small brown birthmark in the shape of the state you live in. "Amazing," you say, and he asks what, and you tell him about the birthmark, and he says it's always been there and how was it you have never noticed before. Seeing the birthmark you feel closer to him. You suppose it's because it probably makes him look more like he did when he was first born. You like to picture him as a boy sometimes, because then he is easier to talk to and you are not so worried he will make fun of your everyday observa-tions. The Betadine paste is brown and translucent and makes you look as though you've been seriously hurt. After he screws the top back on the paste, he tells you the best thing for the rash is time. Of course, he is right, and you nod. You stand up and take the Be-tadine and put it away on the shelf in the bathroom. He still stands and looks at you, but after a while he walks away. You can hear his feet on the staircase and his footsteps are so familiar you think how you could never mistake them for anyone else's. You know ev-eryone's footsteps in the house. You know the sound of Sofia, who wears slippers that are too big for her feet and drag on the floor. You know the sound of Alex, the way she walks quickly and lightly. You can hear Thomas sitting down at the kitchen table, opening up a magazine, entering, probably, the universe, the solar system, the human body, the mind.

CHAPTER FORTY-FOUR

T he meet this weekend is a home meet and you have signed up to time. Your girls are in many individual events because the coach has decided there will be no relays, which, by the official rules, lets the swimmers swim in more events. You are thankful for this because it means there will be plenty of individual races to watch your girls in. What's new are energy drinks in the form of a gel, and your girls, of course, want you to buy some for the meet. You sit in on the required timers' meeting before the race begins. You have heard the talk that is given at this meeting maybe a hundred times before, but still you are required to attend the meeting and listen. The assistant coach, when describing the stopwatch to parents who have never timed before, likes to tell them that the right button starts and stops the watch, the left button clears the watch, and the middle button will blow the whole place up. New parents always laugh at this joke and you smile, not wanting to send the message that you think the joke is tired, not wanting to offend the assistant coach, who you are sure is paid very little and puts in long hours. The assistant coach then describes the other timing device, the plunger. One of the parents asks what the plunger looks like, and the assistant coach says, "It looks like a detonator," and suddenly you are wondering how something as mundane as a home swim meet for school-age children keeps having references to explosions. You are relieved when the topic turns to rubber-ducky prizes for heat winners, and how the timers will not be responsible for distributing the prizes because a heat-winner volunteer will keep track of that.

Paul is timing also, only you're not in his lane. He waves to you when he sees you at the meeting, and you smile and nod, and you make yourself not reach up to your hair and smooth it down, even though you can see out of the top corner of your eye that it's messy, because you are no longer in the business of making yourself attractive for him, you are in the business of every day making sure you save your daughter's life. The kissing and the touching you did with Paul are no longer important. So many things are in the past now, even your brother and his blood and his brains on his carpet are gone. No longer will the thoughts of him seem to suck you down into crevices in your house, through floorboards and chair seats.

You are in a lane with Dinah, and when her daughter swims in your lane Dinah screams, "Go, Baby, go!" and stands on the gutter, her toes in her sandals almost dipping into the pool water. You think how Dinah, if the killer ever threatened her daughter, would probably never let him get near her daughter. You think how you should be a little bit more Dinah, a little tougher, a little louder, a little more almost in the water with your daughter, pushing her along. Dinah, thankfully, is not talking to you about Paul or anything else except the meet. Her daughter has a chance to qualify for age groups at this meet, and that's all she's concerned with. She has agreed to work the plunger, and you write down the times. You are in an end lane, where, in a heat, the slower swimmers are placed, and these swimmers are not as good as others at making streamlined dives, so as an end-lane timer, you are wetter than the middle-lane timers from being splashed so many times by near belly flops and sloppy entries. The pages on the clipboard where you record the times are also very wet, and even the pencil is hard to write with. A Gunga Din, at least that's what you call them—volunteers who pass out plastic water bottles to the timers and officials who can't step away from their posts—comes by with a water bottle. You always need water to drink when timing because the air in the pool is hot and makes you thirsty. You store the bottle under the block, and hope that a swimmer doesn't accidentally kick it into the water.

Dinah's daughter, Jessie, competes in her one-hundred breast, and while she swims, Dinah yells, "Go, Baby, go!" Dinah is yelling, "Finish it! Finish it!" so loudly when her daughter is approaching the wall that you're momentarily deaf in one ear. Jessie's time is fast enough to take her to age groups, the next division. Dinah leaves her post as a timer screaming, "You did it!" and runs to hug her daughter when her daughter comes out of the pool. When Dinah runs back to your side to start the timer for the next race, her front is soaking wet from the hug, and she's so red in the face you worry she's going to collapse.

Alex pokes you from behind. "I'm in heat ten, lane five," she says. You give her the thumbs-up as she walks off to her lane.

When she races you don't watch the swimmer racing in your lane, you watch only Alex, whose entry is tight, whose splash is so light it could be that of a wishing rock thrown into a pond. You start to yell like Dinah yells when Alex comes to do a flip by your end. "Go, Ba—" you yell, catching yourself just in time before you say, "Go, Baby, go!" like Dinah. You yell at the top of your lungs now, because there is another swimmer gaining on your Alex. You can't remember having yelled this loud before. You think how maybe you should have yelled like this when the killer had you in the car, that if you had yelled this loud, it wouldn't have mattered how loud the wind was, or how far away you were from a house. Someone surely would have heard you. You think you are yelling this loud to make up for all the yelling you didn't do with the killer. It feels good to yell so loud. You think it's even making your arms feel better. You can't feel the intense itching. After your daughter wins her heat and you raise both your hands in the air, one holding the clipboard, the other holding the pencil, you feel a hand on your back. You think it's your other daughter, Sofia, come to tell you which heat and lane her next race is in, but when you turn around you see that it's the assistant coach. "Annie, as a timer, it's actually not acceptable to yell so loud for your children," he says. You apologize to him, and when he leaves Dinah says, "Fuck him. Yell all you want to. I'd like to see in the parent handbooks where it says you can't cheer for your own kid. All the money we spend, all the time we spend volunteering—yell till your lungs burst, Annie. Can you believe we made it to age groups? I didn't think Jessie was going to do it there for a second. If she had taken one more stroke, instead of gliding into the wall, we wouldn't have made it. Oh, and sorry about Paul. I can see he's back with his wife.

That must be rough for you, but you look like you're holding up just fine. You're lucky you have Thomas. He's a great guy." You nod. You can't believe Dinah is telling you this. Is she that ecstatic about her daughter making it into age groups? I guess she is, you think. "Hey, after the meet, why don't you and the girls join us at the sushi place?" she says. You stammer, "Thanks, but I have to get back and let the dog out. Maybe another time."

When you ask the girls in the car ride home how well they think they did, your youngest says, "Mom, what were you doing all that yelling for while I was racing? I thought I was doing something wrong and you wanted me to get out. I thought I was in the wrong race or something, you were yelling so loud."

"Sorry," you say, and then, "Hey, I thought you said you could never hear people when they cheered for you."

"I'd have to be dead not to hear you in that race!" she says, and you almost wince when she says the word dead. You wish she hadn't, because suddenly you picture her dead, her throat slit, and you holding her in your arms, trying to support her head to keep it from falling off all the way.

CHAPTER FORTY-FIVE

There are times when you feel like telling Thomas what the killer said. It is like something you've been carrying around that you finally need help with. It is the load of logs in your arms that you're carrying in from the woodpile for the woodstove but just can't make it to the door with, and you know at any second you're just going to have to let them drop to the frozen ground. "Thomas?" you say when he's reading, but he doesn't look up, and you realize you are purposefully trying to get his attention at a time when he's reading, and when you know he won't look up, because deep down you don't really want him to reply. You really don't want to tell him about the killer for fear he'll get up from where he is, go to the gun cabinet, pull out that well-oiled rifle, and go to that school you know the killer works at because you saw his picture in the paper standing by the sheep, and you are afraid Thomas will follow the killer home and shoot him dead, and then Thomas will go to jail for the rest of his life because there's no evidence against the killer, and you cannot have Thomas go to jail. Who would do algebra with your daughters and teach them how two negatives make a positive? Who would cut and chop and split and stack the logs for the fire in the winter? You think maybe there's a way of planting evidence. Maybe you could somehow obtain from Kim's mother an item of Kim's clothing, a strand of hair from her hairbrush, or a swim cap she wore. You could plant the evidence in the killer's house. You imagine this conversation with Kim's mother—"Uh, I was wondering if I could have Kim's old swim cap"—and you lower your head. You do not want to put a woman whose daughter was murdered through this conversation.

This is the night. The dog coming upstairs and lying down at your door. This is Thomas breathing loudly in his sleep. This is Anna Karenina, calling on her friend Princess Betsy, who also has had affairs, but even Princess Betsy won't see her, and Anna is snubbed. This is Vronksy telling Anna not to be seen in public. This is Anna, bereft over Vronksy's coolness toward her, flirting with Levin just to feel better. This is you feeling like Anna, really feeling as if you are she for a moment. This is Anna, believing that Vronsky doesn't love her anymore, that he'll follow his mother's wishes and marry a high-society lady, and this is Anna miserable, thinking the only way to free herself from the torment is to end her life. This is you saying, "Don't do it, Anna," in your room in the night with no one listening but maybe the shapes you see in the knots in the wood. This is the Russian freight train. You cannot stop the train from feeling beneath its wheels the flesh of a woman so sad, broken on the gleaming tracks. This is the moon shining into the room, lighting up the glass gun case and the rifles and guns standing upright inside of it. These are the barrels and triggers of the rifles and guns looking shiny and wet. This is you sighing so loudly that a small sound comes out from inside of your throat. This is moonlight falling on Thomas's forehead, making it shine like the barrels of the guns.

When you see Paul at the next practice he is alone. In the foyer he walks up to you. He touches your shoulder. "Annie, how are you doing?" he says. He tilts his head slightly to the side, and looks long into your eyes, as if he wants you to know that his question is a question full of meaning. You want to step away from him. You wish he would remove his hand. How strange, you think to yourself, that he is repugnant to you now but wasn't a while back, when he was being selfish and not wanting to go to the police with any information about Bobby Chantal. You cannot believe that now you are the one who is being selfish, who could prevent more murders if only you went to the police and told them what you know. When you first told Paul to go to the police you said it like it would be an easy thing for him to do, when obviously it would have been so hard to do. You only realize this now that you are faced with losing your daughter. You have a fear of even being near a police station, because maybe the killer is watching you and maybe he thinks you are about to turn him in. You answer Paul. "Fine," you say, and turn away from him and get ready to swim.

In the locker room you see the older girls from the team, the ones who now drive themselves to and from practice. One of them could easily be the killer's next victim. They are all lively and quick to smile at one another. They laugh easily about things you would laugh at too, and sometimes when you're in the locker room, you smile just listening to them joke with one another while you change into your swimsuit.

This is the coach at a parents' meeting after practice telling you and other parents that swimming is not about the times. This is you thinking, Then what's it about, when every time there's a meet that's all it's about? The expensive timing board up on the wall with the flashing lights that displays swimmers' lanes and times, the expensive timing console and touchpads hung at the ends of lane lines during a meet, the plungers used, the timers using stopwatches, the heat sheets listing seed times and times to beat to advance up into age groups and zones, the announcer, pausing in between races to let everyone know who broke the pool record—these all tell you it's only about the times. It's not as if ribbons and medals are awarded to girls or boys with the prettiest fly, the strongest breast kick, the most elegant backstroke. Ribbons and medals are only given to the kid who touches the wall first. You know you are supposed to embrace the team philosophy. You know you are supposed to realize that it's about the kids challenging themselves and being disciplined and learning to work with others on the team, but it's like saying the involvement of the United States in the Middle East is about human rights and not about oil. Of course it's about oil. You are having one of those moments when you wonder if you are the only one who sees these things clearly. You wonder if the other parents sitting in the room with you, the one with the fashionable scarf maybe, or the one with the dry cough, think it's not about the times.

When Paul comes into the meeting late, you put your purse down on the seat next to you so he won't want to sit down beside you. But he wants to anyway. He smiles and says, "May I?" and you have no choice but to move your purse and put it back on your lap. While the meeting is in progress, you can hear the loud voices of kids yelling to one another during practice, because the door to the room leads right out onto the pool deck. You can hear the coaches blowing whistles and, as always, the splashing of water. You can feel the hot air from the pool deck seeping in under the space at the bottom of the door, and your poison ivy, which has not yet healed, begins to itch.

Throughout the meeting, Paul tries to talk to you. You want to seem polite. You don't want to be rude and talk to the person sitting next to you while the director of the facility is telling you what a wonderful place this is. You like listening to how it is a wonderful place. You wish Paul would be quiet. You like hearing that all of the money you spend every year to keep your daughters on the team goes toward a facility to which no other in your part of the country can compare. You like hearing that because our facility is so nice, we host all the meets, and because we host all the big meets, we don't have to get in the car and travel for miles to a lesser pool, an overly chlorinated, poorly lit hothouse of a pool with only four lanes, for example. We don't have to travel and spend the money on hotels as often as other teams. We don't have to have our kids jumping off the walls in the hotel and not being able to have a restful night's sleep before a big race the next day. Our kids race better in their home pool, you are told. Their times are faster. They're more comfortable. They know exactly when to extend their hand for a backstroke touch and not waste time taking another stroke because they know the position of the backstroke flags in their home pool. The director is trying to make you feel better about having to work all the time at the home meets. Even when your daughters are not racing in some of the sessions, you are expected to help work. On top of that work, there are still positions to fill. Who will be head coordinators? Who will educate the parents? Who will contact the press, the local papers, and let them know there is a meet coming up they should cover? Who will organize the swimathons and car washes? Who will make the pots of chili for the room where the coaches and officials can go to grab something to eat while they're working on deck all day during a meet? Who will make sure the team is social and has dinners together? Who will make sure the granola bars are well stocked at the concessions? Who will decide what to do with all the money the granola bars make? Who will learn how to run the timing console and download the updates, and know how to connect all the wires from the touchpads to the console? Who will put the stickers on the ribbons with the right names and times? This is so much nothingness that you are transfixed. You have even forgotten for a moment that Paul is sitting next to you, nudging you, saying, "Did you hear what I said?" And then you hear. It's all about Bobby Chantal, and you want to get up and leave. Bobby Chantal is like an anchor on your neck you'd like to let drop.

This is the director, looking right at you when Paul is trying to talk to you. This is Paul whispering in your ear, "You're not going to believe this, but the exhumation already took place. Sure enough, they found my DNA on her, or in her, I should say. They found a bunch of hairs and one of them was mine. My lawyer tells me I'll do fine if I have to testify in front of a jury, though. I've got an honest face, he says."

"Didn't you tell him about the red Corvair? About the license plate?"

"Sure, but like I said, those leads were so old they meant nothing."

You leave the meeting early, not wanting to have to listen to Paul anymore. You were hoping there would be some other evidence on Bobby Chantal that would incriminate the killer.

You pass by the swimmers practicing diving off the blocks, their splashes coming up and getting you wet. In the foyer, waiting for your daughters, you feel the need to scratch at your arms again. You lift up your sleeves and examine them. A lifeguard walks by. You see him so often you both smile at each other, even though you don't know his name. He stops when he sees the blisters on your arm. "Oooh, that looks bad. Poison ivy?" You nod. "That's been going around here. A guy who swims here has it in the same place. He says he got it from sheep!"

You cannot believe what he just said. The killer has been swimming here?

"When does he swim?" you ask.

"He comes at night, after swim practice. He should be here soon. Why?"

"Maybe I know him—does he have black hair? About so high? A wrinkled, wide forehead?"

"That's the guy. You know him?"

You look at the clock on the wall behind the front desk. "What's taking my girls so long? I better go check on them," you say to the lifeguard. "See you later." You walk off to the locker room so that you don't have to answer the lifeguard's question about you knowing the killer.

Your girls can't understand why you're having them leave the facility through the side door. You have never left that way before.

It doesn't lead out to the parking lot. It leads to a side yard where metal ventilation ducts stick out from the lawn. Of course, you are hoping to avoid seeing the killer or, more precisely, having the killer see your girls. Your girls are rosy cheeked from having just swum. Your girls smell like flowery shampoo and almond lotion, and the usual faint tinge of chlorine. The killer would be drawn to your girls. Who wouldn't be? They chatter happily about their workout. They talk bathing suits. They say the racing suits long in the leg are meant to shave time off in distance, but not in sprints. For sprints you need a cut-out leg for the sake of mobility, especially for a breaststroke kick. You look left and right once you're outside the facility. Maybe the killer is waiting for you out here in the dark. Suddenly, your poison ivy itches violently. Maybe it senses how near the killer might be. You get to the car without being seen, or so you hope. You're tempted to tell the girls to scrunch down in their seats, to keep their heads from being seen through the windows. Anything to keep the killer at bay.

Driving home, you're speeding. On the turns of the dark, backcountry road, the car feels as if it's going to tip over. "What's the rush?" your girls say. If you had let them read with the light on they wouldn't have noticed, but you have not let them turn the light on, afraid someone will be able to see them. "It's late and you have homework to do," you tell the girls. "Right, so race us home, risking our lives, so we can do it," Sofia says, and you can almost feel her rolling her eyes in the passenger seat next to you. You can almost hear the click her eyeballs make as they turn in their sockets. Listen, I'm saving you from getting your throat cut, you want to tell her, and wipe the sarcasm off her face, but of course you don't. You look straight out onto the road. There is the house that has been burning a brush fire all day, the smoke rising up high and thick behind it, making it look as if the house is on fire. There are the glowing eyes of a raccoon. There are the outlines of horses on the hillside, some owner having not yet put them in their stalls for the night. There are dark clouds speeding by, small ones with one end that tapers into thin strips like a tail, so that the clouds look like rats scurrying by in the sky.

This is the news on the radio. Another woman, a girl still, really, only seventeen, was killed at another rest stop a few exits south. Her throat slashed with a knife. This is you turning the radio off quickly. "Enough, this is enough," you think.

This is Chris in her house, watching the news and listening to the story about the seventeen-year-old girl being killed. She puts her head in her hands. When Paul comes in and hears the news too, she lifts her head and looks at him and says, "I almost wish you were Bobby's killer. Then at least these killings wouldn't still be happening." Paul takes Chris in his arms and they hold each other until Cleo walks in and says, "I guess you're not divorcing. I was kind of hoping you would. I wanted to choose the other house I'd be living in. I was thinking Dad could buy a farm with a pony, a trampoline, and an outdoor swimming pool, with a slide of course."

CHAPTER FORTY-SIX

This is you swimming the next day at the pool by yourself. You told the girls they needed the day off to rest because you didn't want them anywhere near the pool, where the killer might see them. You swim because you have something to think about, and you know you cannot think at home. You swim because you have a feeling the water will tell you what to do. This is you after having swum enough laps that you are finally beginning to relax, and your mind is wandering and you are not even counting your laps any longer. This is the water telling you what to do. The shushing sound the water makes by your ears sounds like so many voices. It sounds like Kim's voice and those of other girls on the team. It sounds like women's voices, like those of the dancing hippos, and men's voices, like those of the trooper and Thomas, and it sounds like the voice of the coach, and the voice of Mandy, and the voice of Pam Chantal. All the voices are telling you the same thing. You understand what they want. When you get out of the pool, it's as if the water is lifting itself up higher so that you can climb out of the pool more easily and go forth and do what you have to do.

This is the water, watching you leave, hoping it's done all it can to convince you. This is the water, winking at you, or so it seems as it glistens and flashes in bright afternoon sunlight streaming in through the windows when you turn your head over your shoulder to look at it one more time to be sure you understand what it wants you to do.

*T*his is the next afternoon. The sounds of cars going up your road are louder now because so few leaves are left on the trees. There are more cars than usual, mostly pickup trucks, it being hunting season, when men make their way up to hunting camps far up your dirt road and stay for a few days in small cabins off the grid, walking the old logging trails, trying their luck in the quiet woods.

If the men in those trucks were to turn their heads and, through the thin maples that border your pond, look up to your house, with its cedar siding turning dark with age from the foundation upward and its copper roof turning green from the base of the chimney, they would see you not sinking into the floorboards and thinking of your brother. They would see you thinking of what's alive. Sofia and Alex.

This is you thinking you'll do anything to keep them alive. It's bad enough that suicides can take place. Those are things you might never be able to stop, but murders, you realize, that's something you can control. That's something you can take care of. This is you rising out of your chair, the menacing floorboards not so menacing now. They are just like the patchwork of land seen from high above, from a flying plane's window, they are that far away, their power to suck you down infinitesimal, nearly gone. This is your walk up to your room with the gun cabinet as if there were some phenomenon taking place that Thomas has read about, some particle attraction in which not only are you walking toward the gun cabinet, but it's coming toward you just as quickly.

This is the rifle you know how to use. Here is where the clip can be taken out and placed beneath the bolt so that when you slide back the bolt, a bullet can be loaded into the chamber. This is the composite Steyr tactical rifle—which feels lighter than it does when you hunt with it in the woods—as you walk to the car to slide it onto the backseat. This is the hunting cap you wear that is Day-Glo orange, and this is the warm coat you wear, with the hunting license you recently renewed folded inside the breast pocket. This is the school the killer works at. This is the large parking lot where at the end of the day the killer gets into his car, a model much newer than his old red Corvair with the Illinois plates, and drives home, and this is your car pulling out after his, following him home. These are the roads, wanting you to follow him, helping you speed along after him. These are the cut fields of corn, just sharp, short stalks left that in the sunlight glow like metal knife blades, so many of them sticking up from the furrowed fields in shining rows. These are other hunters you pass on the road. They drive pickups and wear the same orange caps and nod to you from inside their cabs as you drive by, fellow hunter that you are.

This is the killer pulling into his driveway, a house divided in two so that two families share one inner wall. This is you out of your car that you have parked down the road. This is you with your rifle in your hand as you climb to the top of a ridgeline and look down at him walking through the rooms of his house, starting a load of laundry. This is the hillside, still grassy from summer and comfortable, happy to provide a comfortable place for you to sit and watch. These are the crosshairs in the Zeiss scope of the rifle with the killer at the center of them. These are the crosshairs fixed on his head as he grasps a bar in a doorframe and begins to do pull-ups. This is the safety you switch off with your thumb so that a red dot now shows. This is you exhaling at the same time your forefinger squeezes the trigger. This is you thinking how it is just like using your camera and pressing the shutter to take a portrait of the bride. You want a good shot. This is the bullet that enters his forehead, exploding the wrinkles that look like steps. These are your ears ringing. This is you still looking through the scope, watching the blood begin to flow and soak into his carpet in a long curvy line, as if a snake were coming out from inside his head. This is you walking down from the ridge, the leaves beneath your boots crunching, and the twigs snapping loudly. This is you shaking as you slide your warm rifle into the seat beside you. This is you hearing your name being called. "Annie? Annie is that you? Lord, I didn't know you hunted. Catch anything?" Dinah says, pulling up alongside you in her car.

"No, not a thing," you say.

"Did you know we just moved into that house right there?" Dinah points to the two-family home where you just shot the killer. "It's a two-family home. We have the one on the left, and some other man who's been living there for years has the one on the right. It's so nice to be closer to the pool. I just dropped Jessie off for practice. We're trying to get her time down for age groups so she's in a faster heat. Why don't you come inside for a drink? You look cold. You're shaking."

"Sorry, I've got to get back home to start dinner. Thomas took the girls to practice tonight, and it's my turn to cook."

"Another time, then," Dinah says.

This is you driving away in the pink glow of twilight, a few stars coming out high overhead.

This is the rifle in the seat beside you still giving off heat. You can feel it when you get out of the car and walk toward the house. This is your shoulder, feeling sore now from the kick of the rifle when you took the shot, as you walk in the door and into your warm home. This is Thomas and Sofia doing homework upstairs. This is Alex asking if you saw any deer. This is you saying, "No, not a one." This is Alex removing the clip from beneath the chamber and looking at the bullets.

"You must have shot something. You're missing a bullet," she says.

"No, that clip wasn't full, I checked before I left," you say.

"It was so full. I was the last one to use it. I know."

"Check the chamber, maybe I left one in there," you say, even though you know you haven't left one in there.

This is Alex peering down the chamber. "No, nothing," she says.

"What would you like for dinner?" you ask her. "We can have steak, if you'd like. Hey, how did you do on that history quiz?"

She doesn't answer. You hear her walking up the stairs with your rifle, on her way to putting it back into the gun cabinet. You get out the steaks. You stab potatoes with a knife tip and put them to bake in the oven. You chop broccoli florets from their stalks. Alex comes back downstairs.

"Mom, you shot at something," she says. "I know you did. What did you shoot?"

"Oh, all right, I'll tell you." you say. "I saw a coyote running by—well, actually, I saw what I thought was a buck running by. I think I imagined his antlers even. I took the shot. It turned out to be a coyote. I feel so bad about it, I didn't want to tell anyone. I guess I'm not much of a hunter after all."

"Good thing it wasn't a person you thought was a buck."

"Yes, absolutely. But it shook me up a bit. Just the thought that I could make such a stupid mistake."

"You've got buck fever, Mom. That's what it is. You're dying to shoot one." She speaks in an accent that sounds very New England, and the word "fever" comes out as "fevah."

You laugh. "Yes, I've got the buck 'fevah,' all right." You place the steaks on tinfoil, and your wavy reflection in it makes you look as if you're underwater.

At dinner you are laughing. Your children are funny. They tell good stories about what happened at school and at practice. You are so happy they are safe. You let them turn on all the lights in the living room. It doesn't matter now. No one will be looking in at you. You allow yourself to look at Sofia and imagine what she will look like when she's older. You see her with her braces off and her shoulders back, more confident with age.

That night, in bed, you lean over and start kissing Thomas. The kissing is better than it was with Paul. You know your husband's lips and mouth. You like how when he kisses you in return he strokes your back at the same time. You like how it feels okay to be kissing your husband. You remember your wedding day, how he told you behind the barn to remember that kiss as being the real wedding kiss. It is the same great kiss now. You are free now to go further with him. There is no stopping what the two of you can do together. You hear the howling of the coyotes out there and it is beautiful. You are so glad that it is not really true, that you did not kill one of them with its ruffed silver neck and its dark shining eyes.

This is you a few days later at practice, where Dinah tells you about her neighbor being killed. "Imagine, I was living next to the guy and he was dead for four days before they found him," she says. "I smelled him. Imagine if that shot missed? My daughter or I could have been killed. It's too scary. I'm thinking of moving again. Poor guy, though, he was a school secretary. Who would want to kill him? Probably his ex-wife." She laughs. "I should know," she adds.

"You look great, Dinah," you say. "I can't believe how much weight you've lost, and so quickly. Hey, how did your daughter do in that last meet?" Now you have opened up the floodgates and Dinah begins to talk about every single one of her daughter's events and how she did and how many seconds she took off and how she has been practicing her touches by rolling her hand into the wall for that extra corkscrew momentum. Like the trajectory of a bullet, you think. And Dinah tells you how she has been feeding her daughter those energy blocks, the gels made by Gatorade, and she really thinks those make the difference. She tells you she has looked into colleges already, even though Jessie is a solid four years away from applying. She's been scoping out ones with the best swim teams, the ones that have Division I teams. She tells you she doesn't know which would be better for her daughter, to join a team where she's a big fish in a little pond or one where she's a little fish in a big pond. You sit back against the wall on your bench on the bleachers and let her words cascade over you as you watch the swimmers practicing, swimming back and forth in their lanes. They do a serpentine warm-down. They line up on deck and dive one at a time into one lane, and when they get to the other end they go under the lane line and swim back down a new lane. They wind their way through the entire pool this way, and when they are done they get out of the pool and grab their gym bags and head off to the locker rooms.

This is you in that wobbly phone booth again, calling the police hotline. This is you telling the cop who answers that you've got a tip for him: The killer is the same man who was found dead in his apartment not long ago. Follow the lead, you tell the cop, and hang up.

This is Mandy, at night, after swim practice, mopping the ladies' room and wondering whatever happened to the new member, the man with the dark hair who would watch the swimmers during practice, the one who, when he went into the water himself, lowered himself in with a smile. Perhaps he quit. It happens sometimes—a person joins the facility and then leaves. Maybe they received the membership as a gift and didn't really want it in the first place, or maybe they just preferred to stay at home and run on their own treadmill, or maybe they were too embarrassed by their own body and didn't want to be seen by so many other people every day. Whatever the case, Mandy is glad. The man scared her.

She didn't like how he watched the girls. She felt justified in being leery of him. Too much has happened around here lately, especially with those murders taking place. She was on the verge of reporting him to the director herself, because she didn't like how he watched the girls through the glass wall, but she never felt like the director would have listened to her if she told him. What would she have said anyway? There's a man watching the swimmers in the pool? That would have been absurd. Everyone watches through the glass wall. Even she sometimes stops in the middle of her mopping and leans her hands on her mop and rests her chin on her hands and watches the team workout. The team is impressive to watch. The swimmers unflagging in their two hour swim. The coaches walking up and down the deck, following every lap of their swimmers and stopping at the end of the lanes to give comments and directions. It's like looking into an ant farm where the ants are always moving and working. Mandy scrubs the grout hard on the ladies' room floor. It's satisfying to see the dirt come up, and to see her mop reveal the bright whiteness. Yes, she says to herself, what a relief that man isn't here anymore. She thinks of going up to the lake with her husband this weekend. They would have to dress warmly to sit in the boat, but she doesn't mind. She looks forward to seeing the migrating geese that she knows will fly overhead. She looks forward to hearing the loon's call and seeing the trees onshore, now bare, leaving their jagged images on the water's surface.

CHAPTER FORTY-SEVEN

This is a few months later, the middle of winter. Layers of old snow sit beneath a layer of new snow, covering up what became pocked and riddled with road grime and dirt.

This is Chris at Paul's hearing in a small courtroom, where she sits with her head bowed and a welcome bit of sun coming in through the windows, almost brightly enough to make her feel hopeful. Paul is looking uncomfortable at having to answer all of the questions about his affair with Bobby Chantal, and when asked why he never went to the police afterward with the information about the car he saw in the parking lot, he tells the court honestly that he thought the focus of the case would be shifted to him, and that it would prevent the real killer from being caught. And also, of course, he was afraid he would be implicated and found guilty of a murder he never committed. After the first hearing, Chris and Paul walk arm in arm out to the car to drive back home. "I'm sorry to put you through all of that," he says. "I should have gone to the police years ago, but I didn't want you to know about it then. I thought you'd hate me. I don't know what the courts will decide, but already I feel it was the right thing to do."

When they drive up to the house they can hear the phone ringing and Paul rushes in to answer it, his boots on the lawn sending up powdery snow behind him in an arc. It's his lawyer.

"Looks like you'll be getting off the hook," his lawyer says.

"What? Already?"

"Yep, you don't even have to testify, because they found the guy."

"You're kidding. Who did they find?"

"The murderer. He's some guy who worked at a school all these years. He was found dead not long ago, shot dead. It was a cold case until someone sent in an anonymous tip saying he was the man, not you. Sure enough, they were able to match some carpet fibers found on his clothes to the fibers on the clothes of the last two victims, and they found the same fiber match on Bobby Chantal's body. Guy lived in the same apartment for years. Results just came in. You can sleep easy tonight, buddy."

This is the night, the air frosty and clean. The clouds sailing by, revealing stars so bright one could see by them to walk a wooded trail, and Paul thinking he's the luckiest man in the world. He turns over and settles against Chris, matching his body up to hers, his mouth at her neck, planting kisses in a row.

This is Chris the next day in her studio with one of her biggest buyers from Connecticut. He has been here over an hour, having had tea with her and having admired all of her work, except one that he hasn't seen. It's covered with a cloth. Chatting with her, almost ready to leave after having chosen three paintings he would like to buy, he points to the covered painting. "May I?" he says, wanting to reveal it. Before Chris can say no, the cloth is off, and the face of the killer is staring at them. "Oh, God. Isn't that the face of that serial murderer who was found dead up here?" the buyer says. Chris nods. "I'm sorry, it's not for sale. In fact"—Chris says as she takes her X-Acto knife and rips through the canvas— "pretend like you never even saw it." Later, Chris takes the canvas she ripped out of the frame and burns it in the woodstove, feeling relieved that she'll never have to see the face again. She thinks about Beatrice, how she wishes the killer being caught could somehow have reversed what was done to Beatrice all those years ago, but she knows now nothing can change that. She'll just have to be content with the fact the killer is now dead, and that, she thinks, is something to be very happy about. If they ever found out who killed him, she's going to go up to the person who did it and personally thank them.

CHAPTER FORTY-EIGHT

*T*his is March, when the state championship is held at the facility. The nights are still freezing, but the days are warming up and the ice in the streams begins to melt. From your house you can hear the sound of the rushing water coming from your melting streams and growing higher in your valley. You and the girls have taken morning walks back to the stream on your land. If they could they would spend all day breaking the ice with sticks, standing knee-deep in their boots, and watching the cold water flow around the holes they have made as it bubbles beneath the ice shards.

This is the facility on the weekend of the state championship, where the girls are all heading to the bathrooms after warm-ups to put on their fast suits. The mothers and friends help guide the suits up and over the swimmers' rears. This is you later, on deck, with your hand over your heart. Along with everyone else in the facility—the deck is packed with swimmers, officials, and coaches, the bleachers crowded with parents and grandparents—you face the flag and get ready to hear the recording of the national anthem. This is the anthem, playing for a second and then not playing. This is everyone waiting for the technical problem to be solved by the coach, but the coach is not able to fix it. This is the coach coming back out on deck and beginning to sing it herself in a loud voice. This is everyone else in the facility joining in, even you, and the sound of your voices carries up high and reaches to the glass-paneled ceiling, and you think to yourself that this is the way the anthem should always be sung, by everyone at the meet, because it sounds so much better than the recording.

This is the facility, where everyone seems so much more relaxed now that the killer is gone. This is Paul and Chris, cheering Cleo on from the stands as she's about to take off from the blocks. This is Cleo waving up to them, smiling. This is Chris grabbing onto Paul's hand while Cleo is racing. Her race is that exciting, and Chris never realized before how fast her daughter is. This is Dinah, running after Jessie with a Gatorade chew and telling her to take one exactly three heats before her own, so that it has time to take effect. This is Jessie saying, yes, Mom, sure, Mom, but then giving the Gatorade chew to a teammate, because even though Jessie likes the way the Gatorade chew tastes, and it might help her swim, she knows another girl on the team who has never had them before and wants to try them so badly. This is Dinah, up in the stands, seeing her daughter on deck give away the chew and thinking with great relief how different her girl is than she is, thinking how her daughter, even so young, is and will be a better and more generous person than Dinah is now. And Dinah doesn't care now if Jessie wins her race or not. She doesn't care if Jessie comes in dead last. What she just saw Jessie do was better than winning any swimming race she could imagine.

These are the other parents from the visiting swim teams in the stands; everyone's relaxed, everyone's talking to the person they are seated next to, no one is standing up leaning on the railing to take pictures, getting in the way of all the other parents. You look around you at the facility, and you can see all of the parents you know from your team stationed at their various jobs. You can see the parent of Maria smiling while putting names on the award ribbons. You can see Wes, the father of Ginger, standing guard on the stairs and making sure no one comes up them because it's a fire hazard, but you also see him relaxed, pretending he doesn't see a parent sneak up the stairs to get in a picture. You can see Charlotte working the timing console and stopping for a moment to look up and wave to her son, who walks by her to get to his place in the bullpen. You can see Mandy even. She is behind the glass looking in, holding her mop at rest for a moment, admiring how inviting the pool looks, and thinking how later, when the meet is over, even she might put on a suit and go in. She picked up a suit a few months ago after it was left on a bench in the locker room, and she put it in the lost and found, but no one's come to claim it. It's a suitable suit, she thinks, not too short or deep in the neckline. Now that the killer is gone, she wouldn't be upset if anyone happened to see her in it, anyone who happened to be on the other side of the glass. Yes, the suit would do nicely, she thinks, for her first step into that water she's looked at for so long but never actually experienced.

This is you looking around at everyone, not seeing a likeness to your brother in any of the faces, and thinking that's good.

There was only one him, of course. A him that was damaged and scared and stupid and brave and arrogant and selfish and loving and hurtful and caring and talented and a lousy father and a good father too . . . What is it when someone is everything you can name? Is there a word for that? Because he was all of those things, you think. You'll never know exactly why he killed himself or if someone could have stopped him in time. Maybe that day at the beach when he got up so suddenly and grabbed you and ran with you into the waves it was because what your parents were arguing about, what they were yelling at each other about, was that your father wanted a divorce. Your brother, not wanting to hear how your father wanted to leave the family, then grabbed you and ran with you into the waves. You figure, time-wise, that it was about right, that not long after that day at the beach your father was packing his bags and moving in with his girlfriend. Of course, you'll never know for sure what made your brother grab you then, and it doesn't matter either. What matters is now. What matters is your girls racing right now, shaving off time here and there, and gaining time here and there. What matters is Kim's mother in the stands, now at the point where she's able to watch her other daughter swim and cheer loudly for her. What matters is you right now timing with Thomas. He is telling the swimmers in your lane that they are in the lucky lane. That everyone who has swum in your lane has won their heat. You look over at your daughters standing in line waiting for their heats behind the blocks. They are healthy. You can see the small muscles in their backs move when they move. You can see the color in their cheeks as they talk and laugh with their friends in line. You see Thomas smiling at you. Yes, this is the lucky lane, you think to yourself.

This is after the state championship. The pool is closed. The water is being drained so that the grout and tile can be scrubbed. This is the water leaving through the drains, taking with it the thoughts of Annie, the motion of Kim, the detestable skin of the killer, and this is the new water being pumped in, filling the corners, meeting the gutters. This is the new water, the night before the pool's opening to the public, waiting in moonlight shining in through the windows for the first swimmers, waiting to see whose bodies it will feel moving through it, waiting to hear what thoughts will come from those swimmers and soon become those of the water.

ACKNOWLEDGMENTS

*T*hank you, Maya Ziv, for being a phenomenal editor who knows exactly how to bring out the best in a person's writing and bring a character to life! I'm so grateful for all of the work that you and the staff at Harper Perennial have put into making this novel take shape.

Thank you, Judy Heiblum, for being a stellar agent. Even miles and oceans away, you always take the time to guide me in the right direction and give me brilliant advice.